HE WAS NOT AT ALL THE MAN SHE
HAD MARRIED

They stared at each other, both held motionless in the pregnant pause. Only a few years, and yet it seemed a lifetime had passed. Grayson was no longer a boy, not by any stretch of the imagination. His face had lost that faint remnant of youth, and time had etched its passing in the lines that bracketed his mouth and eyes. Not happy lines, she could see. Frown lines, lines of sorrow. The brilliant blue of his irises that had caused many women to fall in love with him were now a deeper, darker shade. They no longer smiled, and appeared to have seen far more than possible in only a four-year span.

She raised a hand to her bodice. Dismayed by the rapid lift and fall of her chest.

Gray had been beautiful before. Now, there were no words to describe him. She forced her breathing to slow, and fought off a sudden, desperate flare of panic. She had known how to handle the boy, but this . . . this man was not tamable. Had she met him anew, she would know to stay far away.

Also by Sylvia Day

The Stranger I Married

SYLVIA DAY

KENSINGTON PUBLISHING CORP.
http://www.kensingtonbooks.com

KENSINGTON BOOKS are published by

Kensington Publishing Corp.
119 West 40th Street
New York, NY 10018

All Kensington titles, imprints, and distributed lines are available at special quantity discounts for bulk purchases for sales promotion, premiums, fund-raising, educational, or institutional use.

Special book excerpts or customized printings can also be created to fit specific needs. For details, write or phone the office of the Kensington Special Sales Manager: Attn. Special Sales Department. Kensington Publishing Corp., 119 West 40th Street, New York, NY 10018. Phone: 1-800-221-2647.

Kensington and the K logo Reg. U.S. Pat. & TM Off.

ISBN-13: 978-0-7582-9040-3
ISBN-10: 0-7582-9040-3
First Trade Paperback Printing: January 2007
First Mass-Market Printing: August 2009

eISBN-13: 978-0-7582-9066-3
eISBN-10: 0-7582-9066-7
Kensington Electronic Edition: July 2014
10 9 8 7 6 5 4 3 2

Printed in the United States of America

This book is gratefully dedicated to Editorial Goddess Kate Duffy. There are numerous reasons why I think she's fabulous—from the biggies like being the first editor to buy my work, to the smaller (but no less important) things like being generous with her praise.

Kate,
How lucky I am to write for you.
Your enthusiasm for our work together is such a gift. I'm thankful every day to have found you right at the beginning of my career. You have taught me so much, and given me so many opportunities to grow. You allow me to write the stories in my heart, and you've shown me how wonderful the editor/author relationship can be.

Thank you so much.
Sylvia

Acknowledgments

As always, huge thanks and hugs go out to my critique partner, Annette McCleave (*www.AnnetteMcCleave.com*). She keeps me on my toes, and I love her for it.

And the Allure Authors (*www.AllureAuthors.com*) for supporting me and my work. The Allure gals have a true sisterhood, and it means a great deal to me.

Prologue

"**D**o you truly intend to steal your best friend's mistress?" Gerard Faulkner, the sixth Marquess of Grayson, kept his eyes on the woman in question, and smiled. Those who knew him well also knew that look, and its wicked portent. "I certainly do."

"Dastardly," Bartley muttered. "Too low even for you, Gray. Is it not sufficient to cuckold Sinclair? You know how Markham feels about Pel. He's lost his head over her."

Gray studied Lady Pelham with a connoisseur's eye. There was no incertitude about her suitability for his needs. Beautiful and scandalous, he could not have designed a wife more suited to irritating his mother if he'd tried. Pel, as she was affectionately referred to, was of medium height, but stunningly curved, and built for a man's pleasure. The auburn-haired widow of the late Earl of Pelham had a brazen sultriness that was addicting, or so rumor said. Her former lover, Lord

Pearson, had gone into a long decline after she ended their affair.

Gerard had no difficulty seeing how a man could mourn the loss of her attentions. Under the blazing lights of the massive chandeliers, Isabel Pelham glittered like a precious jewel, expensive and worth every shilling.

He watched as she smiled up at Markham with a wide curving of her lips, lips which were considered too full for conventional beauty, but just the right plumpness to rim a man's cock. All around the room, covetous male eyes watched her, hoping for the day when she might turn those sherry-colored eyes upon them, and perhaps select one of them as her next lover. To Gerard, their longing was pitiable. The woman was extremely selective, and retained her lovers for years. She'd had Markham on a leash for nearly two now, and showed no signs of losing interest.

But that interest did not extend to matrimony.

On the few occasions when the viscount had begged for her hand, she refused him, declaring she had no interest in marrying a second time. Gray, on the other hand, had no doubts whatsoever that he could change her mind about that.

"Calm yourself, Bartley," he murmured. "Things will work out. Trust me."

"No one can trust you."

"You can trust me to give you five hundred pounds if you drag Markham away from Pel and into the card room."

"Well, then." Bartley straightened his spine and his waistcoat, neither action capable of hiding his widening middle. "I am at your service."

Grinning, Gerard bowed slightly to his greedy acquaintance who took off to the right, while he made his way to the left. He strolled without haste around the fringes of the ballroom, making his way toward the pivotal object of his plan. The journey was slow going, his way blocked by one mother-and-debutante pairing after another. Most bachelor peers similarly hounded would grimace with annoyance, but Gerard was known as much for his overabundance of charm, as he was for his penchant for mischief. So he flirted outrageously, kissed hands freely, and left every female in his wake certain he would be calling on her with a formal offer of marriage.

Casting the occasional glance toward Markham, he noted the exact moment Bartley lured him away, and then crossed the distance with purposeful strides, taking Pel's gloved hand to his lips before the usual throng of avid admirers could encircle her.

As he lifted his head, he caught her eyes laughing at him. "Why, Lord Grayson. A woman cannot help but be flattered by such a single-minded approach."

"Lovely Isabel, your beauty drew me like a moth to a flame." He tucked her hand around his forearm, and led her away for a walk around the dance floor.

"Needed a respite from the ambitious mothers, I assume?" she asked in her throaty voice. "I'm afraid even my association will not be enough to make you less appealing. You are simply too delicious for words. You shall be the death of one of these poor girls."

Gerard breathed a deep sigh of satisfaction, an action which inundated his senses with her lush scent of some exotic flower. They would rub along famously, he knew. He had come to know her well in the years she had been with Markham, and he had always liked her immensely. "I agree. None of these women will do."

Pel gave a delicate shrug of her bare shoulders, her pale skin set off beautifully by her dark blue gown and sapphire necklace. "You are young yet, Grayson. Once you are my age, perhaps you will have settled down enough to not completely torment your bride with your appetites."

"Or I can marry a mature woman, and save myself the effort of altering my habits."

Arching a perfectly shaped brow, she said, "This conversation is leading somewhere, is it not, my lord?"

"I want you, Pel," he said softly. "Desperately. Only an affair will not suffice. Marriage, however, will take care of it nicely."

Soft, husky laughter drifted in the air between them. "Oh, Gray. I do adore your humor, you know. It is hard to find men so deliciously unabashed in their wickedness."

"And it is lamentably hard to find a creature as blatantly sexual as you, my dear Isabel. I'm afraid you are quite unique, and therefore irreplaceable for my needs."

She shot him a sidelong glance. "I was under the impression you were keeping that actress, the pretty one who cannot remember her lines."

Gerard smiled. "Yes, that's true. All of it." Anne could not act to save her life. Her talents lay in other, more carnal activities.

"And honestly, Gray. You are too young for me. I am six and twenty, you know. And you are . . ." She raked him with a narrowed glance. "Well, you *are* delectable, but—"

"I am two and twenty, and could ride you well, Pel, never doubt it. However, you misunderstand. I have a mistress. Two, in fact, and you have Markham—"

"Yes, and I am not quite finished with him."

"Keep him, I have no objections."

"I'm relieved to have your approval," she said dryly, and then she laughed again, a sound Gray had always enjoyed. "You are quite mad."

"Over you, Pel, definitely. Have been from the first."

"But you've no wish to bed me."

He looked at her with pure male appreciation, taking in the ripe swell of her breasts above the low bodice. "Now, I did not say that. You are a beautiful woman, and I am an amorous man. However, since we are to be bound together, *when* we decide to fall into bed with one another is moot, yes? We shall have a lifetime to make that leap, *if* we decide it would be mutually enjoyable."

"Are you in your cups?" she asked, frowning.

"No, Isabel."

Pel stopped, forcing him to stop with her. She stared up at him, and then shook her head. "If you are serious—"

"There you are!" called a voice behind them.

Gerard bit back a curse at the sound of Markham's voice, but he faced his friend with a careless smile. Isabel's countenance was equally innocent. She truly was flawless.

"I must thank you for keeping the vultures at a distance, Gray," Markham said jovially, his handsome face lit with pleasure at the sight of his paramour. "I was momentarily distracted by something that proved not to be worth my time."

Relinquishing Pel's hand with a flourish, Gerard said, "What are friends for?"

"Where have you been?" Gerard growled a few hours later, as a hooded figure entered his bedroom. He paused his pacing, his black silk robe swirling to a halt around his bare legs.

"You know I come when I can, Gray."

The hood was thrown back revealing silvery blond hair and a beloved face. He crossed the room in two strides and took her mouth, lifting her feet from the floor. "It is not often enough, Em," he breathed. "Not nearly."

"I cannot drop everything to serve your needs. I am a married woman."

"You've no need to remind me of that fact," he grumbled. "I never forget it."

He buried his face in the curve of her shoulder, and breathed her in. She was so soft and innocent, so sweet. "I've missed you."

Emily, now Lady Sinclair, gave a breathless laugh, her lips swollen from his kisses. "Liar." Her mouth turned down morosely. "You have been seen with that actress more than a few times in the fortnight since I saw you last."

"You know she means nothing. It's you I love."

He could explain, but she would not understand his need for wild, unrestrained fucking, just as she had not understood

Sinclair's demands. She was too slight of frame, and genteel in sensibility, to enjoy such fervency. It was his respect for her which led him to seek such release elsewhere.

"Oh, Gray." She sighed, her fingers curling into the hairs at his nape. "Sometimes I think you truly believe that. But perhaps you love me as much as a man like you is able."

"Never doubt it," he said ardently. "I love you more than anything, Em. I always have." Taking a moment to divest her of the cape, he tossed it aside and carried her to the waiting bed.

As he undressed her with quiet efficiency, he seethed inside. Emily was supposed to have been *his* bride, but he had gone away on his Grand Tour, and returned to find his childhood love married. She said her heart had been broken when he left, and rumors of his affairs had reached her ears. She had reminded him that he had never written, which led her to believe he had forgotten her.

Gerard knew his mother had helped to plant the seeds of doubt, and then had watered them daily. Emily had not been worthy in the dowager's eyes. She had wanted him to marry a bride of higher station, so he would do the opposite, to thwart her and pay her in kind.

If only Em had held on to her faith a little while longer, they could have been wed now. This could have been her bed, one she did not have to leave before the sun rose.

Naked, her pale skin glowing like ivory in the candlelight, Emily took his breath away, as she always had. He had loved her as long as he could remember. She was so beautiful. Not in the way Pel was. Pel had an earthy, carnal sensuality. Em was a different kind of beautiful, more fragile and understated. They were as opposite as a rose was to a daisy.

Gerard was very fond of daisies.

His large hand reached out and cupped the slight weight of her breast. "You are still maturing, Em," he said, noting the new fullness.

She covered his hand with her own. "Gerard," she said in her lilting voice.

He caught her gaze, and his heart swelled at the love he saw there. "Yes, my love?"

"I am *enceinte*."

Gerard gaped. He had been careful, and made use of French letters. "Em, dear God!"

Her blue eyes, those lovely eyes the color of cornflowers, filled with tears. "Tell me you are happy. Please."

"I . . ." He swallowed hard. "Of course, sweet." He had to ask the obvious question. "What of Sinclair?"

Emily smiled sadly. "I do not believe there will be a doubt in anyone's mind that the child is yours, but he will not refute it. He gave me his word. In a way, 'tis fitting. He released his last mistress due to pregnancy."

His stomach clenched tight with shock, Gerard laid her down upon the mattress. She looked so tiny, so angelic against the blood red color of his velvet counterpane. He discarded his robe and climbed over her. "Come away with me."

Gerard lowered his head, and sealed his lips over hers, moaning at the sweet taste of her. If only things were different. If only she had waited.

"Come away with me, Emily," he begged again. "We can be happy together."

Tears slid down her temples. "Gray, my love." She cupped his face in her tiny hands. "You are such a passionate dreamer."

He nuzzled the fragrant valley between her breasts, his hips grinding his erection into the mattress in an attempt to temper his desire. With an iron will, he controlled his baser demands. "You cannot deny me."

"Too true," she gasped, caressing his back. "If I had been stronger, how different our lives would have been. But Sinclair . . . the dear man. I have shamed him enough."

Gerard pressed loving kisses into her tight belly, and thought of his child who had taken root there. His heart raced in near panic. "What will you do then, if you will not have me?"

"I depart tomorrow for Northumberland."

"Northumberland!" His head lifted in surprise. "Bloody hell, why so far away?"

"Because that is where Sinclair wishes to go." With her hands under his arms, she tugged him over her, her legs spreading wide in welcome. "Under the circumstances, how can I refuse?"

Feeling as if she were drifting away, Gerard rose over her, and slid his cock slowly into her, groaning his lust as she closed hot and tight around him. "But you will come back," he said hoarsely.

Emily's golden head thrashed softly in pleasure, her eyes squeezed shut. "God, yes, I will return." Her depths fluttered along his shaft. "I cannot live without you. Without this."

Holding her tightly to him, Gerard began to thrust gently. He stroked into her in the way he knew brought her the most pleasure, while restraining his own needs. "I love you, Em."

"My love," she gasped. And then she came apart in his arms.

Tink.
Tink.

Isabel awoke with a groan, knowing by the soft purplish color of the sky and her exhaustion that it must be just after dawn. She lay there a moment, her mind groggy, trying to determine what had disturbed her sleep.

Tink.

Running her hands over her eyes, Isabel sat up and reached for her night rail to cover her nakedness. She glanced at the large-faced clock on the mantel and realized Markham had departed only two hours before. She had hoped to sleep until late afternoon, and still intended to do so, once she dealt with her recalcitrant swain. Whoever he was.

She shivered as she made her way to the window, where tiny pebbles hitting the glass provided the annoying sound.

Isabel pushed up the sash and looked down at her rear garden. She sighed. "I suppose if I must be disturbed," she called out, "it is best that it be for a sight as handsome as you are."

The Marquess of Grayson grinned up at her, his shiny brown hair disheveled and his deep blue eyes red-rimmed. He was missing his cravat and the neck of his shirt gaped open, revealing a golden throat and a few strands of dark chest hair. He appeared to be lacking a waistcoat as well, and she could not help but smile back at him. Gray reminded her so much of Pelham when she had first met him nine years ago. Those had been happy times, short-lived as they were.

"O Romeo, Romeo!" she recited, taking a seat on the window bench. "Wherefore art thou—"

"Oh, please, Pel," he groaned, cutting her off with that deep laugh of his. "Let me in, will you? It's cold out here."

"Gray." She shook her head. "If I open my door to you, this incident will be all over London by suppertime. Go away, before you are seen."

He crossed his arms stubbornly, the material of his black jacket straining to contain his brawny arms and broad shoulders. Grayson was so young, his face as yet unlined. Still a boy in so many ways. Pelham had been the same age when he'd swept her off her seventeen-year-old feet.

"I am not leaving, Isabel. So you may as well invite me in, before I make a spectacle of myself."

She could tell by the stubborn set of his jaw that he was serious. Well, as serious as a man such as him could be.

"Go to the front, then," she relented. "Someone will be awake to admit you."

Isabel rose from the window seat, and retrieved her white satin dressing robe. She left her bedroom and walked into her boudoir, where she opened the curtains to let in the now pale pink light. The room was her favorite, decorated in soft shades of ivory and burnished gold, with gilt-edged chairs and chaise, and tasseled drapes. But the soothing color scheme was not what most moved her. That distinction went to the only spot of obtrusive color in the space—the large portrait of Pelham that graced the far wall.

Every day she gazed upon that likeness, and allowed her heartbreak and loathing to rise to the surface. The earl was impervious, of course, his seductively etched mouth curved in the smile that had won her hand in marriage. How she had loved him, and adored him, as only a young girl could. Pelham had been everything to her, until she had sat at Lady Warren's musicale and heard two women behind her discussing her husband's carnal prowess.

Her jaw clenched at the memory, all her old resentment rushing to the fore. Nearly five years had passed since Pelham met his reward in a duel over a paramour, but she still smarted from the sting of betrayal and humiliation.

A soft scratching came to the door. Isabel called out and the portal opened, revealing the frowning countenance of her hastily dressed butler.

"My lady, the Marquess of Grayson requests a moment of your time." He cleared his throat. "From the service door."

Isabel bit back a smile, her dark mood fleeing at the image she pictured of Grayson standing haughty and arrogant, as only he could be, while semi-dressed and at the delivery entrance. "I am at home."

A slight twitching of a gray eyebrow was the only indication of surprise.

While the servant went to fetch Gray, she went around the room and lit the tapers. Lord, she was weary. She hoped he would be quick about whatever was so urgent. Thinking of their earlier odd conversation, she wondered if he might not need some help. He could be a bit touched in the head.

Certainly they had been unfailingly friendly with one another, and beyond mere acquaintances, but never more than that. Isabel had always rubbed along well with men. After all, she liked them quite well. But there had been a respectful distance between her and Lord Grayson, because of her ongoing affair with Markham, his closest friend. An affair she had ended just hours ago, when the handsome viscount had asked her to marry him for the third time.

In any case, despite Gray's ability to arrest her brain processes for a moment with his uncommon beauty, she had no further interest in him. He was Pelham all over again—a man too selfish and self-centered to set aside his own needs for another's.

The door flew open behind her, startling her, and she spun about, only to be met head-on with over six feet of powerful male. Gray caught her around the waist and spun her about, laughing that rich laugh of his. A laugh that said he'd never once had a care in the world.

"Gray!" she protested, pushing at his shoulders. "Put me down."

"Dear Pel," he cried, his eyes alight. "I've had the most wondrous news told to me this morn. I'm to be a father!"

Isabel blinked, growing dizzy from lack of sleep and the spinning.

"You are the only person alive I could think of who might be happy for me. Everyone else will be horrified. Please smile, Pel. Congratulate me."

"I will, if you put me down."

The marquess set her on her feet and stepped back, waiting.

She laughed at his impatient expectation. "Congratulations, my lord. May I have the name of the fortunate woman who is to become your bride?"

Much of the joy in his blue eyes faded, but his charming smile remained. "Well, that would still be you, Isabel."

Staring up at him, she tried to discern what he was about, and failed. She gestured to a nearby chair, and then sat herself.

"You really are quite lovely with sex-mussed hair," Gray mused. "I can see why your lovers would mourn the loss of such a sight."

"Lord Grayson!" Isabel ran a hand over the tangles in her

long tresses. The present fashion was close-cropped curls, but she preferred a longer length, as did her paramours. "Please, I must hasten you to explain the purpose of your visit. It has been a long night and I am tired."

"It has been a long night for me as well, I have yet to sleep. But—"

"Might I suggest you sleep on this wild idea of yours? Rested, I think you might see things differently."

"I will not," he said stubbornly, twisting to drape one arm over the back of the chair, a pose that was sultry in its sheer artlessness. "I've thought it through. There are so many reasons why we would be perfect for one another."

She snorted. "Gray, you have no notion of how wrong you are."

"Hear me out, Pel. I need a wife."

"I do not need a husband."

"Are you certain about that?" he asked, arching a brow at her. "I think you do."

Isabel crossed her arms, and settled into the back of the chaise. Whether he was insane or not, he *was* interesting. "Oh?"

"Think on it. I know you grow rather fond of your paramours, but you have to dismiss them eventually, and not due to boredom. You are not that type of woman. No, you have to release them because they fall in love with you, and then want more. You refuse to take married men to your bed, so all of your lovers are free and they all wish to marry you." He paused. "But if you were already married . . ." Gray let his words hang in the air.

She stared at him. And then blinked. "What the devil do you gain out of such a marriage?"

"I gain a great deal, Pel. A great deal. I would be free of the marriage-minded debutantes, my mistresses would understand that they will receive no more from me, my mother—" He shuddered. "My mother would cease presenting marital prospects to me, and I shall have a wife who is not only charming and likeable, but one who doesn't have any foolish notions of love and commitment and fidelity."

For some strange, unaccountable reason, Isabel found herself liking Lord Grayson. Unlike Pelham, Gray wasn't filling some poor child's head with declarations of undying love and devotion. He wasn't making a marital bargain with a girl who might grow to love him and be hurt by his indiscretions. And he was thrilled to have a bastard, which led her to believe he intended to provide for it.

"What of children, Gray? I am not young, and you must have an heir."

His famous, heart-stopping grin burst forth. "No worries, Isabel. I have two younger brothers, one of whom is already wed. They will have children, should we neglect the task."

Isabel choked out a half-crazed little laugh. That she would even consider the ridiculous notion . . .

But she had said good-bye to Markham, much as she regretted that end. He was mad for her, the foolish man, and she had selfishly tied him up for almost two years. It was time for him to find a woman worthy of him. One who could love him, as she could not. Her ability to experience that elevated emotion had died with Pelham on a field at dawn.

Looking at the earl's portrait again, Isabel hated that she had inflicted pain on Markham. He was a good man, a tender lover, and a great friend. He was also the third man whose heart had been broken by her need for physical closeness and sexual release.

She often thought of Lord Pearson, and how emotionally destroyed he had been by her dismissal. She was weary of the hurt feelings, and often berated herself for causing them, but knew she would go on as she had been. The human need for companionship would not be denied.

Gray was right. Perhaps if she were already married, she could find and enjoy a true sexual friendship with a man without him hoping for more. And she would never have to worry about Gray falling in love with her, that much was certain. He had professed a deep love for one woman, but maintained a steady string of paramours. Like Pelham, constancy and the ability to deeply love was beyond him.

But could she engage in similar infidelity after experiencing the pain it could bring?

The marquess leaned forward, and caught up her hands. "Say yes, Pel." His stunning blue eyes pleaded with her, and she knew Gray would never mind her affairs. He would be too occupied with his own, after all. This was a bargain, nothing more.

Perhaps it was exhaustion that stunted her ability to think properly, but within the space of two hours, Isabel found herself in the Grayson traveling coach on the way to Scotland.

Six months later . . .

"Isabel, a moment of your time, if you would, please."

Gerard watched the empty open doorway until his wife's curvaceous form, which had just passed by, filled it again.

"Yes, Gray?" Isabel stepped into his study with an inquisitively raised brow.

"Are you free Friday evening?"

She gave him a mock chastising look. "You know I am available whenever you need me."

"Thank you, vixen." He leaned back in his chair and smiled. "You are too good to me."

Isabel moved to the settee and sat. "Where are we expected?"

"Dinner at the Middletons'. I agreed to speak to Lord Rupert there, but Bentley informed me today that Lady Middleton has also invited the Grimshaws."

"Oh." Isabel wrinkled her nose. "Devious of her to invite

your inamorata and her husband to an event you are attending."

"Quite," Gerard said, rising and rounding the desk to take a seat next to her.

"That smile is so wicked, Gray. You really should not let it out."

"I cannot restrain it." He tossed his arm over her shoulders and pulled her close, breathing in the exotic floral scent that was both familiar and stirring. "I am the luckiest man alive, and I am smart enough to know it. Can you imagine how many peers wish they had a wife like mine?"

She laughed. "You remain deliciously, unabashedly shameless."

"And you love it. Our marriage has made you a figure of some renown."

"You mean 'infamy,'" she said dryly. "The older woman starved for the stamina of a younger man."

"Starved for me." He fingered a loose tendril of fiery hair. "I do like the sound of that."

A soft knock on the open door had them both looking over the back of the settee at the footman who waited there.

"Yes?" Gerard asked, put out to be interrupted during a rare quiet moment with his wife. She was so often occupied with political teas and other female nonsense that he was hardly ever afforded the opportunity to enjoy her sparkling discourse. Pel was infamous, yes, but she was also unfailingly charming and the Marchioness of Grayson. Society may speculate about her, but they would never shut their doors to her.

"A special post arrived, my lord."

Gerard held out his hand and crooked his fingers impatiently. As soon as he held the missive, he grimaced at the familiar handwriting.

"Heavens, what a face," Isabel said. "I should leave you to it."

"No." He held her down by tightening his arm on her shoulder. "It's from the dowager, and by the time I am done reading it, I will need you to pull me out of the doldrums, as only you can."

"As you wish. If you want me to stay, I will. I am not due out for hours yet."

Smiling at the thought of hours to share with her, Gerard opened the letter.

"Shall we play chess?" she suggested, her smile mischievous.

He shuddered dramatically. "You know how much I detest that game. Think of something less likely to put me to sleep."

Turning his attention to the letter, he skimmed. But as he came to a paragraph written as if it were an afterthought, but which he knew to be a calculated strike, his reading slowed and his hands began to shake. His mother never wrote without the intent to wound, and she remained furious that he had married the notorious Lady Pelham.

> . . . *a shame the infant did not survive the birthing.*
> *It was a boy child, I heard. Plump and well-formed*
> *with a dark mane of hair, unlike his two blond parents.*
> *Lady Sinclair was too slightly built, the doctor said,*
> *and the baby too large. She bled out over hours. A grue-*
> *some sight, I was told . . .*

Gerard's breathing faltered, and he grew dizzy. The beautifully handwritten horrors on the page blurred until he could no longer read them.

Emily.

His chest burned, and he started in surprise as Isabel thumped him on the back.

"Breathe, damn you!" she ordered, her voice worried, but filled with command. "What the devil does that say? Give it to me."

His hand fell slack, the papers falling to flare out on the Aubusson rug.

He should have been with Em. When Sinclair had returned his letters unopened, he should have done more to support her than merely sending friends with secondhand greetings. He had known Em his whole life. She was the first girl he'd kissed, the first girl he had given flowers to, or wrote poetry about. He could not remember a time when the golden-haired angel had not been in the periphery of his existence.

And now she was gone, forever, killed by his lust and selfishness. His darling, sweet Emily, who deserved so much better than he had given her.

Faintly, he heard a buzzing in his ears, and thought it could be Isabel, who held one of his hands so tightly within her own. He turned and leaned against her, his cheek to her bosom, and cried. Cried until her bodice was soaked, and the hands that stroked his back shook with worry. He cried until he could not cry anymore, and all the while he hated himself.

They never made it to the Middletons'. Later that night, Gerard packed his bags and headed north.

He did not return.

Chapter 1

Four years later

"His Lordship is at home, my lady."

For a great many women such a statement was a common utterance and nothing of note, but for Isabel, Lady Grayson, it was so rarely heard, she could not remember the last time her butler had said the same to her.

She paused in the foyer, tugging off her gloves before handing them to the waiting footman. She took her time with the task, taking the extra brief moments to collect herself, and ascertain that her racing heart was not outwardly visible.

Grayson had returned.

Isabel could not help but wonder why. He'd rejected every missive she sent to his steward, and had sent none to her. Having read the dowager's letter, she knew what had broken him that day he'd left both London and her. She could imagine his pain, having seen his initial excitement and subsequent pride at becoming a father. As his friend, she wished Gray had allowed her to provide him more than just that one hour of comfort, but he'd turned away from her, and years had passed.

She smoothed her muslin skirts, and touched a hand to her upswept hair. When she caught herself checking her appearance, Isabel stopped with a muttered curse. This was Gray. He would not care how she looked. "The study?"

"Yes, my lady."

The scene of that day.

She nodded, and squared her shoulders, shoring up her nerve. As ready as she would ever be, Isabel passed the curving staircase and turned into the first open door on the right. Despite her mental and physical preparations, the sight of her husband's back struck her like a physical blow. He stood silhouetted in the window, appearing taller and definitely broader. His powerful torso tapered to a trim waist, beautifully curved ass, and long, muscular legs. Framed by the dark green velvet curtains, the perfect symmetry of his form stole her breath.

But there was a somber, oppressive air that surrounded him that was so distant from the carefree man she remembered. It forced her to take another deep breath before opening her mouth to speak.

As if he felt her presence, Gray turned before she managed a word. Her throat closed tight as a fist.

He was not at all the man she had married.

They stared at each other, both held motionless in the pregnant pause. Only a few years, and yet it seemed a lifetime had passed. Grayson was no longer a boy, not by any stretch of the imagination. His face had lost that faint remnant of youth, and time had etched its passing in the lines that bracketed his mouth and eyes. Not happy lines, she could see. Frown lines, lines of sorrow. The brilliant blue of his irises that had caused many women to fall in love with him were now a deeper, darker shade. They no longer smiled, and appeared to have seen far more than possible in only a four-year span.

She raised a hand to her bodice, dismayed by the rapid lift and fall of her chest.

Gray had been beautiful before. Now, there were no words to describe him. She forced her breathing to slow, and fought off a sudden, desperate flare of panic. She had known how to handle the boy, but this . . . this *man* was not tamable. Had she met him anew, she would know to stay far away.

"Hello, Isabel."

Even his voice had changed. It was deeper now, slightly raspy.

Isabel had no notion of what to say to him.

"You have not changed at all," he murmured, striding toward her. The previous cockiness of his bearing was gone, replaced by the type of confidence one gained from walking through hell and surviving it.

Sucking in a deep breath, she was inundated with the familiar scent of him. A little spicier, perhaps, but he smelled like Gray, nevertheless. Staring up at his impassive face, she could do no more than shrug helplessly.

"I should have written," he said.

"Yes, you should have," she agreed. "Not just to warn me of your intent to visit, but before, if only to say that you were well. I have been worried about you, Gray."

He gestured with his hand toward a nearby chair, and she sank into it gratefully. As he moved to the settee across from her, Isabel noted his quaint garb. While he wore trousers with jacket and waistcoat, the garments were plain, and of common materials. Whatever he had been doing these last years, it apparently had not required the latest fashions.

"I apologize for your worry." One side of his mouth curved upward in a ghost of his former smile. "But I could not tell you I was well, when I was far from it. I could not bear to look at letters, Pel. It was not because they were from you. For years I avoided any sight of correspondence. But now . . ." He paused, and his jaw tightened, as if with determination. "I am not visiting."

"Oh?" Her stomach fluttered. Their camaraderie was gone.

Instead of the easy comfort she had once enjoyed with him, she now felt decidedly nervous.

"I have come here to live. If I can remember how to do that."

"Gray—"

He shook his head, his slightly-longer-than-fashionable locks drifting about his neck. "No pity, Isabel. I do not deserve it. What's more, I don't want it."

"What *do* you want?"

His met her gaze directly. "I want many things, but mostly I want companionship. And I want to be worthy of it."

"Worthy?" She frowned.

"I was a dreadful friend, as are most selfish people."

Isabel stared down at her hands and noted her gold wedding band—a symbol of her lifelong commitment to a veritable stranger. "Where have you been, Gray?"

"Taking stock."

So he was not going to tell her. "Very well, then. What do you want from me?" She lifted her chin. "What service can I provide?"

"First, I will need to be made presentable." Gray waved a careless hand down the length of his body. "Then I will need to hear the latest *on dit*. I have read the papers, but you and I both know that gossip is rarely the truth. Most importantly, I will require your escort."

"I am not certain how much assistance I can offer you, Gray," she said honestly.

"I am aware." He stood and moved toward her. "The gossips have been unkind to you in my absence, which is why I have returned. How responsible can I be, truly, if I cannot take care of my own wife?" He dropped to a crouch beside her. "It is a great deal to ask of you, Pel, I know. It was not what you agreed to when we made our bargain. But things have changed."

"*You* have changed."

"God, I can only hope that's true."

Gray caught up her hands, and she felt calluses against her fingertips. She looked down, and saw his skin dark from the sun and reddened from work. Next to her smaller, paler ones, the contrast was like night to day.

He gave a gentle squeeze. Isabel lifted her gaze, and was stunned again by the comeliness of his features.

"I will not coerce you, Pel. If you wish to live your life as you have been, I will respect that." That faint hint of his remembered smile shined through again. "But I am not above begging, I warn you. I owe you much, and I am quite determined."

It was that brief glimpse of the old Gray that soothed her. Yes, the outer shell had changed, perhaps even much of the interior, but there was still some of the scapegrace charmer she knew in there. For the moment, it was enough.

Isabel smiled back, and his relief was tangible. "I will cancel my engagements for this evening and we can strategize."

Grayson shook his head. "I need to gather my bearings, and familiarize myself with being home again. Enjoy yourself tonight. You shall be burdened with me soon enough."

"Perhaps you would agree to have tea with me, in an hour or so?" Maybe then she could compel him to tell her about his absence.

"I would enjoy that."

She stood, and he rose with her.

Heavens, he was tall. Had he always been? She could not recall. Pushing aside her surprise, Isabel turned toward the door, and found one hand still caught in his.

Gray released it with a sheepish shrug. "See you in an hour, Pel."

Gerard waited until Isabel departed the room before sinking onto the settee with a groan. During his absence, insomnia had been a recurring torment. Needing physical exhaustion to sleep, he'd worked the fields of his many properties and in doing so he had become accustomed to muscle aches and pains. Never had his body hurt in quite the manner it did now. He hadn't realized how tense he was until he was alone and the seductive floral fragrance that was his wife's alone had dissipated.

Had Isabel always been so beautiful? He could not remember. Certainly he had used the word "beautiful" to describe her in his thoughts, but the reality was beyond what the mere utterance could convey. Her hair had more fire, her eyes more sparkle, her skin more glow than he had remembered.

Over the last few years he had said "my wife" hundreds of times as he paid her accounts and handled other matters relating to her. However, until today, he had never actually put the appellation together with the face and body of Isabel Grayson.

Gerard ran a hand through his hair, and wondered at his sanity when he'd made this marriage bargain with her. When Pel had walked into the room, all the oxygen had left. How had he never noted that corollary before? He had not lied when he said she looked the same. But for the first time, he *saw* her. Truly *saw* her. Then again, during the last two years, he had begun to see a great many things he had been blind to before.

Like this room.

He glanced around and grimaced. Dark green with dark walnut paneling. What in hell had he been thinking? A man could not peruse accounts properly in this gloomy place. And reading was out of the question.

Who has time to read when there are drinks to be had, and women to woo?

The words of his youth came back to taunt him.

Rising to his feet, Gerard walked to the bookshelves and withdrew random volumes. Every one he opened creaked in protest at the bending of its bindings. None of them had ever been read.

What kind of man surrounded himself with beauty and life, and then never spared a moment to appreciate any of it?

Filled with self-disgust, he sat at his desk and began a list of things he wanted changed. Before long he had filled several sheets.

"My lord?"

He lifted his head to see the lackey in the doorway. "Yes?"

"Her ladyship inquired after you. She wishes to know if you have decided against tea?"

Gerard glanced at the clock in surprise, and then pushed away from the desk and stood. "The dining room, or the parlor?"

"Her ladyship's boudoir, my lord."

Every muscle tensed again. How had he forgotten that, too? He had enjoyed sitting in that bastion of femininity and watching her prepare for her evenings out. As he climbed the stairs, he thought back on what time they'd spent together and admitted it had been filled with very little meaningful discourse. But he knew he had liked her, and that she had been a confidant to him.

He needed a friend now, since he no longer had any. He determined that he would rekindle the friendship he had once enjoyed with his wife, and with that expectation in mind, he lifted his hand and knocked on her door.

Isabel took a deep breath at the sound of the soft knock, and then called out permission to enter. Gray came in, pausing on the threshold, a telling moment of hesitation she had not seen from him before. Lord Grayson never waited. He leapt into action the moment he thought of something, which is how he often landed into mischief.

He stared at her, long and hard. Enough to make her regret the decision to receive him in her dressing gown. She had debated internally for almost half an hour, and in the end had decided to act as much as possible like she had before. Surely, the sooner they settled into their usual routine, the more comfortable they both would be.

"I believe the water is most likely cold by now," she murmured, turning away from the gilded vanity to sit on the nearby chaise. "But then I was always the one who drank tea."

"I preferred brandy."

He closed the door, giving her a brief moment to savor the sound of his voice. Why she should notice its slight rasp now, when she hadn't before, puzzled her.

"I have it here." She gestured toward the low table where a china tea set, brandy decanter, and goblet waited.

Gray's mouth widened in a slow smile. "You are always thinking of me. Thank you." He looked around. "I am pleased to find the space exactly as I remember it. With the walls and ceiling draped with white satin, I have always felt like I am standing in a tent when I am in here."

"That was the effect I wanted," she said, relaxing into the low back and curling her legs next to her.

"Is that so?"

He sat across from her, tossing his arm across the back of the settee. Isabel could not help but remember how he used to do the same to her shoulders. At that time, she had thought nothing of it. That version of Grayson had merely been exuberant.

He also hadn't been quite so large.

"Why a tent, Pel?"

"You have no notion of how long I've waited for you to ask that," she admitted with a soft chuckle.

"Why didn't I ask before?"

"We did not talk about such things."

"No?" His eyes laughed at her. "What did we talk about then?"

She moved to pour him a brandy, but he shook his head. "Why, we talked about you, Gray."

"Me?" he asked with raised brows. "Surely, not all the time."

"Nearly all the time."

"And when we weren't talking about me?"

"Well, then we were talking about your inamoratas."

Gray grimaced, and she laughed, remembering how much fun she used to have in simple discourse with him. Then she noted how he looked at her, as if he could not quite put his finger on something about her. Her laughter faded away.

"How insufferable I was, Isabel. How did you ever tolerate me?"

"I quite liked you," she said honestly. "There never was any guessing with you. You always said exactly what you meant."

He looked past her shoulder. "You still hang Pelham's portrait," he mused. Gray returned his gaze to hers. "Did you love him so very much?"

Isabel turned, and looked at the painting behind her. She tried, truly tried to dredge up some remnant of the love she had once felt for him, but her bitter resentment was too deep. She could not reach below it. "I did. I cannot remember the feeling now, but once I loved him desperately."

"Is that why you avoid commitment, Pel?"

She looked back at him with her lips pursed. "You and I did not discuss personal things, either."

Gray's arm left the back of the chair and he leaned forward, resting his forearms on his knees. "Could we not be better friends now, than we were then?"

"I am not sure that would be wise," she murmured, once again glancing at her wedding band.

"Why not?"

Isabel rose and stood at the window, needing to put distance between herself and his new intensity.

"Why not?" he asked again, following her. "Do you have other, closer friends who you share things with?"

He set his hands atop her shoulders, and it took only a moment for his touch to heat her skin, and his scent to reach her nostrils. When next he spoke, his voice came close to her ear. "Is it too much to ask that you add your husband to your list of trusted friends?"

"Gray," she breathed, her heart racing with her distress. Her restless fingers brushed the satin billowing beside the window frame. "I do not have friends such as you describe. And you say the word 'husband' with an import we never gave to it."

"How about your lover, then?" he pressed. "Does he hear your thoughts?"

Isabel attempted to pull away, but he held her fast.

"Why a tent, Pel? Can you tell me that, at least?"

She shivered at the feel of his exhale against her nape. "I like to imagine it is a part of a caravan."

"A fantasy?" Gray's large hands slid down her arms. "Is there a sheik who occupies this fantasy? Does he ravish you?"

"My lord!" she protested, thoroughly alarmed by the way her skin was prickling with sensual awareness. There was no way to ignore the hard male body that bracketed hers.

"What do you want, Gray?" she asked, her mouth dry. "Have you suddenly decided to change the rules?"

"And if I have?"

"We would end up apart, our friendship ruined. You and I are not the type of people who find love ever after."

"How would you know what type of man I am?"

"I know you kept a mistress while professing to love another."

His hot, open mouth pressed against the side of her throat, and her eyes slid closed at the seductive touch.

"You said I have changed, Isabel."

"No man changes *that* much. Regardless, I . . . I have someone."

Gray turned her to face him. His hands around her wrists were hot, his gaze hotter. Lord, she knew that look. It was the look Pelham had brought her to heel with, the look she made certain none of her lovers gave to her. Passion, desire—she welcomed those. But carnal hunger was something to be avoided at all costs.

That famished gaze swept over her body from head to toe and back again. Her nipples ached and tightened as his heated examination passed them, until she knew they must be visible even through her gown. His perusal paused there on the upward journey, and a low growl rumbled in his throat. Her lips parted on a panting breath.

"Isabel," he rasped, his hand lifting to cup her breast, his thumb brushing across the tight peak. "Could you not give me a chance to prove my worth?"

She heard her own needy moan, felt her blood heat and grow sluggish. His mouth lowered to hers, and she tilted her head back, waiting.

And wanting.

A soft scratching at the door broke the moment. She stumbled backward, breaking free of his slackened hold. Her fingers covered her lips, pressing hard to hide their quivering.

"My lady?" came the soft query of her abigail from the hallway. "Should I return later?"

Gray waited, his breathing harsh, the crests of his cheekbones flushed. There was no doubt in Isabel's mind that if she sent her maid away, she would be flat on her back and mounted within moments.

"Come in," she called, wincing at the note of panic that she could not hide.

Damn him. He'd made her want him, this new spouse of hers. Want him with the type of need that made her ache, a need she had thought herself too old and too wise to ever feel again.

It was her worst nightmare come to life.

Her husband closed his eyes a moment, collecting himself, as Mary swept in and went straight to the armoire.

"Shopping tomorrow, Pel?" he asked, his voice maddeningly calm. "I do need new garments."

The most she could manage was a jerky nod.

Grayson sketched an elegant bow and retreated, but his presence lingered in her mind long after he had gone.

Gerard made it to the hallway that led to his rooms before pausing to rest against the damask-covered wall. He closed his eyes and cursed himself. His plan to renew relations with his wife had gone horribly awry the moment he had opened the door.

He should have been prepared, he should have known how his body would react to the sight of Pel draped in black satin, one creamy shoulder bared as she lounged on a chaise. But how could he have known? He had never felt that way about her before. At least, not that he could recollect. But during those previous meetings in her boudoir, he had been so in love with Em. Perhaps that was what had granted him immunity from his wife's abundant charms.

Banging the back of his head lightly against the wall, Gerard could only hope that it would knock some sense into him. To lust for one's wife. He groaned. For most men, that would be so convenient. Not for him. Isabel had been frightened by his interest.

Though not uninterested, a voice whispered in his mind.

Yes, his seduction skills were a bit dusty, but he hadn't completely forgotten everything. He knew the signals a woman's body gave when she lusted in return.

Isabel may be correct in saying they were not the type of people who found love ever after. Lord knows they had both stumbled badly in that pursuit before. But perhaps it did not have to be a grand love affair. Perhaps it could simply be an affair of indefinite duration. A marriage of friendship, and a shared bed. As much as he liked Pel, they had the foundation. He loved the sound of her laugh—that rich, throaty purr that warmed a man from the inside. And her smile, with its teasing hint of wickedness. The sexual attraction was there in bushels. Besides, they were married, after all. Surely that gave him a leg up.

Gerard pushed away from the wall, and went to his rooms. Garments tomorrow, then a slow reintroduction to Society, and a heated seduction of his wife.

Of course, there was her paramour to attend to.

He grimaced. That would be the most difficult part. Isabel did not love her amours, but she cared a great deal for them, and was fiercely loyal. Winning her would take cunning and time, the latter being something he was not accustomed to investing in the pursuit of women.

But this was Pel, and as many would attest, she was worth the wait.

Chapter 2

"You do not look happy, Isabel," John, the Earl of Hargreaves, whispered in her ear. "Perhaps you would care to hear a bawdy joke? Or move along to another party? This one *is* dreadfully boring."

Isabel sighed inwardly and offered a bright smile. "If you wish to leave, I have no objections."

Hargreaves set his gloved hand at the small of her back and gave a soft caress. "I did not say I wanted to leave. I suggested it as a cure for your ennui."

At the moment, she almost wished she were bored. To have her head filled with nothing of import would be infinitely better than having it filled with thoughts of Gray. Who was the man who had moved into her home today? She truly had no notion. She knew only that he was very dark, shadowed with torments she could not understand, because he would not share. He was also very dangerous. As her husband, he could demand anything of her that he desired and she would be helpless to deny him.

Deep in her heart, Isabel could not help but long for the Marquess of Grayson she had once known. The younger Gray with the ready wit and careless disdain. He had been so simple to manage.

"Well, Isabel?" Hargreaves pressed.

She hid her slight irritation. John was a kind man, and had been her paramour for over two years, but he never voiced an opinion, never gave a hint of what he would prefer. "I would like you to decide," she said, turning to face him.

"Me?" He frowned, which did nothing to lessen his appeal.

Hargreaves was very handsome with his aquiline nose and dark eyes. His black hair was graying at the temples, a distinguishing feature that only served to increase his attractiveness. A renowned swordsman, his body displayed the lanky grace of one who was expert in the sport of fencing. The earl was well-liked and well-respected. Women wanted him, and Isabel was no exception. A widower with two sons, he had no need for a wife, and he was good-natured. She usually enjoyed his company. In bed, and out.

"Yes, you," she said. "What would you like to do?"

"Whatever you desire," he said smoothly. "As always, I live for your happiness."

"It would make me happy to know what you want," she retorted.

Hargreaves' smile faded. "Why are you so out of sorts this evening?"

"Asking for your opinion does not make me out of sorts."

"Then why are you snapping at me?" he complained.

Isabel closed her eyes, and tamped down her frustration. Her irritation with John was Gray's fault. She looked at Hargreaves, and caught up his hand in hers. "What would you like to do? If we could do anything at all, what would give you the most pleasure?"

His scowl lifted as his lips curved in a sultry smile. He reached out and stroked the tiny bit of skin that was visible between her short sleeve and long glove. Unlike Gray's touch, it did not make her burn, but it did spread a gentle warmth that Hargreaves could stoke into a fire. "Your company gives me the most pleasure, Isabel. You know this."

"Then I will join you at your home shortly," she murmured.

He departed immediately. Isabel waited a discreet amount of time, and then she made her egress as well. During the carriage ride to Hargreaves House, she brooded over her situation and considered what, if any, options she had. John noted her preoccupation the moment she entered his bedroom.

"Tell me what troubles you," he murmured as he removed her cloak.

She sighed and admitted, "Lord Grayson has returned."

"Bloody hell." Hargreaves circled her and faced her head-on. "What does he want?"

"To live in his home, to regain his social life."

"What does he want *with you*?"

She noted his distress, and sought to soothe him. "Obviously I am here with you, and he is at home. You know how Grayson is."

"I know how he *was*, but that was four years ago." He moved away, pouring himself a drink. When he held the decanter up to her, she nodded gratefully. "I do not know how to feel about this, Isabel."

"You should not feel anything. His return does not affect you." Not like it affected her.

"I would be foolish not to see how it could affect me in the future."

"John." She accepted the proffered glass and kicked off her slippers. What could she say? Perhaps Gray's advances toward her had not been an anomaly. It was possible her husband would still want her in the morning. Then again, perhaps the stress of returning had addled him in some way. She could only hope that the latter was true. A girl should only have to live with one man like Pelham in a lifetime. "No one knows what the future will bring."

"God, Isabel. Do not spout phrases like that." He tossed back his drink and poured another.

"What would you like me to say?" she asked, hating that she could offer no words of comfort and still tell the truth.

He set his snifter down so hard the reddish liquid sloshed over the sides. Hargreaves ignored it, and came to her. "I want you to tell me it does not matter that he has returned."

"I cannot." She sighed, and lifted to her tiptoes to kiss the clenched line of his jaw. His arms came around her, and squeezed her tight. "You know I cannot. I wish I could."

Taking the glass from her, Hargreaves set it on the end table, and pulled her toward the bed. She shook her head.

"You deny me?" he asked, clearly incredulous.

"I am confused, John, and distressed. Both of which rather dampens my ardor. It is no reflection on you. I promise."

"You have never turned me away. Why did you visit? To torment me?"

Isabel pulled back, her lips pursed. "My apologies. I was unaware that I was only invited to fornicate." She tugged her hand from his, and moved away.

"Pel, wait." Hargreaves caught her about the waist, and buried his face in the curve of her neck. "Forgive me. I feel a gulf between us that was not there before, and I cannot bear it."

He turned her to face him. "Tell me truthfully. Does Grayson want you?"

"I don't know."

John released a frustrated breath. "How in hell can you not know, Isabel? You, of all women, should know if a man desires to be in your bed or not."

"You have not seen him. His garments are odd—coarse and overly simple. Wherever he has been, it has not been anywhere he would socialize. Yes, he lusts, John. I recognize that much. But is it *me* he lusts for? Or a woman in general? That is what I do not know."

"Then we must find your husband his own paramour," John said grimly. "So that he will leave mine alone."

She gave a weary laugh. "What an odd conversation to have."

"I know." Hargreaves grinned, and cupped her cheek in his hand. "Shall we sit, and plan a dinner, then? We can make a list of all the women we think Grayson would enjoy, and invite them."

"Oh, John." Isabel smiled her first genuine smile since Gray had returned. "That is such an inspired enterprise. Why could I not have thought of it?"

"Because that's what you have me for."

Gerard read the morning's newspaper over coffee, and attempted to ignore his anxiousness. He would be seen today, Society would know that he had returned. Over the next few days, old acquaintances would come to call, and he would have to decide which friendships to renew, and which would remain in the past.

"Good morning, my lord."

He looked up at the sound of Isabel's voice, and took a sharp, quick inhale as he stood. She was dressed in pale blue, her bodice low and displaying the generous curves of her breasts, while the waist was high and banded with darker blue ribbon. Her gaze would not meet his directly until he returned her greeting. Then she looked at him, and managed a smile.

Pel was obviously nervous, and it was the first time that he had ever seen her less than utterly confident. She stared at him a moment. Then her chin lifted, and she approached him. She pulled out the chair next to him before he could unlock his muscles and do it for her. He cursed inwardly. He had not been a monk for four years, but it had been a good while since his last liaison. Too long.

"Gray," she began.

"Yes?" he prodded when she hesitated.

"You need a mistress," she blurted.

He blinked, and then dropped back into his chair, holding his breath to avoid smelling her. One whiff of her perfume, and he would be hard, no doubt. "A mistress?"

She nodded, and bit her luscious bottom lip. "I doubt you will have any difficulty acquiring one."

"No," he said slowly. Good God. "With the proper attire, and a reintroduction to Society, I could manage the task, I'm sure." Gerard stood again. He could not talk about this with her. "Shall we go, then?"

"Eager, are we?" She laughed, and he grit his teeth at the lusty sound. The wariness that had stiffened her frame when she first entered was gone, leaving behind the Pel of old. A Pel who expected him to contract a mistress, and leave her alone.

"You ate upstairs, did you not?" He backed up a step, and breathed through his mouth. How in hell would he make it through the afternoon? Or the next week, or month? Or— bloody hell—years, as she often invested in her affairs.

"Yes." She stood. "Let's be off then, Lothario. Far be it for me to delay the discovery of your next amour."

Gerard followed at a safe distance, but doing so was not effective in quelling his lust due to the lamentable fact that he now had an excellent view of Isabel's gently swaying hips and lush derriere.

The landau ride was a bit better, as the open top helped to dissipate the scent of exotic flowers. And the walk on Bond Street was better than that, since he could no longer think about his errant cock while being gaped and pointed at. Pel walked beside him, chatting merrily, her lovely face shaded by a wide-brimmed straw hat.

"This is ridiculous," he muttered. "You would think I had risen from the dead."

"In a way, you have. You left without a word, and kept in touch with no one. But I think they are just as interested in the changes to your appearance."

"My skin is sun-darkened."

"Yes, it is. I quite like it. Other women will like it, too."

He glanced down at her in the course of his reply, and realized that from his vantage he had a prime view of her breasts.

"Where is the damned tailor's?" he growled, frustrated beyond measure.

"You *do* need a woman," she said, shaking her head. "Here we are. This is the establishment you listed in your old schedule, is it not?"

The door opened inward with a soft ring of bells, and within moments they were in a private fitting room. He was divested of his clothing, which Pel ordered away with a toss of her hand and a wrinkling of her nose. Gerard stood there in his smalls, and laughed. Until she turned to face him. Then the way she looked at him tightened his throat and choked off his merriment.

"Good heavens," she breathed, while circling him. Her fingertips brushed lightly across the ridges of his abdomen. He bit back a groan. The entire room smelled like her. Now she was touching him intimately.

The tailor entered, and gaped a moment in surprise. "I believe I will have to take new measurements, my lord."

Isabel stepped back quickly at the intrusion, her cheeks flushed. The tailor began to work, and she recovered quickly, directing her attention to talking the tradesman into parting with finished garments ordered by another customer.

"Surely, you would not wish His Lordship to leave your establishment in any manner other than suitably attired?" she asked.

"Of course not, Lady Grayson," came the ready reply. "But these are the closest to finished that I have, and they will not fit His Lordship. But perhaps I could add some extra material here."

"Yes, and let it out a little more there," she said, when the tailor pinned the material at his shoulder. "Look how broad he is. You can remove the padding. First and foremost, he must be comfortable."

Her hand drifted down his back, and Gerard clenched his fists to fight off a shudder. He was anything but comfortable.

"Do you have smalls that will fit him?" she asked, her voice lower and huskier than usual. "This material is too coarse."

"Yes," the tailor said quickly, eager to sell as much as possible.

The jacket was whisked away, and Gerard pulled on the matching trousers. They stood behind him, the tailor and Isabel, and he was grateful. He was holding off a cockstand by dint of will alone. He could not help being aroused. Pel's gaze was so hot, he felt it, and she continued to touch him and say admiring things about his body. A man could only take so much.

"Do not alter this," she breathed, her breath hot against his bare back. Her hand cupped the curve of his ass. "Is it too tight back here, my lord?" she asked him softly, caressing him. "I hope not. It looks wonderful."

"No. The back is fine." Then he lowered his voice so only she could hear. "But you have made the front damned uncomfortable."

The curtain moved to the side, and an assistant entered with the smalls. Gerard closed his eyes in misery. Everyone would see his condition now.

"Thank you," Isabel murmured. "Lord Grayson will need a moment."

He stood in surprise as she shooed the others out. Only when they were alone did he turn to face her. "Thank you, Isabel."

Her eyes were riveted to the placket of his trousers. She swallowed hard, and hugged the smalls to her chest. "You should remove those before you burst the seams."

"Will you help me?" he asked gruffly, hoping.

"No, Gray." She handed him the smalls, and looked away. "I told you, I have someone."

Gerard was tempted to remind her that she also had a

husband, but that would not be fair, considering how he had coerced her into marriage. Selfishly, he had wanted her as his wife to irritate his mother, and save himself from overly ambitious mistresses. He had paid no regard to the censure she would face by taking lovers without first providing him an heir. This was his repayment for his narcissism—to desire what belonged to him, but was not his to take.

He nodded, swallowing the bitterness of his regret. "Give me some privacy. If you would, please."

She did not look at him as she left.

Isabel stepped out of the fitting room, and closed the curtain behind her. Her hands shook terribly, incited by the sight of Gray's body as he dressed and undressed, teasing her with his male perfection.

He was in the prime of his life, retaining the power and strength of youth, while adding the maturity of tough times and a few years. He rippled with muscle everywhere, and she knew from being held against him yesterday that he wielded that power carefully.

Honestly, Gray. You are too young for me.

Why had she not stayed the straight course? Looking at him now, seeing all of his vigor and vitality, Isabel collected how wrong she had been to bind his life to hers.

He needed a lover to take up his time and attention. A man of his age was bursting with lust, and the primal desire to sow his oats. She was convenient and attractive, and so he wanted her. She was the only woman he knew, for the time being. But one does not have an affair with one's spouse.

Isabel groaned inwardly. God, why had she married again? She had made the ultimate commitment to avoid commitment, and look where that foolishness had landed her.

Men who looked like Gray were not constant. She had learned that lesson with Pelham. The dashing earl had needed a wife, and he'd lusted for her. A perfect combination in his mind. But once his infatuation had faded, he had moved on to the next bed, completely disregarding how in love with him she was. Grayson would move on as well. Certainly, he was more somber now, more grounded than when they had wed, but his age was undeniable.

Isabel could bear the rumors of his sexual prowess, and the innuendoes that she was too old to satisfy him or provide him an heir, as long as she felt no claim to him. She was faithful to her lovers, and expected the same in return for the duration of the affair. And therein lay the rub. Affairs were meant to be ended, while marriages lasted until death.

Isabel walked away, determined to find something to distract her from her thoughts. Moving toward the main room, she was intent on looking at the latest renderings, but the sliver of open curtain caught her eye. She paused. Then took a step back.

Against her will, she peeped through that tiny gap, and was arrested by the sight of Gray's fine derriere. Why had God given so much beauty to one man? And that ass! It was fiendish to have a man who looked as good from the back as he did from the front.

The firm cheeks were pale, especially in contrast to the deep tan of his torso. Where had he been, and what had he been occupied with to have developed those muscles and gained that skin color? He was glorious—his back, buttocks, and arms flexing with rhythmic power.

She released her held breath. It was then she noted *why* he was making those repetitive motions.

Gray was masturbating.

Christ! Isabel sagged against the wall as her knees went weak. She could not look away, even as her nipples tightened into aching points, and a slow trickle of arousal began deep inside her. Had she pushed him to this with a simple touch and a heated glance? The thought of holding so much power over such a glorious creature made her ache. Customers and employees scuttled behind her, and there she stood, obviously a voyeur. A woman of the world, she was nevertheless devastated by lust.

He was panting, his thighs straining, and she wished she could see the front of him. What did that beautiful face look like in the heat of passion? Was the lacing of muscle on his abdomen taut with tension? Was his cock as well built as the rest of him? Her imaginings were worse than the watching.

His head fell back, his dark hair drifting across his shoulders, and then he shuddered with a low, pained moan. Isabel moaned with him, sweat misting her skin, and then she turned away before he saw her. Before she saw him, in all his glory.

What the devil was she to do now?

Yes, she was a sensual woman, and the sight of a man pleasuring himself would titillate her, regardless. But never to this extent. She could barely breathe, and the need to climax was near maddening. It would be foolish to tell herself otherwise.

She recognized the tendrils of heat that curled low in her belly. Some called it desire. She called it destruction.

"Lady Grayson?" he called, in that deep raspy voice.

She placed that tone now that she had heard it enough. It was a bedroom voice, the sound of a man who had just cried out his pleasure. Why he should have that voice all the time, to torment women with the desire to give him reason to sound that way, was simply wrong.

"Y—yes?" She took a deep breath, and entered.

Gray faced her wearing the new smalls. His cheeks were flushed, his eyes knowing. She had not gone undetected.

"I hope one day you do more than watch," he said softly.

She covered the lower half of her face with a gloved hand, mortified and anguished. Yet he was unashamed. He stared at her intensely, his gaze taking in the outline of her hardened nipples.

"Damn you," she whispered, hating him for coming home

and turning her life upside-down. She ached all over, her skin too hot and too tight, and she detested the feeling and the memories it brought with it.

"I am damned, Pel, if I must live with you and not have you."

"We had a bargain."

"This," he gestured between them, "was not there then. What do you propose we do about it? Ignore it?"

"Spend it elsewhere. You are young and randy—"

"And married."

"Not truly!" she cried, ready to tear out her hair in frustration.

Gray snorted. "As truly as marriage can be without sex. I intend to correct that lack."

"Is that why you came back? To fuck your wife?"

"I came back because you wrote to me. Every Friday the post would come and there would be a letter, written with soft pink parchment and scented of flowers."

"You sent them back, every one of them. Unopened."

"The contents were not important, Pel. I knew what you did and where you went without your recounts. It was the thought that mattered. I had hoped you would desist, and leave me to my misery—"

"Instead you brought the misery to me," she snapped, pacing the length of the small room to ease the feeling of confinement. "It was my obligation to write to you."

"Yes!" he cried, triumphant. "Your obligation as *my wife*, which in turn forced me to remember that I had a like obligation to you. So I returned to quell the rumors, to support you, to correct the wrong I did you by leaving."

"That does not require sex!"

"Lower your voice," he warned, grabbing her arm and tugging her closer. He cupped her breast, his thumb and forefinger finding her erect nipple, and rolling it until she whimpered in helpless pleasure. "*This* requires sex. Look how aroused you are. Even in your fury and distress, I would wager you are wet between the thighs for me. Why should I take someone else, when it is you I want?"

"I have someone."

"You persist in saying that, but he is not enough, obviously, or you would not want me."

Guilt flooded her that her body should be so eager for him. She never entertained the idea of another man while attached to one. Months passed between her lovers, because she mourned the loss of each one, even though she was the party who said good-bye.

"You are wrong." She yanked her arm from his grip, her breast burning where he had touched her. "I do not want you."

"And I used to admire your honesty," he jeered softly.

Isabel stared at Gray, and saw his determination. The slow, dull ache in her chest was so familiar, a ghost of the hell Pelham had left her in.

"What happened to you?" she asked sadly, lamenting the loss of the comfort she once felt with him.

"The blinders were torn from me, Pel. And I saw what I was missing."

Chapter 3

Once appropriately attired, Gerard moved aside the curtain and stepped out into the short hall. He caught sight of Isabel immediately. Standing by the window, her auburn hair caught stray rays of sunshine and turned to fire. The contrast of those silken threads of flame against the ice blue of her gown was stunning, and very apropos. The heat of her desire had scorched him, even as she chilled him with her words. In fact, he was surprised she had remained the two hours it had taken to alter the pilfered garments. Gerard had half-expected her to leave. But Pel was not one to hide from things unpleasant. She may avoid discussing them, but she would not actually run from them. It was one of the quirky traits he rather liked in her.

He sighed, damning himself for pushing too hard, but he could do nothing differently. He did not understand her, and he could not make amends without comprehension. Why was she so determined to have nothing of importance between them? Why desire him, know he craved her in return, and refuse to act upon it? It was not like Isabel to deny herself the pleasures of the flesh. Did she perhaps love her present amour? His hands clenched into fists at the thought. Gerard was well aware that it was possible to love one person, and yet physically require the attentions of another.

At that thought, he cursed inwardly. He had obviously not changed all that much to have pawed and groped at his wife. What in hell was the matter with him? A gentleman did not treat his spouse in that fashion. He should be wooing her, not salivating to rut in her.

He called out as he approached so as not to startle her. "Lady Grayson."

Pel turned to face him with a winsome smile. "My lord. You look very dashing."

So it was that way, was it? Pretend as if nothing had happened.

He smiled with all the charm he possessed, and lifted her gloved hand to his lips. "A husband must, to escort a wife as fair as you, my lovely Isabel."

Her hand shook a little in his, and her voice when she spoke had a slight catch. "You flatter me."

He wished to do a great deal more to her, but that would have to wait. He tucked her hand around his arm, and led her to the door.

"Even I cannot do you justice," she said, as he retrieved her flowered straw hat from the clerk and set it on her head, pinning it in place with the ease of familiarity. The door chimes rang, and he stepped closer, his back to the street, to allow the new customer to pass. The air sweltered between him and Pel, flushing her skin and tensing his frame.

"You need a lover," she breathed, those sherry eyes wide and held by his gaze.

"I have no need of one. I have a wife who desires me."

"Good afternoon, my lord," the clerk called out, rounding the counter.

Gerard moved to her side, and offered his arm again. Now facing the doorway, he saw the distinguished-looking gentleman who wore an expression of such horror it did not take but a moment to register who it must be. And what he must have heard.

"Good afternoon, Lord Hargreaves." His fingers closed over Pel's on his arm, staking an irrefutable claim. Never having been a possessive man, he frowned and tried to examine why he should feel this way now.

"Good afternoon, Lord and Lady Grayson," the earl said tightly.

Isabel straightened. "Lord Hargreaves, a pleasure."

But it was not, not for any of them. The tension was palpable. "Excuse us," Gerard said when Hargreaves continued to block the doorway. "We were on our way out."

"Lovely to see you again, my lord," Isabel murmured, her voice unusually somber.

"Yes," Hargreaves muttered, stepping aside. "Quite."

Opening the door, Gerard gave one last studious look at his rival, and then led his wife out with a hand at the small of her back. They walked slowly down the street, both lost in their thoughts. Several pedestrians attempted to approach, but a narrowed glance was effective at keeping them away.

"That was awkward," he muttered finally.

"You noted that, did you?" she said, refusing to look at him.

In a way, he missed the overconfidence of his youth. Four years ago, he would have brushed off the encounter as amusing. In fact, he had done that very thing on several occasions, as social engagements had brought him face to face with Pel's lovers, and she with his. Now he was all too aware of his flaws and shortcomings, and to his knowledge the popular and respected Hargreaves had none.

"I've no notion of how I will explain your comment to him," she said, obviously upset.

"He knew the risks when he chose to dally with another man's wife."

"There were no risks! No one could predict that you would come home daft."

"It is not daft to desire your spouse. Pretending you don't, however, is ridiculous."

He stopped abruptly as a merchant door swung inward, and a customer ran out directly before them.

"My apologies, my lady!" the man cried to Pel, tipping his hat before he strode away quickly.

Gerard looked at the establishment, curious about the reason for the man's excitability. His mouth curved as he reached for the door.

"A jeweler's?" Isabel asked with a frown.

"Yes, vixen. There is something I should have attended to years ago."

He urged her inside, and the clerk lifted his head from the sales record book with a smile. "Good afternoon, my lord. My lady."

"That was a happy man who just departed," Gerard noted.

"Ah yes," the clerk agreed. "A bachelor embarking on an offer of marriage, which is strengthened by the lovely ring he purchased today."

In search of equal pleasure, Gerard perused the offerings in the glass cases.

"What are you looking for?" Pel asked, bending over beside him. Her scent appealed to him so deeply, he wished he could lay amongst satin sheets infused with it. With her graceful limbs entwined with his, it would be heaven.

"Have you always smelled so wonderful, Pel?" He turned his head to look at her, and found her almost nose to nose.

She pulled back with a blink. "Gray, really. Can we put off a discussion on perfumery, and find what you want?"

Smiling, he caught her hand, and glanced up at the hovering clerk. "That one." He pointed to the largest ring in the case—a massive ruby surrounded by diamonds, and supported by a filigreed band of gold.

"Heavens," Pel breathed, as it came out from behind its glass shield and sparkled in the light.

Gerard lifted her hand, and sized the ring on her finger, pleased to see it fit snugly, but not too tightly, over her glove. Now, she looked like a married woman. "Perfect."

"No."

He arched a brow, and discerned his wife's distress. "Why not?"

"It . . . it's too large," she protested.

"It suits you." He lounged against the case, and smiled, keeping her hand trapped firmly within his own. "While I was in Lincolnshire—"

"You were?" she asked quickly.

"Amongst other places," he said, stroking her palm. "I would watch the sunset, and think of you. There were times when a ribbon of red clouds in the sky would exactly match the highlights in your hair. When the light catches that ruby, it reflects almost the same color."

She stared at him as he lifted her hand to his mouth. He kissed first the stone, and then the middle of her gloved palm, relishing the opportunity to be close to someone again.

The sunrises, with all their warm golden beauty, had brought memories of Em. He'd dreaded them at first. Each morning reminded him that another day had come, and Emily would not be living it. Later, the warmth the sun brought had been a benediction, a reminder that he had another opportunity to become a better man.

The sunsets, however, had always belonged to Pel. The darkening sky and the welcoming blanket of night that disregarded his imperfections—that was Isabel, who never pried. The sensuality of a bed, and the moments when he could release the stress of the day—that was Isabel, too, lying on her chaise in her boudoir. How odd that her lighthearted companionship had come to mean so much to him, and yet he'd never noticed it when it had been his to enjoy.

"You should save your silver tongue for a woman less jaded than I."

"Dear Pel," he murmured, smiling. "I adore that you are jaded. You hold no illusions about my less-than-sterling character."

"I have no idea what your character is anymore." She pulled away, and he released her. Straightening her spine, Isabel glanced around the small store. When she saw the clerk busy recording their transaction, she said, "I don't understand why you would say such things to me, Gray. You never had any romantic notions, nor sexual ones, to my knowledge."

"What color are the flowers in front of our house?"

"I beg your pardon?"

"The flowers. Do you know what color they are?"

"Certainly, they're red."

He arched a brow. "Are you certain?"

She crossed her arms, and arched her own brow. "Yes, I'm certain."

"And the ones in the planters by the street?"

"What?"

"The planters by the street have flowers in them. Do you know what color those blooms are?"

Isabel chewed her lower lip.

Gerard tugged off his glove, and then tugged that lush bottom lip out of her teeth. "Do you?"

"They are pink."

"They're blue."

He moved his hand to her shoulder, and stroked the creamy expanse of skin with his thumb. The heat of her flesh burned through his fingertips, and spread up his arm, igniting a hunger such as he had not felt in years. For so long he had been numb and frozen inside. To feel this heat, to desire to burn with her touch, to want so desperately to be scorched inside her . . . He relished all of it.

"Blue flowers, Pel." His voice was huskier than he'd like. "I've found people tend to take for granted the things they see every day. But just because one fails to see something, does not mean it isn't there."

Goose bumps prickled her skin. He felt them, even through the calluses on his fingertips.

"Please." She brushed his hand away. "Don't lie, and say pretty things, and attempt to make the past into what you wish it to be in the present. We were nothing to each other, nothing. And I wanted it that way. I *liked* it that way." She tugged off the ring, and set it on the counter.

"Why?"

"Why?" she parroted.

"Yes, my lovely wife, why? Why did you like our marriage as a sham?"

Her eyes shot daggers at him. "You liked it as a sham, too."

Gerard smiled. "I know the reasons why I liked it, but we are talking about you."

"Here you are, Lord Grayson," the clerk said with a wide smile.

Cursing inwardly at the interruption, Gerard dipped the proffered quill in ink and signed the bill. He waited until the ring was boxed and tucked into his inner coat pocket before glancing at Isabel. As she had in the tailor's, she stood staring out the window with a ramrod straight spine, every inch of her voluptuous form betraying her anger. He shook his head, and could not help but think that all the restrained passion in her was untapped. What the devil was Hargreaves doing, or more likely *not* doing, that left her so volatile? Another man might see the rigidness of her spine, and be discouraged. Gerard took it as a sign of hope.

He walked to her, drawn to the vibrancy that attracted everyone. Coming to a stop directly behind her, he breathed her in, and then whispered, "Can I take you home with me?"

Startled by Gray's husky voice in her ear, Isabel spun about so quickly, he was forced to arch backward to avoid being whacked in the face with the brim of her hat. The near miss made him laugh, and once he started, he could not stop.

She gaped at him, awed by how young he looked when lost in merriment. His laugh sounded rusty, as if it had not been let out in awhile, and she loved the sound of it—deeper and richer than it had been before, and she had adored it even then. Unable to resist, she smiled, but when he grabbed his ribs and gasped, she had to laugh with him. Then he caught her about the waist, and spun her around, just like he used to do.

Setting her hands on his broad shoulders for balance, Isabel hung on, and remembered again how she enjoyed being with him.

"Put me down, Gray!" she cried.

With his head tilted back, he looked at her and said, "What will you give me if I do?"

"Oh, that's not fair. You are making a spectacle of us. Everyone will hear of this." She thought of Hargreaves' expression when he'd seen them in the tailor's, and her smile faded. How awful she was to cavort with Gray, when it would hurt John.

"A boon, Pel, or I will carry you around until you agree. I am quite strong, you know. And you are light as a feather."

"I am not."

"Are so." His lip made that little pout of his. It would look ridiculous on any other man, but on Gray it made women want to kiss him. It made Isabel want to kiss him.

"You think too much," he complained when she stared at him mutely. "You rejected my gift. Offering me a boon is the least you can do."

"What do you want?"

He considered it a moment, and then said, "Supper."

"Supper? Can you be more specific?"

"I want to have supper with you. Stay home tonight, and share a meal with me."

"I have commitments."

Gray moved to exit the shop. "My good man," he called out to the clerk. "The door, if you would please."

"You would not carry me outside like this."

"Do you truly believe I wouldn't?" he asked with a devilish smile. "I may have changed, but a leopard cannot completely lose its spots."

Isabel glanced over her shoulder, and saw the street approaching and the multitude of pedestrians who strolled there. "Yes."

He paused mid-step. "Yes, what?"

"Yes, I will have supper with you."

His grin was triumphant. "You are such a generous soul, Pel."

"Stuff," she muttered. "You are a blackguard, Grayson."

"Perhaps." He set her down, and then tucked her hand around his arm, leading her out to the street. "But really, would you want me any other way?"

Looking at him, seeing the lightening of the oppressive air that had surrounded him the day before, she knew she liked him best as a scoundrel. It was when he was most happy.

Just like Pelham.

Only a fool would make the same mistake twice.

Recognizing the voice of reason, Isabel reminded herself to heed it, and keep her physical distance from him. As long as he remained at least three feet away from her, she was fine.

"Lord Grayson!"

They both sighed as a rather large woman approached them wearing a monstrosity of a hat, and an even worse pink ruffled concoction of a dress.

"That is Lady Hamilton," Isabel whispered. "A lovely woman."

"Not in that garment," Gray replied through his smile.

It took everything she had not to laugh aloud.

"Lady Pershing-Moore told me she saw you with Lady Grayson," Lady Hamilton said, panting as she came to a halt before them. "I said she must be daft, but it seems she was correct." She beamed. "So wonderful to see you again, my lord. How was . . . wherever you were?"

Gray accepted the offered hand, bowed over it, and said, "Miserable, as any locale would be without the company of my charming and beautiful wife."

"Oh." Lady Hamilton shot Isabel a wink. "Of course. Lady Grayson accepted an invitation to my rout, which will be held the week after next. I do pray that you intend to accompany her."

"Certainly," Gray said smoothly. "After my extended absence, I intend to never be away from her side for even a moment."

"Wonderful! I now look forward to the event with even greater anticipation."

"You are too kind."

Saying her farewells, Lady Hamilton retreated quickly.

"Gray," Isabel began with a sigh. "Why stir up gossip in this way?"

"If you think there is any possibility that we will not be gossiped about, you are delusional." He continued down the street toward their waiting landau.

"Why add fuel to the fire?"

"Do they teach women how to speak in riddles in finishing school? I vow, you all do it so well."

"Damn you, I agreed to be your escort until you find your footing, but that will not take long, and once you go your own way—"

"We are going the same way, Pel," he drawled. "We're married."

"We can separate. After the last four years it would merely be a formality."

Gray took a deep breath, and looked down at her. "Why would I want to do that? Better yet, why would you?"

Isabel kept her eyes ahead. How could she explain, when she wasn't certain she knew the answer? She shrugged help-lessly.

His hand over hers, he gave a soft squeeze. "A great deal has happened in the last twenty-four hours. Give both of us some time to adjust to one another. I admit, things between us have not progressed the way I anticipated."

He assisted her into the landau, and then directed the driver home.

"What *did* you anticipate, Gray?" Perhaps if she knew his aim, she could find some understanding. Or at the very least ease some of her worry.

"I thought I would return, you and I would sit down with a few bottles of excellent vintage, and become reacquainted. I imagined slowly finding my way in this world, and settling into the comfort you and I once knew together."

"I would like that," she said softly. "But I doubt the possi-bility unless we can find a way to be like we were."

"Is that truly what you desire?" He twisted in the seat to face her, and her gaze dropped, noting how muscular and powerful his thighs were. She could not seem to cease taking note of such things now. "Do you love Hargreaves?"

Isabel's brows shot up. "Love him? No."

"Then there is hope for us." He smiled, but the determi-nation in his voice was unmistakable.

"Not that I don't care quite a bit for him, because I do. We have many interests in common. He is of a like age. We—"

"Does my age bother you, Isabel?" He studied her from beneath the brim of his hat, his blue eyes narrowed and con-sidering.

"Well, you *are* younger, and—"

Gray caught her about the neck, and pulled her close, tilt-ing his head to duck under her hat. His mouth—that sculpted mouth that could dazzle or sneer with equal effectiveness—brushed across hers.

"Oh!"

"I will not accept a sham anymore, Pel." He licked across her lips, and groaned softly. "God, the way you smell drives me insane."

"Gray," she gasped, pushing at his shoulders and discovering just how hard he was. Her lips trembled and burned. "People can see us."

"I don't care." He swiped his tongue quickly into her mouth, and she shivered at the taste of him. "You belong to me. I can seduce you if I want to." As his hand at her nape stroked softly, his voice lowered. "And I definitely want to."

He sealed his lips over hers, a brief tease, and then he pulled away, whispering, "Shall I demonstrate what a younger man can do for you?"

Her eyes drifted shut. "Please . . ."

"Please what?" His free hand rested next to her thigh, and kneaded her, sending waves of yearning through her body. "Please show you?"

She shook her head. "Please don't make me want you, Gray."

"Why not?" He tugged off his hat, and set his mouth to her throat, licking across her racing pulse.

"Because I will hate you forever if you do."

He pulled back quickly in surprise, and she took the opportunity to shove hard, which effectively knocked him over. He fell to his back, his arms flailing outward in an attempt to halt his descent. She flinched as his shoulders hit the side with a loud thump, leaving him nearly prone.

"What the devil?" Gray stared at her, wide-eyed.

She scrambled over to the rear-facing squab.

"Yes, you can have your way, Gray," she said grimly. "Much to my shame. But while my body may be all too willing to indulge, I happen to have morals, and a care for Hargreaves, who does not deserve to be set aside after nearly two years of companionship just for a rut."

"A *rut*, madam?" he growled, cursing as he nearly fell off

the seat in his attempt to sit up. "One does not 'rut' with their spouse."

Once he'd managed to resume his perch, the full extent of his arousal was revealed by the stretching of material between his legs. Isabel swallowed hard, and looked away quickly. *Good God.*

"What else could it be?" she said crossly. "We know nothing of one another!"

"I know you, Pel."

"Do you?" She snorted. "What is my favorite flower? Favorite color? Favorite tea?"

"Tulips. Blue. Peppermint." Gray snatched his hat off the floorboards, shoved it on his head, and crossed his arms.

She blinked.

"Thought I wasn't paying attention?"

Isabel bit her lower lip, and rifled through her memories. What were his favorite flowers, color, and tea? She was ashamed to realize she did not know.

"Ha!" he said triumphantly. "All well and good, Isabel. I shall give you the time you require to come around, and during that time you can learn all about me, and I about you."

The landau rolled to a halt outside their home. She glanced at the planters by the street, and saw the blue flowers. Gray leapt down, and then assisted her. He walked her up the steps, bowed, and then turned about.

"Where are you going?" she called after him, her skin still tingling from his touch, her stomach clenched at the determined set of his shoulders.

He paused, and looked back at her. "If I go in the house with you, I will take you, whether you will it or no." When she said nothing, his mouth curved mockingly. Within moments, he was gone.

Where would he go? He was obviously aroused, and virile enough that his release in the tailor's shop would not affect his ability to perform again. The thought of him occupied in carnal pursuits prodded her in a horribly familiar way. She knew what he looked like unclothed, and she knew that any other woman who saw him similarly would be putty in his hands. An ache she had thought to never feel again gnawed at her belly. A twinge from the past. A reminder.

Entering her home of nearly five years, Isabel discovered, to her dismay, that it already felt almost empty without Gray's vital presence. She cursed him for the upheaval he had wrought in only a few scant hours, and she took the stairs to her room determined to rectify the matter. Detailed planning of her dinner party was in order. She also needed to study her spouse, and ascertain his likes and dislikes.

Then, once she knew him, she would find the perfect mistress for him. She could only hope that Hargreaves' plan would work, and work quickly.

Experience had taught her that men like Gray could not be resisted for long.

Chapter 4

As Gerard ascended the steps to the double doors of Remington's Gentleman's Club, he knew that if it weren't for his frustration, he would be nervous. Inside the popular establishment, there would be at least several gentlemen whose wives or paramours had been sampled by him. In the past, he would have felt no awkwardness. *Rules do not apply in love or war,* he would have said. Now, he knew better. Rules applied everywhere, and he was not exempt from following them.

He handed his hat and gloves to one of the two attending footmen, and passed through the main gaming areas to the great room beyond. Seeking a deep armchair and a libation of some sort, he glanced around the room as he entered. He found comfort in the familiar surroundings. The smell of leather and tobacco reminded him that some things were timeless. A pair of light blue eyes met his, and then they looked away in a deliberate snub. Gerard sighed, accepting his due, then moved forward to make the first of what he knew would be an endless number of apologies to an equally infinite number of recipients.

He bowed, and said, "Good afternoon, Lord Markham."

"Grayson." The man who was once his closest friend did not even look at him.

"Lord Denby, Lord William," Gerard greeted the other two gentlemen who sat with Markham. He turned his attention back to the viscount. "I beg a moment of your time, Markham. If you would grant me that much, I would be eternally grateful."

"I do not think I can spare it," Markham said coldly.

"I understand. I will have to apologize to you here, then," Gerard said, unwilling to be denied.

Markham's head swiveled toward him.

"I am sorry my marriage caused you discomfort. As your friend, I should have had a care for your interests in the matter. I also offer my felicitations on your recent marriage. That is all I wished to say. Good day, gentlemen."

Gerard tilted his head slightly, and then turned about. He found his own small table and leather armchair, releasing his pent up breath as he sat. A few moments later, he opened the paper brought to him, and attempted to relax, a task made more difficult by the stares directed his way, and the peers who approached with greetings.

"Grayson."

He stiffened, and lowered his paper.

Markham stared at him for a long moment, and then gestured to the seat opposite him. "May I?"

"Certainly." Gerard set aside his reading, as the viscount settled into his chair.

"You look altered."

"I would like to think I am."

"I would say so, *if* your apology was sincere."

"It was."

The viscount ran a hand through his dark blond locks, and smiled. "My marriage is pleasant, which eases the sting immeasurably. But tell me this, as I've wondered for years, did she set me aside for you?"

"No. Honestly, you were our only connection up until the moment we spoke our vows."

"I fail to understand. Why deny my suit, but accept yours, if there was nothing between you?"

"Does any man discuss the reasons why his wife married him? Does any man ever know? Whatever her impetus, I am a most fortunate man."

"Fortunate? You have been absent for four bloody years!" the viscount cried, studying him. "I almost did not recognize you."

"A great deal can happen in that time span."

"Or *not* happen," Markham said. "When did you return?"

"Yesterday."

"I spoke with Pel the day before, and she said nothing to me."

"She was not aware." Gerard gave a mirthless laugh. "And, unfortunately, she is not as pleased as I would wish."

Markham settled more comfortably into the big chair, and gestured to a nearby footman for a drink. "I am surprised to hear that. You two always rubbed along famously."

"Yes, but as you noted, I have changed. My tastes are different, as are my goals."

"I wondered how it was that you were immune to Pel's charms," the viscount said, laughing. "Fate does have a way of balancing the scales, if given enough time. I would be lying if I said I wasn't pleased to see you suffer a bit."

Gerard gave a reluctant smile. "My wife is a mystery to me, which deepens my dilemma."

"Isabel is a mystery to everyone. Why do you think so many wish to possess her? The challenge is irresistible."

"Do you remember her marriage to Pelham?" Gerard asked, wondering why he had never bothered to inquire before. "I would like to hear of it, if you do."

Markham accepted the mug offered to him by the attendant, and nodded. "There is not a peer my age who has forgotten Lady Isabel Blakely as she was in her youth. She is Sandforth's only daughter, and he doted on her. Still does, as far as I know. It was known that her dowry was substantial, which attracted the fortune hunters, but she would have been popular, regardless. We all awaited her coming out eagerly. I had plans to offer for her even then. But Pelham was wily. He did not wait. He seduced her fresh out of the schoolroom, before any of us had a chance at wooing her."

"Seduced?"

"Yes, seduced. It was obvious to everyone. The way they looked at one another . . . Theirs was a grand passion. Whenever they were in close proximity, the heat was palpable. I envied him that, the worship of a woman so obviously ripe and willing. I had hoped to have that with her, but it wasn't to be. Even after he began to stray, she still adored him, although it was clear it pained her greatly. Pelham was a fool."

"Hear, hear," Gerard muttered, silently examining the flare of jealousy he felt.

Markham chuckled, and took a long drink. "You remind me of him. Or rather, you did before. He was two and twenty when he married her, and just as cocky as you. In fact, Pel used to note often how much you reminded her of Pelham. When you married, I assumed that was why. But then you kept on with your distractions, and she with hers. You confounded all of us, and angered more than a few. It seemed a waste to have Pel finally remarried, only to have it be to a man who had no interest in her."

Gerard stared down at his hands, which were reddened and callused from hard work. He twisted the thin gold band he wore, a piece of jewelry he and Pel had bought as a lark, jesting that it would never see the light of day. He wasn't quite sure why he wanted to wear it, but now that it was on, he found he liked it. It was an odd feeling, the feeling of belonging to someone. He wondered if Pel had felt it when she wore the ring he'd bought her this afternoon, and if that was why she had rejected it so summarily.

The viscount laughed. "I really should hate you, Gray. But you make it damn difficult."

Gerard's brows lifted into his hairline. "I've done nothing to stop you from hating me."

"You're thinking, and brooding. If those are not signs that you have changed, I've no notion what would be. Cheer up. She's yours now, and unlike myself or Pearson or any of the others, she cannot set you aside."

"But there is Hargreaves," he reminded.

"Ah yes, there is that," Markham said with a broad grin. "As I said, fate does have a way."

"I am horribly disappointed that your errant spouse is not at home," the Duchess of Sandforth complained.

"Mother." Isabel shook her head. "I cannot believe you hastened here simply to ogle Gray."

"As if I wouldn't." Her Grace smiled with the wide grin of a naughty cat. "Bella, you should know by now that over-whelming curiosity is one of my vices."

"One of many," Isabel grumbled.

Her mother ignored that. "Lady Pershing-Moore came to call, and you cannot imagine how dreadful it was that she knew every minute detail of Grayson's appearance, while I did not even know he was in town."

"The only dreadful thing is that woman." Isabel paced the length of her boudoir. "I'm certain she has filled as many gossip-hungry ears as she could manage in one day."

"Is he as fine as she says?"

Sighing, Isabel admitted, "Yes, I'm afraid so."

"She swore the way he looked at you was indecent, is that true as well?"

Isabel paused, and stared at her mother, gazing into eyes of rich, dark brown. The duchess was still considered a great beauty, though her auburn hair was now liberally shot with silver strands. "I am not discussing this with you, Mother."

"Why not?" Her Grace replied, affronted. "How delicious! You have a stunning lover, and a young husband who is even more stunning. I envy you."

Pinching the bridge of her nose, Isabel sighed. "You should not envy me. This is a disaster."

"Ah ha!" Her mother leapt to her feet. "Grayson does want you. About time, if you ask me. I was beginning to wonder if he wasn't a bit touched."

He *was* touched in the head, in Isabel's opinion. They had known one another for years, and lived together for six months with nary a spark. Now it was a conflagration whenever she merely laid eyes on him. On second thought, perhaps she was touched, too. "I need to find him a woman," she muttered.

"You are not a woman? I was certain the doctor assured me you were."

"Mother, good grief. Be serious, please. Grayson needs a mistress."

Moving to the window, Isabel moved aside the sheers, and stared out at the small side garden. She could not help but remember the morning he'd stood below the window of her townhouse, and begged her to admit him. Then begged her to marry him.

Say yes, Pel.

Another memory, one fresher in her mind, was from yesterday afternoon when Gray had stood behind her in this exact spot, and made her want him, which had ruined everything.

"How does his need for a mistress relate to his wish to bed you?" the duchess asked.

"You would not understand."

"You are correct about that." Her mother came over, and set her hands on her shoulders. "I thought you had learned something from Pelham."

"I learned *everything* from Pelham."

"Do you not miss that passion, that fire?" Her Grace

spread her arms wide, and spun around with the exuberant carelessness of a young girl, her dark green skirts twirling around her. "I live for it, Bella. I crave those indecent looks, and thoughts, and actions."

"I know you do, Mother," Isabel said dryly. Her parents had long ago decided to find their romances outside the marital bed, a state of living they both seemed quite content with.

"I thought perhaps you had set aside those silly dreams of lifetime love when you began to take your own lovers."

"I did."

"I don't believe so." Her mother frowned.

"Simply because I think fidelity is a sign of respect, does not mean I attach it to love, or the hope for love." Isabel moved back toward her escritoire, where she had been working on menus and a guest list for her upcoming dinner.

"Bella, my sweet." Her mother sighed, and returned to the chaise where she poured a cup of tea. "It is not in a husband's nature to be faithful, especially handsome and charming husbands."

"I wish they would not lie about it," Isabel said crossly, shooting a glance at the portrait on the wall. "I asked Pelham if he loved me, if he would be true to me. He said, *'All women pale in comparison to you.'* And foolish chit that I was, I believed him." She threw up her hands.

"Even if they have the best of intentions, it is impossible for them to resist all the light-skirts who fall into their beds. Wishing for beautiful men to act against their nature will only lead to heartbreak."

"Obviously I have no desire for Gray to act against his nature, or I would not be actively working toward procuring him a mistress."

Isabel watched her mother drop three lumps of sugar and a ridiculous amount of cream into her tea. She shook her head when her mother lifted the pot in silent query.

"I fail to see why you do not enjoy his attentions while he

is willing to give them to you. Good heavens, the way Lady Pershing-Moore persisted about his appearance, I think I would take him myself if he were interested."

Closing her eyes, Isabel released a long-suffering sigh.

"You should take lessons from your brother, Bella. He is far more practical about such matters."

"Most men are. Rhys would be no exception."

"He has made a list of marriageable females and—"

"A list?" Isabel's eyes flew open. "Now that is too much!"

"It's perfect. Your father and I did the same, and look how happy we are."

Isabel held her tongue.

"Is it tenderness for Hargreaves that holds you back?" her mother asked softly.

"I wish it were. This would be so much simpler." Then she could disregard Gray's sudden preoccupation with her, and deal with him the way she dealt with any overzealous swain—with a smile and a dash of humor. She found it very hard to smile and be humorous when her nipples ached and she was damp between the thighs.

"We rub along well, Gray and I. I like him, he's great fun. I could live with great fun, Mother. For a lifetime. I could not live with a man who had wounded me in some fashion. I am softer than you, and bear scars from Pelham."

"And you think finding Grayson a mistress will make him less appealing? No, don't answer that, darling. I know you find attached men unattractive. An admirable scruple." Her Grace rose, and came to her, setting her slender arm around her daughter's waist and perusing the notes. "No, no. Not Lady Cartland." She gave a delicate shudder. "I would wish a pox on a man before I'd wish her on him."

Isabel laughed. "Very well." She dipped the quill and drew a slash across the name. "Who then?"

"Was he not with someone when he left? Besides Emily Sinclair?"

"Yes . . ." Isabel thought for a moment. "Ah, I remember. Anne Bonner, an actress."

"Invite her. He left for reasons other than boredom, so perhaps there is still something there."

A sharp pang of loneliness took Isabel off guard, and her hand paused above the parchment long enough to create an ink drop. "Thank you, Mother," she said softly, grateful, for once, to have her parent with her.

"Of course, Bella." The duchess leaned over, and pressed their cheeks together. "What are mothers for, if not to help their daughters find mistresses for their husbands?"

Isabel lay on her bed and attempted to read, but nothing could hold her attention. It was just after ten, and she had remained at home as Gray had asked. The fact that he had not redeemed his requested boon was his error, and if he thought he could collect later, he was sorely mistaken. She would not be affording him the option again. Canceling her plans for one evening was enough of an imposition, especially when he didn't have the courtesy to show up.

This was, of course, what she had hoped for, that he would find his pleasures elsewhere. This was exactly what she wanted. Everything was going well. Perhaps she wouldn't need to hold a homecoming dinner after all. What a relief. She could set aside the planning, and direct her attentions to living her life as she had before her husband returned.

She released her breath, and considered retiring when she heard a sound from the boudoir. Surely it wasn't excitement she felt, as she tossed aside the book. She was simply investigating. Anyone would if they heard strange noises in their suite.

Isabel ran into the next room, and threw open the hallway door. Then gaped.

"Hello, Pel," Gray said, standing in the gallery in only his rolled-up shirtsleeves and trousers. Bare feet, bare throat, and bare forearms. With his thick, dark hair damp from a recent bath.

Dastardly.

"What do you want?" she grumbled, upset that he would come to her dressed, or undressed as the case may be, in that fashion.

He arched a brow, and lifted his arm, bringing a small basket up to her eye level. "Supper. You promised. You cannot withdraw now."

She stepped back to allow him entry, and attempted to hide her blush. Failing to see the obvious basket because she was ogling him was mortifying. "You missed dinner."

"I didn't believe you would want me." The double entendre was clear. He stepped into her room, and she could not help but breathe in his scent as he walked by. The size of her satin-draped boudoir shrank to embrace him, and enclosed them together. "Supper, however, was guaranteed."

"Are your only pursuits those that are guaranteed?"

"Obviously not, or I wouldn't be here." Gray sat on the floor by the low table, and opened the basket. "You shan't chase me away with your ill-humor, Isabel. I waited all day for this meal, and I intend to enjoy it. If you've nothing charming to say to me, put one of these pheasant sandwiches in your mouth, and just let me look at you."

She stared at him, and then he lifted his gaze and winked one of those blue eyes at her. Her descent to the floor was only partially due to courtesy. The rest was due to suddenly weak knees.

He pulled out two glasses and a bottle of wine. "You look lovely in pink satin."

"I thought you reconsidered." She lifted her chin. "So I changed."

"No need to worry," he said dryly. "I had no illusions that you dressed to entice me."

"Rogue. Where have you been?"

"You never used to ask me that."

Isabel had never cared before, but she would not say that aloud. "You used to volunteer information, now you share nothing."

"Remington's," he said around a bite.

"All evening?"

He nodded, and reached for his glass.

"Oh." She knew of the courtesans there. Remington's was a bastion of male iniquity. "D–did you enjoy yourself?"

"You aren't hungry?" he asked, ignoring the question.

Lifting her wine, she took a large swallow.

Gray laughed, the sound pouring over her like warm liquid. "That's not food."

She shrugged. "Did you enjoy yourself?" she asked again.

His look was pure exasperation. "I would not have stayed as long as I did if I were miserable."

"Yes, of course." He'd bathed, and changed his clothes. Isabel supposed she should be grateful that he did not come to her reeking of sex and perfume, as Pelham had done on several occasions. Her stomach roiled at the thought, though the image in her mind was of Grayson and not Pelham, and she moved up to the chaise, lying on her back to stare at the tented ceiling. "No. I am not hungry."

A moment later she was inundated with the smell of Gray— that of starched linen and sandalwood soap. He sat on the floor beside her, and caught up her hand in his own.

"What can I do?" he asked softly, his callused fingertips drifting over her palm, sending heated frissons across her skin. "It pains me that my presence distresses you so, but I cannot stay away, Pel. Do not ask me to."

"And if I did?"

"I could not oblige you."

"Even after tonight's amusements?"

His fingers stilled, and then he gave a low chuckle. "I

should be a good husband, and set your mind at ease, but I have just enough of the rapscallion left in me to want you to suffer a bit, just as I will be suffering."

"Men who look like you never suffer, Gray," she retorted with a snort, turning her head to meet his gaze.

"There are men who look like me? How disheartening."

"See how our relationship alters when you change your role from friend to husband?" she complained. "Lies, evasions, things left unsaid. Why do you want us to live in that manner?"

Gray ran a hand through his hair, and groaned.

"Can you answer me that, Gray? Please help me to understand why you wish to ruin our friendship."

His eyes met hers, filled with the bleakness she had felt around him yesterday. Her heart swelled with emotion at the sight. "God, Pel." He set his cheek against her thigh, his dark hair dampening the satin. "I don't know how to discuss this, and not sound maudlin."

"Try."

He stared at her for a long time, his long eyelashes shielding his thoughts and casting shadows upon his cheekbones. The fingers that stroked her palm stopped, and entwined with hers. The simple intimacy was like a physical blow. For a moment, she found it difficult to breathe.

"After Emily died, I despised myself, Isabel. You've no notion of how I wronged her—so many ways, so many times. What a waste it was for a woman like her to perish due to a man like me. It took me a long while to accept the self-loathing, and realize that while I could not change the past, I could honor her by changing who I was in the future."

She tightened her grip on his hand, and he squeezed back. It was then she felt the unrelenting curve of a ring on his finger. Grayson had never worn his wedding band before. That he wore it now gave her a jolt that made her shiver violently.

He nuzzled his face against her, making her gasp at the

resulting flare of longing. Misunderstanding her distress, he said, "This is dreadful. I apologize."

"No . . . Continue. Please. I want to know everything."

"It is a miserable task attempting to change one's character," he said finally. "I think whole years passed without finding anything worth smiling about. Until you walked into the study yesterday. Then, in that one moment, I saw you and felt a spark." He lifted their joined hands, and kissed her knuckles. "Then later, in this room, I smiled. And it felt good, Pel. That spark turned into something else, something I have not felt in years."

"Hunger," she breathed, her eyes riveted to his impassioned face. She knew the feeling, because it gnawed at her now.

"And desire, and *life,* Isabel. And that is from the outside. I can only dream about what it would be like from the inside." Gray's voice deepened, and turned husky with want, his eyes now free of the abject torment she had witnessed in them when he'd first arrived. "Deep inside you, as far as I can go."

"Gray . . ."

His head turned, his hot, open mouth pressing against her upper thigh, burning through the pink satin of her robe and night rail. She tensed all over, her spine arching gently in a silent plea for more.

Tormented, Isabel pushed his head away. "After you have slaked that hunger, what happens to us then? We could not go back to what we had before."

"What are you talking about?"

"Have you never found that you can no longer eat a food you used to crave? Once hunger is appeased, the dish you gorged on becomes unappetizing." She sat up, and slipped past him. Rising to her feet, she began to pace, as was her wont when agitated. "We would be truly estranged then. I would most likely choose a different property in which to reside. Social events where we meet would become uncomfortable."

He rose to his feet, and followed her with his gaze. A gaze that was tactile in its intensity. "You see your former lovers every day. They are sociable with you, and you with them. What makes me different?"

"I do not look at them over coffee in the morning. I do not rely on them to settle my accounts, and see to my welfare. They do not wear my ring!" She paused, and closed her eyes, shaking her head at the foolishness of her errant mouth.

"Isabel," he began softly.

She held up her hand, and stared at the portrait on the wall. A golden god stared back at her, forever arrested in his prime. "We will find you a paramour. Sex is sex, and another woman would be far less messy."

Her husband moved with such grace, she failed to hear him approach. Gray's encircling arms came as a surprise—one banding her waist, the other crossing her torso so a large hand could cup her breast possessively. She cried out as her feet left the floor, and he buried his face in her neck. The feel of his body was so hot and hard behind her, filled with strength, yet tender in its clasp.

"I do not require your assistance to find sex. I require *you*." He licked and nipped at the tender skin of her throat, and then he breathed her in, his arms tightening around her with a low groan. "I want messy. And sweaty and dirty. God give me strength, for I have been cursed with wanting that from my wife."

Isabel burned at the feel of his erection, and then melted in his embrace when he ground it against her in near desperation. "No."

"But I can be gentle, Pel. I can love you well." His grip lightened, his fingertips softly teasing her nipple. She writhed in his arms, the ache between her legs nearly unbearable.

"No . . ." she moaned, wanting him with every breath in her body.

"See your ring on my finger," he growled, obviously frustrated. "Know that I am yours. That I am different from the others." Gray licked the shell of her ear, and then bit the lobe. "Want me, damn you. The way I want you."

Grayson set her aside with a curse, and left the room, leaving Isabel to the warring halves within her—the part of her that knew an affair with Gray could not last, and the part of her that did not care if it didn't.

Chapter 5

Gerard stood in his parlor, and silently cursed the crowd that gathered there. The daylight hours were his time to spend with Pel and work on building their rapport. Tonight, he knew she would venture out and dazzle the peerage with her charm and beauty. Isabel was a social creature who enjoyed time spent in the company of others, and until he had acceptable garments he could not escort her. So he had determined to make the most of the time he was afforded, perhaps take her on a picnic. But then the callers had begun to arrive. Now their home swarmed with curious visitors who wanted to see both him, and the state of his scandalous marriage.

Resigned, he watched his wife pour tea for the women around her. Isabel sat in the middle of the settee, surrounded by blondes and brunettes who paled in comparison, her auburn hair striking and distinguishing. She wore a high-waisted gown of cream-colored silk, a shade uniquely suited to her pale skin and radiant tresses. In his parlor, which was decorated in striped blue damask, she was in her element, and he knew that despite the reasons why they had married, Pel had been an excellent choice as a bride. She was charming and gracious. He could find her easily, simply by following the sounds of laughter. People were happy in her presence.

As if she felt the weight of his regard, Isabel lifted her gaze and caught his eye. A soft pink flush swept up her chest to color her cheeks. He winked at her and smiled, just to watch her blush deepen.

How had it ever escaped his notice how she stood apart from all other women?

He could not help but note it now. Simply being in the same room with her made his blood thrum in his veins, a feeling he had once thought to never feel again. Isabel had attempted to keep her distance by moving from room to room, but he followed her, needing the flare of awareness he felt only in proximity to her.

"She is lovely, is she not?"

Gerard turned to the woman at his side. "Indeed, Your Grace." A smile curved his mouth at the sight of Pel's mother, a woman of renowned beauty. It was obvious his wife would age just as well. "She takes after her mother."

"Charming, and dashing," Lady Sandforth murmured, returning his smile. "How long will you be staying this time?"

"As long as my wife is here."

"Interesting." She arched a brow. "May I be so bold as to ask why you have had a change of heart?"

"The fact that she is my wife is not enough?"

"Men desire their wives in the beginning, my lord. Not four years later."

He laughed. "I am a little slow, but I'm catching up."

A movement caught his eye, and Gerard turned his head to discover Bartley at the door. He took a moment to think, trying to decide how he should proceed. They had once been friends, but only in the most mercenary sense of the word. He made his excuses, and moved to meet the baron, offering a genuine smile of welcome.

"Bartley, you look well." And indeed he did, having lost a good portion of the weight that had thickened his waistline.

"Not as well as you, Gray," Bartley returned. "Although I

admit, you appear to have the chest of a laborer. Have you been working your own fields?" He laughed.

"Occasionally." Gerard gestured down the short hallway by the stairs. "Come. Have a cigar with me, and tell me what trouble you've occupied yourself with in my absence."

"First, I have brought you a present."

Gerard's eyebrows rose. "A gift?"

Bartley's florid complexion was mitigated by a broad grin. "Yes. Since you've just returned, and have yet to truly socialize, I knew you would be a tad . . . shall we say, lonely?" He gestured toward the front door with a jerk of his head.

Curious, Gerard's gaze followed the prodding, and he saw the dark-haired beauty by the front door—Barbara, Lady Stanhope. Her mouth curved in a smile so carnal, it could only be called wicked. He remembered that smile, remembered how it had incited his lust and a torrid nine-month affair. Barbara liked her fucking sweaty and messy, too.

He moved to greet her, lifting her proffered hand to kiss the back. Her long nails raked his palm with sensual deliberation.

"Grayson," she said, in a girlish voice that did not suit her disposition. That had turned him on, too, hearing that innocent angel's voice while he used her lush body. "You look divine, at least from what I can see of you with your clothes on."

"You also look well, Barbara, but then you knew that."

"When I heard you had returned, I came quickly, before another woman snatched you up."

"You should not have come to my home," he admonished.

"I know, darling, and I'm leaving. I just knew I would have a better chance at you if you saw me in person. A note is so impersonal, and not nearly as fun as touching you." Her eyes, clear as jade and just as beautifully colored, sparkled with amusement. "I would like us to be friends again, Gray."

Gerard arched a brow, and his mouth curved in an indulgent smile. "A lovely offer, Barbara, but I must decline."

She reached out and brushed a hand down his stomach, giving a soft purr. "I heard the rumors of you and Lady Grayson reconciling."

"We were never estranged," he corrected, taking a small step backward.

Barbara gave a soft pout. "I do so hope you will reconsider. I've procured a room at our favorite hotel. I will be there for the next three days." She blew a kiss to Bartley, then she looked up again. "I hope to see you there, Grayson."

He bowed. "I wouldn't wait up."

As the footman closed the door behind his lascivious guest, Bartley came to his side. "You can thank me with brandy and a cigar."

"I have never required your services in this particular regard," Gerard said dryly.

"Yes, yes, I know. But you've just arrived, and I wanted to save you a spot of trouble. No need to keep her when you're done with her."

Shaking his head, Gerard led Bartley away from the door to his study. "You know, Bartley. I doubt there is a chance in hell of reforming you."

"Reforming me?" the baron cried, horrified. "Good God, I should hope not. How dreadful."

The hour was nearly six before their home was empty of visitors. As Isabel stood in the foyer beside Grayson and watched the last callers depart, she could not contain her sigh of relief. The entire day had been a study in misery and clenched teeth. She could swear that every one of Gray's former paramours had come calling today. At least the peeresses had, the ones who knew she could not turn away. And Gray had been charming and witty, making every one of those odious women infatuated with him all over again.

"Well, that was trying," she muttered. "Despite what a

scoundrel you are, you remain popular." She turned, and took the stairs. "Of course, the majority of visitors were women." *Young* women.

The soft chuckle beside her was maddeningly smug. "Well, you do wish me to contract a mistress," Gray reminded.

She shot him a sidelong glance, and found that lusciously etched mouth twitching with a withheld smile. She snorted. "Shameless of them to come to *my* home, and ogle you within my view."

"Perhaps scheduled interviews would please you better?" he suggested.

Coming to an abrupt halt on the next-to-last stair, Isabel set her hands on her hips and glared at him. "Why are you deliberately trying to provoke me?"

"Sweetheart, I loathe being the one to point this out to you, but you were already provoked." He let that smile out, and she gripped the railing to support herself at the sight of it. "I must admit, it warms my heart to see you so jealous."

"I am *not* jealous." Isabel took the last stair, and turned down the hallway. "I simply require a little respect to be afforded to me in my own home. And, I learned long ago that any man who makes a woman jealous is not worth having."

"I agree."

The softly spoken acknowledgment startled her, and her steps faltered just before she reached her door.

"I hope you keep in mind, Pel," he murmured, "that I did not enjoy those visitors any more than you did."

"Liar. You adore fawning women. All men do."

It is not in a husband's nature to be faithful, especially handsome and charming husbands, her mother had said, and Isabel knew that firsthand. Of course, Gray had not lied to her. He made no promises to be faithful, only to be a good lover, a fact she did not doubt.

"I adore fawning women only when they are temperamental marchionesses with satin-draped boudoirs." He reached around her, turning the brass knob, his arm brushing against the side of her breast. "What vexes you, Isabel?" he asked, his mouth to her ear. "Where is that smile I long for?"

"I am trying to be pleasant, Gray." She hated being ill-humored. It was not in her nature.

"I had other plans for today."

"You did?" She did not know why it bothered her that he had somewhere to go, a task to accomplish that did not include her.

"Yes." He licked the shell of her ear, his broad shoulders blocking out everything but him. "I had hoped to spend the day wooing you, and showing you my charming side."

Isabel pushed against his chest, tamping down the little quiver his words and nearness gave her. He leaned closer, resting one hand against the jamb, surrounding her with his scent and hard body. A thick lock of his dark hair fell over his brow, making him look relaxed and very much like a six-and-twenty-year-old man.

"I have seen quite enough of your charming side." And his passionate side. She shivered at the memory of his arms around her, and his lips at her throat.

"Are you cold, Isabel?" he asked, his voice low and intimate, his gaze half-lidded. "Shall I warm you?"

"Frankly," she whispered, her hands brushing over the top of his shoulders, which made him shudder. "I am very hot at the moment."

"Me, too. Stay home with me tonight."

She shook her head. "I really must go out." Stepping back into her room, she expected him to follow, but he did not.

"Very well." Gray sighed, and ran a hand through his hair. "Will you be taking dinner in your room?"

"Yes."

"I have some tasks to attend to, then I will return and watch you prepare. I hope you have no objections. A man must find his pleasures where he can."

"No, I have no objections." She was beginning to realize that the thought of him finding pleasure elsewhere was highly disturbing.

"Until later then." He pulled the door closed, and Isabel stared at the portal for long moments after he had departed.

Over the course of the next few hours, she bathed and ate a light meal. Normally she would gossip with Mary during her toilette. Servants knew the prime bits, and she liked to hear them. Today, however, Isabel was quiet. Her mind was occupied with the events of the afternoon. She knew some of the women in her home today were intimately familiar with her husband. Over the last four years, she had met those same women many times and thought nothing of it. Now it bothered her to such an extent, she could not stop thinking about it.

Worse than that, though, were the new women, the ones not in his past, but in his future. The ones who had come to bat their eyelashes, touch his arm, and smile with carnal promise. Every one of them so certain Isabel would not mind. Why would she? She had Hargreaves, and she had never minded before. Fact was, she did mind. Knowing one of those women would soon share Gray's bed made her blood simmer. Dressed only in her chemise and underbust corset, she was nevertheless overheated by her thoughts and frustration.

She closed her eyes as her abigail swept her hair up, and arranged it in the popular style of short curls around her face. There was a slight knock at the door, and then it opened without further ado. The presumptive move was slightly disturbing, but what bothered her most was the direction from whence the sound came. Opening her eyes, she looked to the side, and watched Gray enter from the adjoining bedroom.

"What . . . ?" she sputtered.

He took a deep breath, and then sprawled on her favorite chaise. "You look ravishing," he said, as if it were perfectly normal for him to enter from the master suite. "Or more aptly, ravishable. Is that a word, Pel? If not, it should be, with your likeness rendered next to it."

From the time they had married, he had kept a room down the hall and around the corner from hers. She had offered to take a suite in the guest area, since this was his home and their marriage a sham, but he had pointed out how much more time she spent at home than he did. Which was true. She slept in her bed every night. Gray sometimes did not sleep in his room for days on end.

The thought sparked her temper. "What were you doing in there?"

He blinked innocently. "Whatever I felt like. Why?"

"There is nothing in there besides empty furniture."

"On the contrary," he drawled. "Most of my possessions are in there. At least the ones I use on a regular basis."

Her fingers curled around the edge of her vanity. The thought of Gray sleeping mere feet from her, with only a door to separate them, was instantly arousing. She pictured his body nude, as she had seen it in the tailor's. She wondered if he slept facedown, with those powerful arms wrapped around a pillow and that luscious, tight ass bare to her view. Or perhaps faceup? The feel of his cock was imprinted on her derriere from last night. The long, hard heat of him . . . Bare . . . Gray's beautiful body sprawled in sleep . . . Tangled in sheets . . .

Oh Lord . . .

Swallowing hard, she looked away from him before he could read her thoughts or see her turmoil.

"Bartley inherited a chicken."

"Beg your pardon?" Isabel's eyes moved to her husband's again. As he had the night before, he was dressed in loose trousers and shirtsleeves, a tempting sight, which she was certain he knew. They would have to deal with his changing rooms eventually, but she did not have the heart to tackle the argument now. She already had an altercation ahead of her when she met with Hargreaves.

"Bartley's aunt was an eccentric," he replied, his voice directed upward as he moved to lie on his back. "She kept a chicken as a pet. When he last visited her, she was so pleased with her chicken he felt it best to agree and say that it was the handsomest chicken he had ever seen."

"A handsome chicken?" Her lips twitched.

"Quite." She could not miss the smile in his voice. "When she passed on, she bequeathed portions of her estate to her many relatives and—"

"Bartley was given the chicken."

"Yes." Gray's laughing eyes met hers in the mirror as she stood to don her gown. "No, don't laugh, Pel. This is serious, you know."

Her abigail smothered a giggle.

"Oh, of course," Isabel said gravely, schooling her features.

"The poor creature is mad for Bartley. But then I do believe chickens have pea-sized brains."

"Gray!" she cried, laughing.

"Apparently he cannot go into his rear garden any longer. The moment he steps outside, she begins screeching for him." Gray leapt to his feet in a fluidly graceful motion, and held out his arms. "She runs at him with her wings spread in joy, and flies into her lover's arms."

Both she and her abigail laughed aloud.

"You are fabricating that tale!"

"I am not. While I do admit to having a wild imagination," he said, coming toward her, "even I could not imagine any female mad for Bartley, poultry or otherwise."

Gray smiled at her maid. "I can take over from here."

Mary curtsied, and left.

Isabel's smile faded as he came up behind her, and began to work on the tiny row of cloth-covered buttons that ran up her spine. She held her breath, trying not to smell him. "We were doing so well, Gray," she complained. "For a moment,

I felt the friendship we had before. Why ruin it by reminding me of this damned attraction?"

His fingertips drifted over her chemise-covered upper back. "Gooseflesh. You have no notion of how difficult it is for a man to stand this close to a woman he desires, to feel that desire returned, and then not act upon it."

"Friends," she insisted, secretly amazed at the steadiness of her voice. "That is the only way to make this marriage work."

"I can be your friend, as well as your lover." His hot, open mouth pressed against the top of her shoulder.

"And what will become of us when we are no longer lovers?"

Wrapping his arms around her waist, Gray set his chin on her shoulder and stared at their reflection. He was so much taller than she was. He had to hunch over her, surrounding her completely.

"What do you want me to say, Isabel? That we will always be lovers?"

His hands pushed down her loose bodice and cupped her breasts, kneading gently, his hips swirling against her derriere. The fierce evidence of his desire was unmistakable, and heat spread instantly across her skin. She was primed for sex, her body repeatedly aroused by his seductions, and her eyes slid closed on a low moan.

"Look at us," he urged. "Open your eyes. See how flushed we are, how needy." Strong, nimble fingers tugged at her nipples. "I know I could make you come like this, still fully clothed. Would you like to come, Isabel?" He licked her sweat-misted skin. "Of course, you would."

Afraid to see herself in his arms, she shook her head.

Gray shifted, his hips aligning so he could rub his cock against her, up and down, the hard length making her sob in near desperation. He worked her nipples, elongating them, pulling and twisting until she cried out in pleasure. She felt every motion of his fingers as if they were between her legs, her cunt creamy and aching for him.

"I cannot say we will always be lovers." His gruff voice skittered across her skin, making her nipples tighten further. He groaned. "But I can tell you that if my lust for you were half the measure it is now, I would still want you desperately."

She knew he would still want someone else, too. Even when he'd been in love, he had not been steadfast. Despite this knowledge, her back arched, thrusting her breasts into his hands and her buttocks against his bone-hard erection. Gray growled—a deep, throaty warning. "Stay home with me."

The temptation to do so was nearly overwhelming. She wanted to push him to the floor, sink her body onto his cock, and ride out this agitation.

"I never once wanted you," she moaned, undulating in his embrace, every part of her straining. She was almost mad with desire, prepared to throw aside everything she held dear to take him. But some of her reasoning would not be denied. "Not once did I ever look at you, and think about sharing your bed."

Now she could not stop thinking about it.

Forcing her eyes to open, Isabel stared at the mirror and watched herself writhe between his skilled hands and hard body. At that moment she hated herself, hated seeing an echo of the girl she had been almost a decade ago, helpless in the grip of a desire skillfully crafted for a man's pleasure.

Gray's arms tightened, pinning her tightly to his chest. His mouth, hot and wet, nuzzled all over her throat and shoulder. "God, I want to fuck you," he rasped, the clasp of his fingers becoming a hard pinch. "I want that so badly I'm afraid I will tear you apart."

The crudeness of his speech was more than she could tolerate. With a cry, she climaxed, her cunt spasming so hard her knees nearly gave way. Gray held her upright, his hold strong and steady.

Panting, Isabel turned her gaze away from her wanton reflection and sought out Pelham's likeness. She looked into dark eyes that had once drawn her into sexual decadence, and she called to mind every one of his mistresses. She remembered every occasion where she had been forced to sit across from one of them at a social function or to smell their perfume on her husband's skin. She thought of all the women who had been in her home today with their come-hither smiles, and her stomach roiled violently, dousing her ardor instantly.

"Release me," she said, her voice low and determined. She straightened, shrugging him off.

He stiffened behind her. "Listen to your breathing, and the rapid beat of your heart. You want this as badly as I do."

"I do not." She struggled in near panic until he released her with a curse. Then she spun on him with her fists clenched, every cell in her body working to turn her raging desire into just plain rage. "Keep your distance from me. Move back to your room. Leave me alone."

"What in hell is the matter with you?" He ran both hands through his thick, dark hair. "I do not understand you."

"I don't want a sexual relationship with you. I have said that many times."

"Why not?" he said crossly, beginning to pace.

"Do not push me anymore, Grayson. If you continue forcing yourself on me, I will have to leave."

"*Forcing* myself on you?" He pointed a finger at her, a wealth of frustration betrayed by the rigidity of his body. "We will sort this out. Tonight."

Lifting her chin, Isabel held her gown to her breasts and shook her head rapidly. "I have plans for this evening. I told you that."

"You cannot go out," he scoffed. "Look at you. You are shaking all over with the need for a hard tumble."

"That is not your concern."

"Damned if it isn't."

"Gray—"

Gray's eyes narrowed dangerously. "Do not bring Hargreaves into this, Isabel. Do not go to him to sate the needs I arouse."

She gaped. "Are you threatening me?"

"No. And well you know it. I am promising you, that if you go to Hargreaves to ease cravings brought on by *my* touch, I will call him out."

"I cannot believe this."

He threw up his hands. "Neither can I. There you stand, aching for me. Here I stand, ready to fuck you until neither of us can walk. What is the problem, Isabel? Can you tell me that?"

"I do not want to ruin our marriage!"

Gray took a deep, calming breath. "I must point out to you, dear wife, that marriage, by nature, includes sex. Between the spouses, not third parties."

"Not our marriage," she said firmly. "We had a bargain. You must find someone else."

"That blasted bargain! Christ, Pel. Things have changed." He stepped toward her with arms outstretched, the tense line of his jaw softening.

She ran to her escritoire, and put the piece of furniture between them. If he touched her, she would crumble.

His jaw clenched again. "As you wish," he bit out. "But this is not what you want. I saw you today, the way you looked at every woman who walked in the door. The truth is, whatever your reasoning is for not wanting me in your bed, you don't want me in any other woman's bed either." Gray bowed. "However, your wish is my command. You can collect your error on your own."

Before she could react, he was gone. And while she regretted her words immediately, she did not chase him down and tell him not to go.

Chapter 6

Gerard strode the length of the hallway that led to Lady Stanhope's hotel room, and cursed his stubborn wife.

There were benefits to doing as Isabel urged. His desire for her was nigh unbearable, causing him to push her too quickly and frighten her. He understood this, and he appreciated that he was not giving her enough time to become accustomed both to his new interest and his return to her life. It was true that fucking Barbara would take the edge off his hunger, but *damn it!* He did not want to take the edge off. He wanted to experience the aching, burning, intoxicating passion with Isabel, not a substitute for her.

But the thought of his wife with Hargreaves was so infuriating, his blood boiled. He would be damned if she eased her needs while he suffered with his own. Gerard knocked on Barbara's door, and walked right in.

"I knew you would come," she purred, nude on the bed, wearing only a black ribbon around her throat. He hardened instantly, as any man would at the sight of her. Barbara was a beautiful woman with a ravenous sexual appetite, enough to incite his anger and frustration into adulterated lust.

Shrugging out of his jacket and unfastening the buttons

of his waistcoat, he approached the bed with grim determination.

Barbara came up on her knees, and moved to help him. "Grayson," she breathed in her girlish voice, her eager hands shoving his garments off his shoulders to pool on the floor. "You are so hot for it tonight."

He crawled over her, pinning her to the bed, then rolled, bringing her over him.

"You know what to do," he muttered, then lay there, staring up at the ceiling, his mind completely disconnected from the meaningless sex that would soon follow.

Tugging his shirt free, Barbara ran her hands across his rippled abdomen. "I think I could orgasm just looking at you." She leaned over him, pressing her breasts against his thigh as she worked to open his trousers. "But, of course, I will do more than look."

Gerard closed his eyes, and longed for Isabel.

Isabel stepped down from her carriage and entered the Hargreaves residence by way of the mews. It was a path she had taken hundreds of times, and one that used to fill her with warm anticipation. Tonight, however, was completely different. Her stomach was knotted, and her palms damp. Gray had left on horseback, and she knew he had gone to another woman.

And she was the one who had driven him there.

At this moment, he was most likely buried deep inside someone, his gorgeous ass tightening and flexing as he thrust his cock into a willing body. She told herself their marriage was best this way. Better he find someone else now, than after she had succumbed. But even knowing this, she did not feel any better. The pictures in her mind tormented her, and the feeling of possessiveness did not abate. As she walked silently along the upper floor hallway, she could not fight her feelings of guilt and betrayal.

She knocked softly on John's bedroom door, then entered.

Hargreaves sat before the fire. Dressed in a multi-colored silk robe, and holding a snifter in his hand, he stared broodingly into the fire. "I did not think you would come," he said without looking at her. His voice was slightly slurred, and she noted the near-empty decanter on the table next to him.

"I am sorry," she murmured, sinking to the floor at his feet. "I know the gossip hurts you. It pains me deeply."

"Have you slept with him?"

"No."

"But you want to."

"Yes."

His eyes met hers, and he cupped her cheek in his hand. "Thank you for your honesty."

"I sent him away tonight." She nuzzled into his touch, relishing the peace and familiar comfort she found in his presence. "He went."

"Will he stay away?"

Leaning her cheek against his knee, she stared into the fire. "I'm not certain. He seems quite determined."

"Yes." John's fingers slipped into her hair. "I remember that age. The barest periphery of your mortality hits you, and the need to sire an heir becomes nearly overwhelming."

Isabel stiffened. "He has two younger brothers. He does not need an heir."

John's laugh held no humor. "When did he tell you this? When you married? When he was two and twenty? Of course he was not interested in children at that time. Most men are not. Fucking is primary, and pregnancy does put a damper on that."

She thought of Gray's boyish excitement over Emily's pregnancy, and her blood ran cold. He had shown a strong desire for children before.

"He is a marquess, Isabel," Hargreaves said, his lips on the rim of his glass, his fingers in her hair. "He needs an heir, and while he may have brothers, a man does like to produce his own issue. What other reason did he give you for returning?"

"He said he felt guilt for leaving me to face the rumors alone."

"I would not have thought Grayson was capable of such altruism," Hargreaves said dryly, setting his empty glass aside. "He would have to be a completely different man than the one I knew of only four years ago."

Staring into the fire, Isabel suddenly felt very foolish and very hurt. She sat there for a long time watching the flames dance.

Later, John's hand drifted, weighing heavily on her shoulder. She turned her head, and found him sleeping. Torn, and terribly confused, she rose and fetched a blanket. Once she knew he was comfortable, she left.

Gerard turned his head away when Barbara attempted to kiss him. Her perfume was cloying, a musky scent he had once found attractive and now found sadly lacking. His cock was rock hard and aching in her hand, his body responding to her expert ministrations despite his emotional and mental disconnections. She whispered shocking, depraved things in his ear, and then she straddled him, preparing to mount him.

"I am so glad you came home, Grayson," she breathed.

Home.

The word swirled through his head, and made his stomach clench tight. He had never had a home. As a child, his mother's bitterness had poisoned everything around him. The only time he had felt relaxed and accepted was with Pel. That had changed with their new attraction, but he would do whatever was necessary to have that accord again.

And his present encounter was not the way to go about it. This was not home. This was a hotel, and the woman preparing to fuck him was not his wife. Gripping her waist, Gerard turned quickly, tossing her to the bed next to him.

Barbara squealed in delight. "Yes!" she cried. "I wondered when you would enter into the spirit of things."

Gerard thrust his hand between her legs, and stroked her to orgasm. He knew just what she liked, and where she liked it. Within moments Barbara was coming, and he was free to depart this sordid encounter.

Releasing a frustrated breath, he rolled from the bed, refastened his trousers, and moved to the washstand in the corner.

"What are you doing?" she purred, stretching like a cat.

"Washing. Then leaving."

"No, you are not!" She sat up. With her flushed cheeks and pouty red mouth, she was lovely. But not at all what he wanted.

"Sorry, sweet," he said gruffly, scrubbing his hands in the basin. "I am not in the mood this evening."

"You lie. Your cock is hard as a poker."

Gerard turned, and collected his coat and waistcoat.

Barbara's shoulders slumped. "She's old, Grayson."

"She is my wife."

"That never bothered you before. Besides, she has Hargreaves."

He stiffened, his jaw clenching.

"Ah. A direct hit." Her smile was as wicked as always. "Is she with him now? Is that why you came to me?" Spreading her legs, she leaned against the pillows and ran her hands between her thighs. "Why should she have all the fun? I can offer the same entertainments."

Buttoning the last button, Gerard moved to make his egress. "Good night, Barbara."

He was only a few feet down the hall when he heard something fragile shatter against the door. Shaking his head, he descended the stairs quickly, eager to go home.

* * *

Comfortably ensconced in her own bedroom, Isabel dismissed Mary as soon as she had undressed. "But bring me some Madeira," she murmured as the abigail curtsied.

When she was alone, she sank into the wingback in front of the fire and thought of Hargreaves. This situation was so unfair to him. He had been good to her, she adored him, and she hated herself for being so confused. Her mother would say there was no monopoly on desire, and life had proved that to be true. The duchess would find nothing at all wrong with desiring two men at one time. Isabel, however, would always believe that a person should be strong enough to resist baser demands, if they cared enough.

Several minutes later, a knock drew her attention to the open door, and she gestured the maid in. The servant balanced the bottle of Madeira and a glass on a tray in one hand. The other was loaded with towels.

"What are those for?" Isabel asked.

"Forgive me, my lady, Edward requested them for His Lordship's bath."

Edward was Gray's valet. It was nearly dawn. Her husband was bathing away the scents of his carnal exertions and she sat here, morose and guilty. Suddenly furious at the unfairness, she stood and collected the towels. "I will see to this."

The girl's eyes widened, but she curtsied, and set down the bottle and glass before departing.

Isabel crossed her boudoir to the dressing room and then, without any warning, opened the door to the bathing room. Gray lay in steaming water, his head resting against the lip of the tub with his eyes closed. He did not move at all when she entered, and she took a brief moment to absorb the sight of his dark chest and long, powerful legs. All of his beauty was visible through the clear water, including the impressive cock she had felt only briefly. She was instantly aroused, which further incited her temper. A narrow-eyed glance at Edward sent the valet fleeing from the room.

Gray took a deep breath, and then stiffened all over. "Isabel," he breathed, his eyes drifting open. He stared at her with impossibly blue eyes framed with wet lashes, and made no effort to cover himself.

"Did you enjoy your evening?" she bit out.

His lips pursed at her tone. "Did you?"

"No, I did not, and I blame you entirely."

"Of course you would." The silence stretched out, the air between them thick with things left unsaid and a desire that went unappeased. "Did you fuck him, Pel?" he asked finally, his voice gruff.

Her gaze roamed over the length of his body.

"Did you?" he repeated when she said nothing.

"Hargreaves was deep in his cups, and miserable." *While Gray spent a pleasurable evening in some woman's bed.* The thought so enraged her, she threw the towels in his face, and spun on her heel. "I hope you fucked enough for all of us."

"Bloody hell. Isabel!"

Hearing a splash, she began to run. Her bedroom was near, she could make it. . . .

Gray caught her by the waist, and lifted her feet from the floor. She flailed, kicking and elbowing, slipping in his wet grasp and her satin night rail.

"Cease," he growled.

"Release me!"

She reached back, and yanked on his wet hair.

"Ow, damn it!"

He stumbled, then dropped to his knees, pressing her facedown upon the floor and covering her body with his own. Her gown was soaked in the back, her breasts flattened into the rug. "I hate you!"

"No, you don't," he muttered, stretching her arms over her head.

She squirmed as much as she was able with his weight atop her. "I cannot breathe," she gasped. He slid to the side, keeping one heavy leg across hers and her arms pinned. "Desist, Gray. You have no right to accost me like this."

"I have every right. Did you fuck him?"

"Yes." She turned her head to glare at him. "I fucked him all night. In every way imaginable. I sucked his—"

Gray's mouth took hers so hard she tasted blood. His tongue slid into her mouth, thrusting in a brutal rhythm, his lips slanting across hers. He held both of her wrists in one hand, while the other reached for the hem of her gown and yanked it upward.

Her blood raced through her veins, her heart pounded furiously against her rib cage. Incited beyond bearing, she bit down on his bottom lip. His head jerked backward with a curse.

"Unhand me!"

Her night rail was trapped beneath her, halting its upward progress, and Gray moved his weight to finish the job. The slight ease in pressure gave her room to buck, and she did, knocking him off guard. She scrambled on her hands and knees.

"Isabel," he snarled, lunging toward her.

He caught the trailing end of her gown and held it tight, causing the thin ribbon ties at her shoulders to rip away. She crawled right out of the ruined garment, intent on reaching her room. Hope flared the moment before her ankle was caught in a vicelike grip. Kicking out with her free leg, she fought desperately, but Gray was too powerful. He climbed over her, subduing her arms, and shoving his thigh between her legs.

Tears of frustration coursed down her cheeks. "You cannot do this," she cried, writhing, fighting against the craving within her more than she fought against him. As she struggled, the heavy heat of his erection was an unmistakable weight against her buttocks.

He once again pinned her arms over her head with one hand. The other brushed gently down her side, and then between her legs. He parted the folds of her sex, slipping two fingers deep inside.

"You're wet," he groaned, his fingers drifting through the evidence of her excitement. She twisted her hips in an attempt to escape his probing. "Calm down." Gray buried his face in the back of her neck. "I fucked no one, Isabel."

"You lie."

"That is not to say that I failed to make the attempt. In the end, however, I only wanted you."

She shook her head, crying silently. "No. I do not believe you."

"Yes, you do. You know a man's body well enough. I could not be this hard if I had been coming all night."

His fingertips, slick with her cream, found her clitoris and circled over it. Her spine arched helplessly, her blood slowing and becoming sluggish with her desire. He was everywhere, completely surrounding her, his hard body caging hers to the floor. A finger dipped inside her until it was buried. She shivered all over, and drenched his hand.

"Hush," he soothed, his voice low and thick by her ear. "Let me ease you. We are both overwrought."

"No, Gray."

"You want this as much as I do."

"I don't."

"Who is lying now?" His finger left her, his damp hand clutching her thigh and lifting it out of the way. His arm slipped under her head, his biceps pillowing her cheek, his palm cupping her left breast. "I need you."

She attempted to close her legs, but then the tip of his cock was there, just at the slick rim of her sex. He stroked it against her, and pinched her nipple. She whimpered as lust misted her skin with sweat.

"You are hot and creamy for my cock." The edge of his teeth grazed her shoulder. "Tell me you don't want me."

"I don't want you."

His chuckle rumbled against her back. The thick head of his shaft entered her, stretched her, the pressure just what she needed, but still not enough. Her hips moved without volition, straining to take more, but he pulled back enough to keep just that tiny bit of him inside her.

"No," he admonished, suddenly much more in control, as if the carnal connection soothed him in some way. "You don't want me."

"Damn you." She ground her face against his arm, wiping away her tears.

"Tell me you want me."

"I do not." But a moan escaped her, and her hips swiveled restlessly, massaging him inside her.

"Isabel . . ." His teeth sank gently into her shoulder, his hips shifting to slide his cock deeper. "Stop that, before I blow without you."

"You wouldn't dare!" she gasped, the thought of being left in this agony was horrifying.

"Continue, and I will be unable to help myself."

She moaned her misery, and buried her face in his arm. "You want to breed me."

"What?" He stilled. "What the devil are you talking about?"

"Confess," she said hoarsely, her chest tight. "You have returned for an heir."

To her surprise, he shuddered against her. "Ridiculous. But I know you will not believe me, so I promise not to come in you. Not until you want me to."

"You are correct. I don't believe you."

"You shall drive me mad, stubborn wench. Cease making excuses, and simply admit you want me. Then I will give you this." He gave her a shallow thrust. "And not my seed."

"You are horrid, Grayson." She wiggled, desperate to stroke herself to orgasm.

"Actually, I am very good." His tongue entered her ear. "Allow me to prove it."

"Do I have a choice?" She shivered, her skin sticking to his with their sweat. "You will not let me go."

Gray sighed, and hugged her to his chest. "I *cannot* let

you go, Isabel." He nuzzled against her throat, and swelled inside her. "Christ, I love the way you smell."

And she loved the way he felt, thick and hard, his cock as large and virile as the rest of him. Pelham had trapped her with this—this heated, drugging pleasure that made a woman want to languish in her bed and be fucked endlessly. A slave to desire.

She was too weak with craving to protest as his fingers found her clitoris and massaged the surrounding skin stretched wide to accommodate him.

"I am thicker at the root," he murmured wickedly. "Imagine how that will feel while I pump it into you."

Her eyes closed, her legs spreading in silent invitation. "Do it, then."

"Is that what you want?" His surprise was patent.

"Yes!" She thrust her elbow into his ribs, and heard him grunt. "You hateful, arrogant cretin."

Reaching up to lace his fingers with hers, Gray gave a low growl and began to thrust in shallow digs. He forced her to feel every inch, made her stretch to his width, acknowledging his power and possession. She cried out her pleasure and relief, the feel of him so devastating to her heightened senses.

It was a claiming, one she could say she fought until the very end.

Clenching her hands with his, Isabel surrendered to her new addiction with a sob of despair.

Chapter 7

Gerard grit his teeth as he worked his cock into slick, swollen tissues. Crushing Pel to his chest, he struggled to keep his wits while every cell in his body was focused on the heated pleasure of her cunt and the panting cries she welcomed him with. He burned all over, even the roots of his hair, his drying skin misting with sweat until it was damp again.

"Oh Pel," he crooned, pushing her leg aside so he could pump deeper. "It feels like heaven inside you."

She writhed beneath him, the gyrations of her hips a stimulation he could barely stand. "Gray . . ."

The breathy plea made him shudder hard against her. "Damn it, cease wiggling before I lose what little control I have."

"This is control?" she gasped, arching her hips up in silent demand. "What are you like when you have none?"

He released her hands, and hugged her slim body to his.

Many times in his life he had been witless with lust. Many times he had given those baser impulses free rein. Never had the need been as fierce as it was with Isabel. Her flamboyant beauty, blatant sexuality, and lush curves were made for a man as primitive in his desires as he was. She had been too much for him four years ago, though his arrogance would never have allowed him to admit it. Now he was worried he would be too much for her. And frightening her from his bed was not an option.

Releasing her hands, he thrust his hands beneath her, and rolled, bringing her over him.

"W–what?" she gasped, her unbound hair falling over his face and shoulders, drowning him in her scent. His cock grew impossibly harder.

"Ride me," he growled, his hands releasing her as if she burned him. Her ripe body draped over his was nearly his undoing. What he wished to do more than breathe was to pin her beneath him, and shaft her tight cunt without mercy until he was well and truly spent. And then do it again. But she was his wife, and deserved better than that. Since he could not trust himself to take the lead, he had to trust it to her.

Isabel hesitated, and he thought for a moment that she would change her mind and refuse him again. Instead she set her hands to the floor and raised her torso. She slid down, taking more of him inside her, until the drenched lips of her sex kissed the base of his cock. His hands fisted as she moaned plaintively. The positioning of her body angled his cock deliciously.

"God, Gray. You feel so . . ."

Squeezing his eyes tightly shut, Gerard sucked in his breath at her unspoken praise. He understood what went unspoken. There were no words for this.

Perhaps it was simply that she had aroused and rejected him repeatedly, as no other woman ever had. Perhaps it was because she was his wife, and that added bit of true ownership increased the moment's poignancy. Whatever it was, sex had never been like this, and they hadn't even begun.

"You must move, Pel." Opening his eyes, he swallowed hard as she extended her arms straight behind her, the ends of her hair pooling on his chest. He wondered how they would do this. Would she dismount and face him? Watching her come would give him great pleasure, but the thought of separating his cock from her was nigh unbearable.

"Must I?" she purred in a taunting tone, and while he could not see her face, he knew her look would be sly. She lifted one hand, her weight settling more firmly on the other arm, her ass cradled by his loins. He lay frozen with bated breath as she reached between her legs, first giving his drawn up balls a teasingly soft squeeze before stroking higher.

Oh hell. If she masturbated on his cock, he would explode.

"Are you going to—?" he began.

She did.

He grunted as her cunt clenched tight as a fist around him. "Bloody hell!"

Clutching her hips in almost panic, Gerard held her slightly aloft as he thrust upward violently, fucking through her gasping depths like a man possessed.

"Yes!" she cried, her head falling back, burying his throat and mouth in fiery tresses. All the while her body milked his cock, luring his seed, the pulsating spasms nearly brutal in their intensity.

It went on forever, her first heated release, but he bit his lip bloody and held on. Only when she went limp in his arms, did he yank himself free, coming hard, spurting scalding streams of lust and longing across her thigh and the rug.

He had wanted to take the edge off.

They had barely scratched the surface.

Pel lay back over him, gasping for air, and he cupped her breasts and kissed her temple. The scent of her mixed with sex was intoxicating. He pressed his nostrils against her skin and breathed it in.

"You are a horrid, dreadful man," she whispered.

Gerard sighed. Of course, he would have to marry the most obstinate woman in the world. "*You* rushed the business. But I shall be certain to lengthen the process the next time around. Perhaps then you will be more agreeable." He levered them both up to a seated position.

"Next time?"

He could tell she was poised to argue, so he reached between her legs and stroked her clitoris with a soft glide of his fingertips. When she moaned, he grinned. "Yes, next time, which will commence momentarily, once I have cleaned us up a bit and moved this arrangement to a more comfortable venue."

She scrambled to her feet, spinning to face him, a whirl of auburn hair and flushed, creamy skin. Staring up at her, Gerard was struck by the absolute carnal perfection of her form. Purely, beautifully naked, Isabel Grayson was a Venus, a siren—full-breasted with generously curved hips, and a wide mouth framed by full kiss-bruised lips. His cock responded with admirable haste. Isabel's eyes dropped to it, and then widened.

"Good grief. We just attended to that thing."

He shrugged, and bit back a smile as she continued to stare, her gaze blatantly appreciative and only slightly intimidated. Rising to his feet, he caught up her hand and tugged her back into the bathing chamber. "I cannot help but respond. You are quite simply a stunningly attractive woman."

Isabel snorted, but followed him without protest, although she lagged slightly behind. He glanced over his shoulder to see why, and caught her ogling his ass with a riveted gaze. She was too preoccupied to realize he'd taken note, so he flexed his buttocks and then laughed when she blushed. Whatever her objection to marital sexual intimacy, it was certainly not due to lack of interest in him.

"Care to tell me about your night?" he asked solicitously, treading new ground. He was not accustomed to casual conversation in the middle of an amorous interlude. His fully engorged erection was not helping him concentrate either. Not that he could help it. His wife's gaze was burning his skin.

"Why?"

"Because you are upset about it." Gerard turned and pushed her into a chair, taking a moment to brush the lovely hair he so admired over her shoulders.

"This is so awkward," she complained, her arms crossing over her chest modestly as he reached into the tub and pulled out one of the soaked towels. "What are you doing?" she asked, watching him squeeze out the excess water.

"I told you." He dropped to a crouch before her, and with a hand on each knee, forced her legs apart.

"Stop that!" Isabel slapped at his hands. He arched a brow and slapped her back, although with far more gentleness. "Brute," she gasped with wide eyes.

"Wench. Allow me to clean you up a bit."

Sherry-colored eyes shot fire at him. "You have done quite enough, thank you. Now leave me in peace, and I will care for myself."

"I haven't even started," he drawled.

"Nonsense. You've had what you wanted. Let's forget this happened, and go on as we were."

Gerard rocked back on his heels. "Had what I wanted, eh? Don't be daft, Pel." He shoved her clenched thighs apart and thrust the cloth between them. "I have yet to do the things I want. You have not been bent over a piece of furniture and fucked from behind. I have not sucked your nipples or your—" He ran the cloth gently through the lips of her sex, and then followed it with a teasing glide of his tongue, pausing a brief moment to tease her clitoris from its hood. "You have not been flat on your back and ridden properly. In short, we are nowhere near finished."

"Gray." She surprised him by cupping his cheek with her hand. Her gaze was earnest and direct. And very hot. "We started this with a bargain. Let us end this with one."

His eyes narrowed in suspicion. "What kind of bargain?"

"A pleasurable one. If I give you one night, and promise

to do whatever you wish, will you in turn promise to keep to our original agreement from the morning onward?"

His blasted cock raised its head in eager agreement, but Gerard was not so keen. "One night?" She was mad if she thought that would be enough for either of them. He was as hard at this moment as he had been before he'd come, she affected him that much.

He returned his attentions to his ministrations, spreading her lips and cleaning her gently. She was lovely, flushed and glistening, and blessed with a dazzling frame of dark mahogany curls.

Her fingers sifted through his hair, tugging it to draw his gaze back up to her face. Her fingertips glided over his features, following first the arch of his brows before caressing his cheeks, and then his lips. She seemed wearily resigned. "These lines around your eyes and mouth . . . they should age you, diminish your beauty. Instead, they do the opposite."

"It is not a bad thing to want me, Isabel." He dropped the cloth, and embraced her waist, his face buried between her breasts where the scent of her was so strong. She was naked in his arms, and yet a barrier was between them. No matter how tightly he held her, he could not get close enough.

Turning his head, he caught her nipple with his mouth, suckling, seeking intimacy. He licked the distended tip, stroked his tongue around it and relished the velvety softness. She moaned, her hands gripping his head, pulling him closer.

He was aching for her, physically hurting. He released her breast, and caught her up. Her legs wrapped around his waist, her arms around his neck, and he grunted his approval at her longed-for acquiescence. His pace quickened as he walked straight through to his bedroom, a chamber he had stood in only hours before, despondent that he had changed rooms to be closer to Pel and had instead pushed her away.

Now she would scent his sheets, warm his blood, and sate his hunger. As he set her down carefully on the bed, his throat tightened. Above her, the headboard displayed his crest, below her lay his red velvet counterpane. The thought of indulging in his wife's charms in such a proprietary setting aroused him beyond bearing.

"One night," she murmured against his throat.

Gerard shuddered, both from the feel of her breath across his skin, and from the realization that he could not take her as he truly desired. He would have to woo her with his body and show her how gentle he could be, because he had to change her mind and make her crave him.

And she was giving him only one night in which to do it.

Isabel sank into linen-covered pillows on Gray's bed and noted again how much he had changed. He had once preferred silk sheets, she knew. What the change signified, she didn't know, but she wanted to. She opened her mouth to ask, but he took it, his lips firm against hers, his tongue sweeping inside with a slow, deliberate glide. Moaning, she welcomed his weight over hers.

He was hard all over, every inch of his golden skin stretched taut over rippling muscle. In all of her life, she had never seen a masculine body as beautifully formed as her husband's. Considering that Pelham had been exquisite in his own right, it was not a compliment she bestowed lightly.

"Pel." Gray breathed into her mouth, a low seductive burr of sound. "I am going to lick you all over, kiss you everywhere, make you come all night."

"And I will do the same to you," she promised, her tongue swiping soothingly across his damaged lower lip. Having decided on the goal of exhausting their mutual lust, she was now prepared to give her all to the endeavor.

Pulling away slightly to look at her, Gray gave her the opportunity she needed to take the upper hand. She hooked her heel over the back of his calf, and rolled, rising above him. Then she laughed when he rolled again and reclaimed the advantage.

"Oh no, vixen," he chastised, staring down at her with laughing blue eyes. "I gave you the top previously."

"I did not hear you complaining at the time."

His mouth twitched with a withheld smile. "It was over so quickly I didn't have a chance to protest."

She arched a brow. "I think you were simply speechless with pleasure."

Gray laughed aloud, the sound teasing her as it vibrated from his chest to hers. Her nipples peaked tighter in response. The lowering of his lids told her he noticed.

"Whatever I wish," he reminded, as he moved his hand down to lift her leg and spread her wide. With a roll of his hips, the tip of his cock breached her, forced her to open, the size of him almost uncomfortable but highly tantalizing.

Immediately she melted, her cunt softening, growing slick, crowning the broad head of his cock with her cream. Her toes curled, and her chest grew tight. He smelled wonderful, the bergamot that scented his soap diminished by the primitive scent of his sweat and the recent bout of sex.

"Gray." His name was both a request for more and a plea for less. She didn't know how to fight the sudden feeling of connection. In the years since Pelham had passed on, sexual congress had been about gratification, satiation. This, on the other hand, was pure surrender.

His large hands slipped beneath her shoulders, his forearms holding his weight aloft enough to prevent crushing her. "You are handing Hargreaves his congé."

It was a statement, an order, and while she wished she could argue with him just for his arrogance, she knew he was right. To be so attracted to Gray was proof that her interest was not as engaged by John as it once had been.

Still the knowledge saddened her, and she turned her head to hide her stinging eyes.

Gray brushed his mouth across her cheekbone, and pressed a scant inch into her. She groaned and arched upward, eager to forget her hazardous decision to indulge.

"I can make you happy," he promised against her skin. "And you will never lack pleasure, I can assure you of that."

Perhaps he could make her happy, but she could not do the same for him, and once he strayed, contentment would rapidly deteriorate into misery.

She wrapped her legs around his hips and pulled herself upward from the mattress, slowly engulfing his cock. Her eyes slid closed, her focus shifting to her blossoming enchantment with Grayson's lovemaking. He was so long, so thick. No wonder his mistresses tolerated his indiscretions. He would be hard to replace.

"Do you prefer a slow fucking, Pel?" he asked in a strangled whisper, his arms trembling as he sank in a bit more. "Tell me what you like."

"Yes . . . Slow . . ." Her voice was slurred, her nails digging into his broad back. She liked it any way and every way, but was rapidly losing the ability to think coherently.

She sank downward as he took over, his buttocks clenching as he slowly worked his way into her. Despite his recent penetration, her cunt forced him to earn the right to enter again. His cock pushed in and pulled out in a steady rhythm, every downward plunge taking him a little bit deeper.

Sweat from him dripped onto her throat and chest. "God, you are tight," he groaned.

She flexed her inner muscles just to increase his torment.

"Push me too far and you will regret it," he warned darkly. "I don't want to come in you, but I won't stop. Not for any reason. You gave me one night, and I am damn well taking it."

Isabel shivered. *I won't stop.* He would take her whether she willed it or no. The thought aroused her, as evidenced by the sudden rush of cream that allowed him to sink home in one deep glide.

"Open wider." His lips touched her ear. "Take all of me."

She was already so full it was hard to breathe, but she shifted slightly and he slipped in to the root.

"Beautiful," he praised, nuzzling his damp cheek against hers. "Now we can go as slow as you like."

Beginning to move, Gray took her with breathtaking leisure, moving in deliberate undulations of his entire body—his chest flexing against hers, his thighs buffeting hers, his fingers kneading almost restlessly against the tops of her shoulders.

She fought the sounds that struggled to be freed until she was unable to bear it any longer, her head tilting back on a plaintive whimper.

"That's the way," he encouraged, his voice gravelly and strained. "Let me hear how much you like it." He swiveled his hips and thrust, stroking her deep inside. She was so wet it was audible and she cried out, raking his back. He arched into her touch, and ground into her. "My God, Isabel . . ."

She matched his tempo, throwing her hips upward as he came down, the tip of his cock striking some tender spot she hadn't known existed. She mewled and writhed, growing desperate at his steady pace. "More . . . Give me more . . ."

Gray rolled to his side, and anchored her thigh on his hip, the tight roping of his abdominal muscles rippling as he pumped harder, not faster, his pelvis slapping against hers. The position was intimate, their bodies pressed together, their faces just inches from each other. Their panting breaths mingled between them as they strained in unison toward their mutual goal. One bicep pillowed her head, one large hand cupped her buttock holding her in place to take his thrusts. His bright blue gaze stared at her, glittering with his lust, his jaw locked and teeth grinding together. He looked like he was in pain, his cock rigid and impossibly thick.

"Come," he grit out. "Come now!"

The harsh bite of command in his tone was a delicious threat, one that shoved her off the edge with brutal force. She cried out, nearly screamed, her orgasm so powerful her entire body shook with each clenching spasm.

His fingers dug into her, bruising her, his cock slamming

deep. Only when she was finished did he pull out, shoving her leg off his hip so he could fuck through her closed thighs. She held still, awed as he came, his cock jerking between her legs, each pulse met with a grunt, his open lips pressed to her forehead.

Even as Gray emptied himself onto the counterpane, she knew she was ruined. She wanted *this,* longed for this depth of feeling during sex.

She hated him for reminding her of what it could be like, of what she was missing, of what she had avoided for the last several years. He had given her an addicting taste of what he would soon take away.

Already she missed it, and ached for its loss.

It was the sounds of industrious servants in the bathing chamber that first raised Gerard's eyelids, but it was the scent of sex and exotic flowers that raised the rest of him. With a soft grumble at the intrusion, he took a quick inventory of his present circumstance.

His left arm was asleep from acting as a pillow for Pel's head. He lay sprawled on his back, his wife's buttocks against his hip, her back curved into his side. She wore a sheet, he was bare. He had no notion of what time it was, and it did not matter. He was still tired, and if the sound of Isabel's soft snoring was any indication, she was too.

He had been having his way with her for hours, his need slaked only slightly with each successive encounter. Even now his cock stuck straight up in the air, aroused by the feel and smell of her. Although he was exhausted, he knew there would be no sleep with an erection like he had. He rolled into Pel, casting off the sheet that covered her with his working arm and lifting her leg over his. Using gentle fingers, he reached between her legs, cupping her sex, feeling how swollen she was.

He licked the tip of his middle finger and then stroked her

clitoris, circling it, rubbing it, teasing it. She whimpered and halfheartedly attempted to push his hand away.

"No more, damn you," she muttered, her voice husky with sleep and disgruntlement. But when he reached deeper, he found her wet.

"Your cunt disagrees."

"Blasted thing is daft." She pushed his arm again, but he only cuddled closer. "I am exhausted, you horrid man. Allow me to sleep."

"I will, vixen," he promised, kissing the top of her shoulder. He circled his hips against her so that she felt how needy he was. "Let me take care of this, and we can sleep all day."

Isabel groaned into his numb arm. "I am too old for you, Gray. I cannot keep pace with your appetite."

"Nonsense." He reached between her legs and positioned his cock. "You don't have to do anything." He bit her shoulder gently as he forged his way into her with soft, shallow strokes. Half-asleep and intoxicated by the rapturous feel of her, he moved languidly, his fingers circling her clitoris, his face buried in the wild tangle of her hair. "Just lie there and come. As many times as you want."

"Oh God," she breathed, creaming in welcome. She moaned softly, her hand coming to rest on his flexing wrist as he pleasured her.

Too old for him. Even as he scoffed at the notion, the tiny part of his brain not presently lost to their lazy fucking wondered if it was as much of an issue for her, as it was for Society. It was not one for him, certainly. Did that have something to do with her reticence? Did she believe herself unable to satisfy him? Was that why she insisted he acquire a mistress? If so, his constant sexual demands were not helping his cause any. Perhaps he should—

Her cunt fluttered around him, and the thought was lost. He increased the pressure on her clitoris and growled as she fell into orgasm with a soft, startled cry. He would never have his fill of that feeling. Tight as a glove to begin with, when Isabel came, it was in hard, clenching spasms. Like a fist tightening rhythmically. He swelled in response, and her back arched into his chest.

"Christ, Gray. Do not get any bigger."

He bit a little deeper into her soft flesh.

He wanted to drive into her, fuck her senseless, roar out his pleasure. He wanted her nails in his back, her hair soaked with sweat, her nipples marked by his teeth. She drove him insane, and until that ravenous animal within him was freed and fed, he would never be fully sated.

They would quite simply have to fuck a great deal, he thought, his tortured grimace hidden in her tresses. It was a goal he suspected would not be an easy one to attain, given her present state of soreness and exhaustion. Plus her obstinate nature and the ridiculous thought that he was too young for her. And he had no clue as to what any of her other objections might be. There was the bloody bargain, of course. And Hargreaves . . .

As the obstacles between them stacked up, he groaned. It shouldn't be this damned difficult to seduce his own wife.

But as she came apart in his arms, her body shivering against his own, his name on her lips as she cried out, he knew, as he had known from the moment he first saw her, that Isabel was worth it.

Chapter 8

Isabel shut her boudoir door quietly behind her, and made her way to the staircase. Gray remained sprawled in the bathtub, his beautifully etched mouth curved in a triumphant, contented smile. He thought she was well and truly seduced, and perhaps she was. Certainly she moved differently, her body was relaxed and languid. Sated. *Demented*.

She wrinkled her nose. What a dreadful mire.

Now keeping him at bay would be difficult at best. He knew what he could do to her, how to touch her, how to speak to her to make her mindless with lust for him. He would be insufferable from here on out, no doubt. Merely removing herself from the bed had been a chore. The man was insatiable. If Gray had his way, she was certain they would never leave it.

Her sigh came out like a low, pained moan. The first few months of her marriage to Pelham had been similar. Even before they said their vows, he had snared her in a web of seduction. The rakishly handsome earl with the golden hair and wicked reputation had appeared to be everywhere, showing up at all the venues she did. Later, she realized those had not been random acts of fate, as her stupid heart had believed. At the time, however, it seemed they were destined for one another.

The smiles and winks he had given her created a feeling of familiarity, a sense that they shared some secret. She had assumed it was love, silly girl that she was. Fresh from the schoolroom, Pelham's amorous attentions completely overwhelmed her, sweet gestures such as paying her abigail to deliver notes to her.

Those single lines written in a bold masculine scrawl had been devastating.

> *You look ravishing in blue.*
> *I miss you.*
> *I thought of you all day.*

After they wed he fucked her abigail, but at the time Isabel had taken the girl's adoration of the dashing peer as a sign that he was the right choice for a husband.

The week before her coming-out ball, he climbed the elm outside her bedroom balcony, and snuck boldly into her room. She was sure only pure love could goad him to take such a risk. Pelham had whispered to her in the darkness, his voice raw with lust as he stripped away her night rail, and loved her with his mouth and hands. *I hope I am caught. Then you will for certain be mine.*

Of course, I'm yours, she whispered back, awash in the glory of orgasm. *I love you.*

There are no words for what I feel for you, he returned.

A sennight of midnight liaisons and decadent pleasure had garnered her total supplication. The consummation on the seventh night had guaranteed she was his. She had entered her first Season completely off the market, and while her father would have preferred a peer of higher station, he did not gainsay her choice.

Only enough time for the reading of the banns was allowed before they married, and then they'd fled the city for a blissful honeymoon in the countryside. There she had been overjoyed to lie in bed with Pelham for days on end, rising only to bathe and eat, wallowing in carnal delights as Gray wished to do now. The similarities between the two men could not be ignored. Not when the thought of both men made her heart race and her palms damp.

"What the devil are you doing, Bella?"

Isabel blinked, quickly regaining her awareness of her surroundings. She stood at the top of the staircase, her hand on the rail, lost in thought. Her mind was sluggish from lack of sleep, and her body was sore and tired. Shaking her head, she stared down into the foyer and met the scowling countenance of her older brother, Rhys, Marquess of Trenton.

"Is it your intention to hang about up there all day? If so, I consider my obligation to you met, and I will be off to find more pleasant adventures."

"Obligation?" She descended to him.

He smiled. "If you have forgotten, do not look to me to remind you. It's not as if I wish to go."

Rhys' hair was a dark mahogany, an absolutely glorious color that set off his tan skin and hazel eyes. The ladies went a bit batty around him, but occupied with his own pleasures, he scarcely paid them any mind. Unless he found them sexually attractive. The simple fact was, he was very much like their mother when it came to the opposite sex. A woman to him was a physical convenience, and when she was no longer convenient, she was easily discarded.

Isabel knew that neither her mother nor brother had any malicious intent. They simply could not see why any of their lovers would fall in love with an individual who did not return the sentiment.

"Lady Marley's breakfast," she said, as she remembered. "What is the time?"

"Nearly two." His jaded gaze raked her from head to toe. "And you are just rolling out of bed." His mouth curved knowingly. "Apparently, the rumors of your reconciliation with Grayson are true."

"Do you believe everything you hear?" Reaching the marble foyer, she tilted her head back to look up at her brother.

"I believe everything I see. Reddened eyes, bruised mouth, clothing you chose without thinking clearly."

Isabel glanced down at her somewhat simple muslin day gown. It was not what she would have selected had she remembered her schedule for the day. Of course, thinking back on it now, Mary had questioned the garment, but Isabel had been so anxious to leave the room before Gray accosted her again that she had waved off the soft query.

"I will not discuss my marriage with you, Rhys."

"Thank God for that," he said with a shudder. "Deuced annoying when women start discussing their feelings."

Rolling her eyes, she requested her pelisse from the nearby servant. "I do not have feelings for Grayson."

"Quite sensible."

"We are just friends."

"Obviously."

As she secured her hat with a hat pin, she shot him a sidelong glance. "What did I promise you again, in return for your escort? Whatever it is, it is worth more than your company."

Rhys laughed, and Isabel silently acknowledged his appeal. There was something about men who could not be tamed. Thankfully she had grown out of the fascination for such hopeless sport long ago.

"You are introducing me to the lovely Lady Eddly."

"Ah, yes. Under normal circumstances I wouldn't agree to such a blatantly obvious pairing, but in this case I think you two are perfect for one another."

"I definitely agree."

"I am having a dinner party . . . eventually. You and Lady Eddly are both invited as of this moment." Having Rhys there would help to calm her nerves. And she would need all the assistance in that regard as she could muster. The mere thought of surviving a dinner with Gray and a bevy of his former paramours made her stomach roil.

Sighing at her predicament, Isabel shook her head. "Horribly uncouth of you to use your sister in this manner."

"Ha," Rhys scoffed, collecting her pelisse from the returning maid and holding it out for her. "Dreadful of you to drag me along to a breakfast, and at the Marley residence no less. Lady Marley always smells of camphor."

"It is not as if I wish to go either, so cease your whining."

"You wound me, Bella. Men do not whine." With his hand on her shoulder, he spun her to face him. "Why are we attending if you doubt your enjoyment of the event?"

"You know why."

He snorted gently. "I wish you would disregard what others thought about you. I personally find you the least annoying woman I know. Straightforward, pleasant to look upon, and capable of witty discourse."

"I suppose your opinion is the only one that matters."

"Is it not?"

"I wish I could ignore the gossip," she grumbled, "but the Dowager Lady Grayson feels the need to bring it to my attention as often as possible. Those horrid notes she sends infuriate me. I wish she would just spit her venom out, rather than attempt to hide it beneath a thin layer of civility." Isabel stared into her brother's resigned features. "I have no notion how Grayson grew up sane with that harridan as a mother."

"You do realize that women who look as you do often have trouble with other females? Catty creatures that you are. You cannot bear it when one woman attracts excessive masculine attention. Not that you have ever experienced that particular kind of jealousy," he finished dryly. "You are always the woman attracting the regard."

She had experienced other kinds of jealousy though, such as the kind a wife experiences when the bed her husband ruts in is not her own.

"Which is why I associate with men more so than women, though that has its pitfalls, too." Isabel was aware that other women found her appearance off-putting, but there was nothing she could do about that. "Let's be off then."

Both of Rhys' brows rose into his hairline. "I must pay my respects to Grayson. I cannot simply abscond with his wife. The last time I did that, he gave me a brutal pummeling in the pugilist rings at Remington's. The man is much younger than I, take pity on me."

"Write him a note," she said curtly, shivering at the image of her husband with his hair still damp. Just thinking of it reminded her of the night before and the way he had taken her.

"Don't have feelings for Grayson, indeed." Rhys' hazel gaze was blatantly skeptical.

"Wait until you marry, Rhys. The need to escape occasionally will become all too clear." With that in mind, she gestured impatiently toward the door.

"I've no doubt about that." He offered his arm, and retrieved his hat from the waiting butler.

"You are not getting any younger, you know."

"I am aware of my advancing years. Therefore, I have made a list of suitable spousal prospects."

"Yes, Mother told me of your 'list,'" she said dryly.

"A man must be sensible about choosing a bride."

Isabel nodded with mock severity. "Of course, feelings should never be considered."

"Did we not already agree to avoid a discussion of feelings?"

Smothering a laugh, she asked, "And who is at the top of your list, may I ask?"

"Lady Susannah Campion."

"The Duke of Raleigh's second daughter?" Isabel blinked.

Lady Susannah was indeed a sensible choice. Her breeding was exceptional, her deportment flawless, and her suitability for the rank of duchess could not be denied. But the delicate blonde girl had no fire, no passion. "She would bore you to tears."

"Come now," he demurred. "She cannot be as bad as that."

Her eyes widened. "You have yet to meet the girl you are considering marrying?"

"I've seen her! I would not marry a chit sight unseen." He cleared his throat. "I simply have not had the pleasure of speaking with her yet."

Shaking her head, Isabel felt again like she did not quite fit in with her *sensible* family. Yes, falling out of love was a dreadful experience, but falling into it wasn't so bad. She was certainly a far wiser and better-rounded individual than she had been before meeting Pelham. "Thank heaven you are coming with me today, for Lady Susannah will certainly be at the breakfast. Be certain you speak with her."

"Of course." As they left the house and approached his waiting phaeton, Rhys adjusted his long-legged stride to hers. "This might be just the thing to make dealing with an angry Grayson worthwhile."

"He will not be angry."

"Not with you perhaps."

Her throat tightened. "Not with anyone."

"The man has always been a trifle touchy where you are concerned," Rhys drawled.

"He has not!"

"Has, too. And if he has truly decided to exert his husbandly rights, I pity the man who intrudes. Step lightly, Bella."

Releasing a deep breath, Isabel kept her thoughts to herself, but the butterflies in her stomach took flight again.

Gerard gazed at his reflection, and heaved a frustrated breath. "When is the tailor scheduled to arrive?"

"Tomorrow, my lord," Edward replied with obvious relief.

Turning to face his longtime valet, Gerard asked, "Are my garments truly that dreadful?"

The servant cleared his throat. "I did not say that, my lord. However, removing dirt clods and repairing torn knees are not exactly a full utilization of my many talents."

"I know." He sighed dramatically. "I did consider dismissing you on several occasions."

"My lord!"

"But since tormenting you was often my only entertainment, I resisted the urge."

The valet's snort made Gerard laugh. Leaving the room, he mentally arranged his schedule for the day. His plans started with a discussion with Pel about redecorating his study and ended with her once again sharing his bed. He was content with that schedule until his foot met the marble floor of the foyer.

"My lord."

He faced the bowing footman. "Yes?"

"The Dowager Marchioness has arrived."

His hackles rose. He had managed a blessed four years without seeing her, but he would have gone a lifetime if that had been possible. "Where is she?"

"In the parlor, my lord."

"And Lady Grayson?"

"Her Ladyship departed with Lord Trenton a half hour past."

Normally, Gerard would take exception with Trenton, as he did with anyone who deprived him of his wife's company without telling him first, but today he was relieved to spare Isabel his mother's visit. There could be a hundred excuses for why his mother had come, but the truth was simply that she wished to berate him. She took such pleasure in it, and now she had four years' worth of bile to vent. It would be unpleasant, no doubt, and he steeled himself inwardly for the trial ahead.

He also took a moment to acknowledge what he'd avoided

seeing before, that he had always been slightly jealous of those who stole Pel's attentions. The feeling of possessiveness was only exacerbated by his deepened interest in her.

But he did not have time to contemplate what that meant at the moment, so Gerard nodded to the servant, took a deep breath and headed in the direction of the parlor. He paused a moment in the open doorway, studying the silver strands that were now weaved liberally through the once dark tresses. Unlike Pel's mother, whose love for living preserved her beauty well, the dowager marchioness simply looked tired and worn.

Sensing his presence, she turned to face him. Her pale blue gaze raked him from head to toe. Once, that look would have withered him. Now, he knew his own value. "Grayson," she greeted, her voice tight and clipped.

He bowed, noting that she still wore widow's weeds even after all these years.

"Your clothes are a disgrace."

"It is lovely to see you, too, Mother."

"Do not mock me." She sighed loudly, and sank onto the sofa. "Why must you vex me so?"

"I vex you just by breathing, and I'm afraid I am not willing to go to the extent of stopping to please you. The best I can do is to give you a wide berth."

"Sit, Grayson. It is rude of you to stand and force me to strain my neck looking up at you."

Gerard sank into a nearby wooden-armed chair. Sitting directly across from her, he was able to study her in depth. Her back was ramrod straight, painfully so, her hands clenched in her lap until the knuckles were white. He knew he took after her in coloring—his father's portrait was of a man with brown hair and eyes—but her bone-deep rigidity was far removed from his own ability to bend when necessary.

"What ails you?" he asked, only superficially concerned. Everything ailed his mother. She was simply a miserable woman.

Her chin lifted. "Your brother Spencer."

That caught his attention. "Tell me."

"Completely lacking in any sort of male authority, he has decided to adopt your way of living." Her thin lips pursed tighter.

"In what way?"

"In every way—whoring, drinking to excess, complete irresponsibility. He sleeps all day and is out all night. He has made little effort to support himself since leaving school."

Scrubbing his hand across his face, Gerard struggled to reconcile the image she presented with the fresh-faced brother he had known four years ago. It was his fault, he knew. Leaving any child in the care of their mother was bound to lead to a preoccupation with the pursuit of oblivion.

"You must speak with him, Grayson."

"Talking will accomplish nothing. Send him to me."

"I beg your pardon?"

"Gather up his possessions, and send him to me. It will take some time to straighten him out."

"I will not!" His mother's spine stiffened further. How that was possible, he could not say, but it did. "I will not have Spencer under the same roof as that harlot you married."

"Watch your tongue," he warned with ominous softness, his fingers curling around the carved arms of his chair.

"You have made your point and embarrassed me utterly. End this farce now. Divorce that woman for adultery, and do your duty."

"That woman," he bit out, "is the Marchioness of Grayson. And you know as well as I that a successful petition for divorce would include evidence of marital harmony prior to the adultery. It could also be said that my own inconstancy drove her to hers."

His mother flinched. "To wed a mistress. For heaven's sake, could you not have wounded me alone, and not the title as well? Your father would be so ashamed."

Gerard hid the way that statement cut him with an impassive face. "Regardless of my reasons for choosing Lady Grayson, it is a choice I am quite content with. I hope you can learn to live with it, but I am not overly concerned if you do not."

"She has never once honored her vows to you," the dowager said bitterly. "You are a cuckold."

His breath was harshly drawn, his pride stung. "Am I not culpable for that? I have not been a husband to her in anything but a fiduciary capacity."

"Thank God for that. Can you imagine what kind of mother that woman would be?"

"No worse than you."

"Touché."

Her quiet pride made him feel guilty. "Come now, Mother." He sighed. "We are so close to ending this lovely visit without bloodshed."

But as always, she could not quit while they were ahead.

"Your father has been dead for decades, and yet I have been true to his memory."

"Is that what he would have wanted?" he asked, genuinely curious.

"I am certain he would not have wanted the mother of his sons to fornicate indiscriminately."

"No, but a genuine companion, a man who could offer the comforts women long for—"

"I knew what I promised when I said my vows—to do honor to his name and title, to give him and raise fine sons who would make him proud."

"And yet we never do," Gerard said dryly. "As you so often point out to us, we are constantly shaming him."

Her brows drew together in a glower. "It was my responsibility to be both a mother and father to you all, to teach you how to be like him. I realize you think I have failed, but I did the best I could."

Gerard held his retort, his mind filling with memories of whippings with leather straps and hurtful words. Suddenly eager to be alone, he said, "I am more than willing to take

Spencer in hand, but I will do so here, in my house. I have my own affairs to attend to."

"'Affairs' is an apt description," she muttered.

He put his hand to his heart, deflecting her sarcasm with his own. "You disparage me unjustly. I am a married man."

Her gaze narrowed as she assessed him. "You have changed, Grayson. Whether that is a good thing or not remains to be seen."

With a wry smile, he rose. "I have a few arrangements to make in anticipation of Spencer's arrival, so if we are done . . . ?"

"Yes, of course." His mother fluffed out her skirts as she stood. "I have my doubts about this, but I will present your solution to Spencer and if he agrees, so will I." Her voice hardened. "Keep that woman away from him."

His brow arched. "My wife does not have the pox, you know."

"That is debatable," she snapped, departing the room in a flounce of dark skirts and chilly hauteur.

Gerard was left with both relief and a sudden longing for the comfort of his wife.

"I warned you."

Rhys looked down at the top of his sister's head. Standing beneath a tree on the Marley rear lawn, they were alone and apart from the other milling guests. "She is perfect."

"Too perfect, if you ask me."

"Which I did not," he said dryly, but silently he agreed with Isabel's assessment. Lady Susannah was poised and collected. She was a beauty, and yet when he had spoken to her, she reminded him of a moving statue. There was very little life in her.

"Rhys." Isabel turned to face him, her dark red brows drawn together beneath her straw hat. "Can you see yourself being a friend to her?"

"A friend?"

"Yes, a friend. You will have to live with your future wife, sleep with her on occasion, discuss issues relating to your children and household. All of these things are much easier to accomplish when you are friends with your spouse."

"Is that what you have with Grayson?"

"Well . . ." The line between her brows deepened. "In the past, we were close acquaintances."

"Acquaintances?" She was blushing, something he had rarely seen her do.

"Yes." Her gaze drifted, and she suddenly seemed very far away. "Actually," she said softly. "He was a very dear friend."

"And now?" Not for the first time, Rhys found himself wondering what the arrangement was between his sister and her second husband. They had always seemed happy enough before, laughing and sharing private looks that said they knew each other well. Whatever their reasons for seeking sex outside of their marriage, it was not because of lack of charity with each other. "The rumors suggest that you may soon have a marriage that is more . . . traditional."

"I do not want a traditional marriage," she grumbled, her arms crossing beneath her bosom, her attention coming back to the present.

He held up his hands in self-defense. "No need to snap at me."

"I did not snap."

"You did so. For a woman who just rolled out of bed, you are remarkably testy."

Isabel growled. He raised his brows.

Her glare lasted a moment longer and then it faded into a sheepish pout. "I am sorry."

"Is Grayson's return so trying?" he asked softly. "You are not yourself."

"I know it." She released a frustrated-sounding breath. "And I have not eaten since supper."

"That explains a great deal. You were always grumpy when hungry." He held out his arm. "Shall we brave the throng of dour biddies, and fetch you a plate?"

Isabel covered her face with a gloved hand and laughed.

Moments later she stood opposite him at the long food tables, loading her small plate unfashionably high. He shook his head and looked away, hiding his indulgent smile. Moving a short distance from the others, Rhys pulled out his pocket watch and wondered how much longer he would have to bear this odious affair.

It was only three o'clock. He closed the golden door with a click and groaned.

"It is the height of bad taste to look as if you cannot wait to depart."

"I beg your pardon?" He spun about, searching for the owner of the lyrical feminine voice. "Where are you?"

There was no reply.

But the hair at his nape was suddenly on end. "I will find you," he promised, studying the low hedges that lined his left and rear sides.

"To find implies that something is hidden or lost, and I am neither."

Gads, that voice was sweet as an angel's and sultry as a siren's. Without care for his tan-colored breeches, Rhys plunged through the hip-high shrubs, rounded a large elm, and found a small sitting area on the other side. There, on a half-circle-shaped marble bench sat a petite brunette with a book.

"There was a pathway a little further down," she said without looking up from her reading.

His gaze raked her trim form, noting the worn toes of her slippers, the slightly faded hem of her flowered gown, and the too-tight bodice. He bowed and said, "Lord Trenton, Miss . . . ?"

"Yes, I know who you are." Snapping the book closed, she lifted her head and studied him with the same thorough perusal he had given her.

Rhys stared. He could not do otherwise. She was no great beauty. In fact, her delicate features were unremarkable. Her nose was pert and covered with freckles, her mouth just as any other female mouth. She was not young or old. Nearing thirty would be his guess. Her eyes, however, were as pleasing as her voice. They were large and round and a startling blue with yellow flecks. They were also filled with keen intelligence, and even more intriguing, a mischievous sparkle.

It took him a moment to realize she said nothing.

"You are staring," he pointed out.

"So are you," she retorted with a straightforwardness that reminded him of Bella. "I have an excuse. You do not."

His brows raised. "Share your excuse with me. Perhaps I can make use of it as well."

She smiled, and he suddenly found himself uncomfortably hot. "I doubt that. You see, you are quite the handsomest man I have ever seen. I confess it took my brain a moment to reclassify my previous notions of manly beauty, in order to fully process yours."

He returned her smile in full measure.

"Stop that," she said with a chastising wag of an ink-stained finger. "Go away."

"Why?"

"Because you are affecting my ability to think properly."

"Don't think." He moved toward her, wondering what she smelled like and why her clothes were worn and her fingertips stained. Why was she alone, reading, in the midst of a gathering? The sudden flood of questions and the overpowering need to know the answers puzzled him.

As she shook her head, glossy dark curls drifted across her pink cheeks. "You are every bit the rake they say you are. If I did nothing to sway you, what would you do?"

The impertinent chit was flirting with him, but he suspected it was unintentional. She was truly curious, and that unabashed quest for knowledge piqued his jaded interests. "I am not certain. Shall we find out together?"

"Rhys! Damn you," Isabel muttered from a short distance away. "You will not collect from me if you have run off."

He stopped mid-step and cursed under his breath.

"Saved by Lady Grayson," the girl said with a wink.

"Who are you?"

"No one important."

"Is that not for me to decide?" he asked, entirely too reluctant to leave her.

"No, Lord Trenton. That was decided long ago." She stood, and collected her book. "Have a good day." And before he could think of a reason for her to stay, she was gone.

Chapter 9

Isabel paused in the foyer of her home at the sound of masculine voices. One was rushed and urgent. The other, her husband's, was low and unwavering. The door to Gray's study was closed or she would have peeked, out of curiosity. Instead, she looked at the butler who was collecting her hat and gloves. "Who is with Lord Grayson?"

"Lord Spencer Faulkner, my lady." The servant paused a moment, then added, "He arrived with luggage."

She blinked, but in no other way did she betray her surprise. With a nod of dismissal, Isabel went to the kitchen to make certain the cook was aware of the extra mouth to feed. Then she went upstairs to take a short nap. She was exhausted, both from a night spent with very little sleep and an afternoon of chatting inanities with women who spoke unkind things about her behind her back. Rhys was supposed to have been both support and a distraction, but he himself had seemed distracted, his gaze wandering restlessly over the guests as if he were looking for something. Like a way to escape, she imagined.

With the help of her abigail, Isabel stripped down to her stockings and chemise, then took down her hair. Within moments after lying on her bed, she was asleep and dreaming of Gray.

Isabel, he breathed in a voice filled with sin. His mouth, hot and wet, moved across her exposed shoulder. His stroking hand was equally hot, the callused palm causing a delicious friction even through the silk that covered her legs.

Her heart warned her to refuse him, and her arm lifted to push his touch away.

I need you, he said roughly.

Her blood thrummed with eagerness and she whimpered, every nerve ending alive and waiting for the pleasure he could bring. She could smell him and feel his warmth. His ardor radiated outward, igniting hers. It was a dream, and she did not want to wake up. Nothing she did here would affect her.

Her hand dropped away.

Good girl, he praised, his lips to her ear. He lifted her thigh and set it over his. "I missed you today."

She came to consciousness with a start.

And found a very hard bodied, very aroused Grayson at her back.

"No!" Struggling, Isabel squirmed out of his embrace and sat up. She glared at him. "What are you doing in my bed?"

He rolled to his back and tucked his hands under his head, completely unabashed about his obvious erection. Dressed in an open-collared shirt and trousers, his blue eyes sparkling with both devilry and lust, he was unbearably handsome. "Making love to my wife."

"Well, cease." She crossed her arms under her bosom and his eyes dropped to her breasts. Her blasted nipples replied with enthusiasm. "We had a bargain."

"Which I never agreed to."

Her mouth fell open.

"Bring that mouth over here," he murmured, his eyelids lowering.

"You are dreadful."

"That is not what you said last night. Or this morning. I believe you said, 'Oh God, Gray, that is *so* good.'" His lips twitched.

Isabel threw a pillow at him.

Gray laughed and shoved it under his head. "How was your afternoon?"

She sighed and shrugged, her body achingly aware of the man who sat so close to her. "Lady Marley had a breakfast."

"Was it pleasant? I confess, I'm surprised you managed to lure Trenton to such an event."

"He wants a favor."

"Ah, extortion." He smiled. "I love it."

"You would, you wicked man." Catching up one of the pillows, she reclined opposite him. "Perhaps you could fetch my robe?"

"Damnation, no," he said, shaking his head.

"I have no wish to incite your already considerable appetite for sexual congress," she said dryly.

He caught up her hand and kissed her fingertips. "The mere thought of you incites me. At least this way, I also have a charming view."

"Was your day better than mine?" she asked, making every effort to ignore how his touch burned her.

"My brother has come for an extended visit."

"I heard." Gooseflesh spread across her skin as he stroked her palm. "Is something wrong?"

"Wrong? Not precisely. Apparently, he is running amok."

"Hmm . . . Well, he is the age for it." But studying Gray, she could see he was disturbed. "You look so grave. Is he in trouble?"

"No." Gray fell onto his back again and stared up at the ornate ceiling. "He has not yet run up any great debt or angered someone's husband, but he is certainly on a steady course in that direction. I should have been here to guide him, but once again my own needs came before anyone else's."

"You cannot blame yourself," she protested. "Any wildness on his part is natural for boys his age."

Her husband stilled, his head turning to reveal narrowed eyes. "Boys his age?"

"Yes." She recoiled slightly, suddenly wary.

"He is the same age as I was when we wed. Did you think I was a boy then?" He rolled on top of her, pinning her to the bed. "Do you think I am a boy now?"

Her heart raced. "Gray, really—"

"Yes, really," he purred, his jaw set ominously as he thrust his hand under her buttocks and tilted her pelvis to cradle his. He rolled his hips, rubbing his cock against the perfect spot between her legs. "I want to know. Do you think me less than a man because I am younger than you?"

She swallowed hard, her body tense and straining beneath his. "No," she breathed. Her subsequent inhale filled her lungs with his luscious scent. Grayson was virile, temperamental, and most definitely a man.

He stared down at her for a long moment, his cock hardening and swelling between her thighs. Lowering his head, he took her mouth, his tongue licking between her parted lips. "I have wanted to do this all day."

"You did do this all day." Her hands fisted in the counterpane to prevent herself from touching him.

Gray rested his forehead against hers and laughed. "I hope you have no objection to Spencer's visit."

"Of course not," she assured him, managing a smile through her near painful attraction. What the devil was she to do with him? With herself? She could only hope that Lord Spencer would distract him from his single-minded seduction. How long could she truly expect to resist?

"Thank you." He brushed his mouth across hers, then twisted to drape her body over his.

She frowned, puzzled. "No need to thank me. This is your home."

"This is *our* home, Pel." He settled into the pillows. When she tried to slide off him, he caught her waist. "Stay here."

When she opened her mouth to argue, he grimaced, which arrested her. "What is it?" Before she could think better of it, her hand was cupping his cheek. He leaned into her touch and sighed.

"Spencer told me that I am his hero."

Her brows rose. "What a lovely thing to say."

"But it's not. Not at all. You see, to him, I am the brother he knew before. That is the man whom he and his friends emulate. They are drinking in vast quantities, associating with questionable people, and showing no concern whatsoever for the effect of their behavior on others. He said he has yet to manage two mistresses, but he is giving it his best effort."

Isabel winced, her stomach clenching at the reminder of how wild her husband was. His edges might have smoothed some, but he was no less dangerous. So far he had been cocooned with her while awaiting his garments, but soon he would be out and about. Once that happened, everything would change.

He nipped the fleshy part of her palm with his teeth, and held her gaze with his. "I told him he was better off finding a wife such as you. You are more expensive than two mistresses, but worth every shilling."

"Grayson!"

"It's true." His smile was wicked.

"There is no hope for you, my lord." But she had to bite her lip to keep a straight face.

His hands left her waist and followed the curve of her spine. "I missed you, dear Pel, these last four years." He gripped her shoulders, and pulled her gently but firmly to his chest. "I must begin anew. You are all I have at the moment, and I am grateful that you are more than enough."

Her heart welled with tenderness for him. "Whatever you

need—" He chuckled, and her eyes widened in horror. "As far as your brother is concerned, you understand. Not for . . ." She wrinkled her nose as he laughed. "Odious man."

"Not for sex. I collect what you meant." His mouth nuzzled into her hair, and his chest expanded beneath her. "Now, you must understand what *I* mean." Cupping her buttocks, he rocked her against his rigid cock. His lips to her ear, he whispered, "I ache for you—for your body, your scent, the sounds you make when we're fucking. If you think I will deny myself those pleasures, you are mad. A raving lunatic."

"Stop that." Her voice was so thready it had no substance. He was like warm marble beneath her—hard, ridged, solid. She could almost believe he would support her, provide her an anchor, but she knew men of his ilk too well. She did not hold it against him, she simply accepted it.

"I will make a bargain with you, dear wife."

Lifting her head, she caught her breath at the heat that burned in his eyes and flushed his cheeks. "You do not honor your bargains, Grayson."

"I shall honor this one. The day you stop wanting me is the day I will no longer want you."

She stared at him, taking in the wicked arch of his brow, before sighing dramatically. "Can you grow a wart?"

Gray blinked. "Beg your pardon?"

"Or overeat? Perhaps cease to bathe?"

He laughed. "As if I would do anything to make myself less attractive to you." The fingers that combed through her hair were gentle, the smile he gave her tender. "I find you irresistible as well."

"You never paid me any mind before."

"That is not true, and you know it. I am no more immune to your charms than any other man." His jaw firmed. "Which is why Spencer will accompany you when you go out tonight."

"Your brother has no interest in the tame social affairs I attend," she said with a laugh.

"He does now."

Isabel took a moment to absorb the sudden quiet intensity of her husband's tone, before sliding off of him and leaving the bed. The fact that he let her go without argument made her wary. "Must I be home at a certain time as well?" she asked tightly.

"Three." He sat up further on the pillows and crossed his arms. The unspoken challenge was evident in his tone and posture.

She picked up the gauntlet. "And if I fail to return by that time?"

"Why, I will come after you, vixen," he replied with ominous softness. "I've no wish to lose you, now that I have found you."

"You cannot do this, Gray." She began to pace.

"I can, and will, Pel."

"I am not chattel."

"You do belong to me."

"Does that possession apply to you in like fashion?"

He frowned. "What are you asking?"

She paused next to the bed and set her hands on her hips. "Will you always return at three when I am not with you?"

His frown deepened.

"When you do not return in a timely manner, will I have the right to hunt you down? Shall I barge into whatever den of iniquity you happen to be gracing and rip you from the arms of your lover?"

Gray rose from the bed with slow, predatory grace. "Was that your intent? A lover?"

"We are not talking about me."

"Yes. We are." Rounding the bed, he came toward her on bare feet. Somehow she found the sight arousing, which only goaded her temper. The man was everything she did not want, and yet she wanted him more than anything.

"I am not a sex-obsessed female, Grayson, which is what your question implies."

"You can be as sex-obsessed as you like. *With me.*"

"I cannot keep up with you," she scoffed, backing away. "Eventually, you will fill the lack elsewhere."

"Why worry about *'eventually'* now?" His gaze penetrated as he stalked her. "Forget the past and the future. If there is one thing I learned over the last four years, it is that *this* moment is the one that matters."

"How is that any different than how you lived before?" Sidestepping quickly, Isabel nearly ran to the door that led to her boudoir. She gasped as Gray caught her about the waist. The feel of him behind her—hard, aroused—flooded her with memories.

"Before," he said harshly in her ear, "everything in my life could wait until another day. Visiting my estates, meeting with my stewards, seeing Lady Sinclair. Sometimes that other day never comes, Pel. Sometimes today is all there is."

"See how different we are? I will always think of the future and how my actions today will come back to haunt me."

With one arm banded around her waist, he used his free hand to knead her breast. Against her will, she moaned.

"*I* will haunt you." Gray surrounded her, dominated her, teased her with his seductive touch. "I am not fool enough to cage you in, Isabel, not when we are already leg-shackled together." With a curse, he released her. "I will remind you of that as often as is necessary."

She spun to face him, her skin missing the touch of his. "I will not be guarded like a prisoner."

"I've no wish to lessen your freedom."

"Then why?"

"Soon others will know you have dismissed Hargreaves. They will sniff after you, and for the moment, I am unable to do aught about it."

"Staking your claim?" she asked coldly.

"Protecting you." Linking both arms behind his neck, he stretched and suddenly looked weary. "I returned for the express purpose of being a husband to you, I have said that from the first."

"Please. We have run this into the ground."

"Indulge me, vixen," he said softly. "One day at a time, that is all I ask. Surely you can spare that much?"

"I have already—"

"How else can we live together? Answer me that." His voice roughened as his arms fell to his sides. "Each craving the other . . . hungry . . . I am famished for you. Starving."

"I know," she whispered, feeling the great distance between them, even though they stood so close. Shivering with lust, her nipples hardened. She grew moist for him despite her soreness. "And I cannot sate you."

"I did not sate you either. We spent mere hours together. Not nearly enough time." Gray moved toward the door to make his egress.

"We have not finished discussing your three o'clock rule, Grayson."

He stilled, but did not face her. In the candlelight, his hair gleamed with the vitality that defined him. "You stand there clad only in chemise and stockings, your body creamy and begging for a fucking. If I stay here a moment longer, that is what you will get, Pel."

She hesitated, her arm lifting toward his tense back, a momentary sign of weakness before she could control it.

How else can we live together?

They couldn't. Not for much longer.

Her hand dropped. "I shall be home by three."

Gray nodded and left without looking back.

Gerard looked across his desk at Spencer and released a weary breath. There was too much turmoil in his life at the moment. The only time he felt remotely at peace with his return to London was when he was talking with Pel.

Not arguing. Talking.

He wished to God he understood her. Why was she so focused on the unraveling of a relationship that had yet to truly begin? To him that made as much sense as wearing a fur-lined coat in warm weather just because it would one day rain.

"This is not what I anticipated when I agreed to come here," Spencer grumbled, shaking his head. His hair was over-long, and a thick lock fell over his forehead in a way Gerard knew would urge women to touch it. He knew because it was a style he once sported for that very reason. "I thought you and I would be going about town together."

"And we shall, once I am suitably attired. In the meantime, I envy you an evening spent in Lady Grayson's company. You will enjoy yourself, I can assure you."

"Yes, but I was hoping to spend my evening with a woman I can fuck."

"You will escort my wife home no later than three, and after that you are free to do as you please." Gerard almost advised him to enjoy himself, since it was the last such late night Spencer would have in a while. But he held his tongue.

"Mother hates her, you know," Spencer said, pausing briefly in front of the desk. "Truly detests her."

"And you?"

Spencer's eyes widened. "Do you truly wish to hear my opinion?"

"Certainly." Gerard leaned back in his very uncomfortable chair and reminded himself to toss it out when the study was overhauled. "I'm curious to learn how you feel about my wife. You will be sharing a residence with her. Your thoughts, therefore, concern me."

Spencer shrugged. "I cannot decide if I envy you or pity you. I've no notion how a peeress came to have a body like that. Pel's beauty is not genteel in any fashion. That hair. Her skin. Her breasts. And for God's sake, where in hell did she get those lips? Yes, I would give up a fortune for a woman like that in my bed. But to take one to wife?" He shook his head. "And yet both you and Pelham sought your pleasures outside the marriage bed. Can you tell me why?"

"Idiocy."

"Ha!" Spencer laughed and strolled to the array of decanters. After pouring himself a drink, he turned and rested his hip against the mahogany table. His body was lean with youth, and Gerard studied him, trying to see how Pel must have seen him when they'd wed. Perhaps the contrast between himself and Spencer would facilitate his cause with his wife. Surely she could not fail to note how different he was now.

"And I've no wish to provoke you, Gray, but I prefer women who prefer me."

"Perhaps that would have been possible, had I been here to see to her."

"True." Tossing back his drink, Spencer set his glass down and crossed his arms. "Will you be bringing her into line now?"

"She was never out of line."

"If you say so," Spencer said skeptically.

"I do. Now, I expect you to stay with Lady Grayson for the duration of your evening. Stay out of the card rooms and rein in your libidinous inclinations until she is home safely."

"What, exactly, do you expect to happen to her?"

"Nothing, because you will be there."

Gerard rose as Pel's lush form filled the doorway. She wore pale pink, a color that should have made her look sweetly innocent; instead it emphasized her worldliness and vibrant sensuality. Her full breasts were beautifully showcased in the loving embrace of her high-waisted gown. The overall effect, to him, was of a sugar-coated treat. One he wished to nibble and consume until he was gorged.

He blew out his breath; his response to the mere sight of her was both primitive and instinctual. He wished to toss her over his shoulder, run up the stairs, and fuck like rabbits. The image was so absurd, he could not help but chuckle through a tortured groan.

"Come now," she murmured with a slight smile. "I cannot look as bad as all that."

"Good God," Spencer cried out, moving forward to capture her hand and lift it to his lips. "I shall need a small sword to hold them off. But never fear, my dearest sister-in-law, I shall serve you until the very end."

Isabel's soft, husky laughter drifted through the study and weakened Gerard's already shaky resolution to allow her to go. He was not a jealous man by nature, but Isabel resisted the connection he sought and his tenuous position in her life caused him a rare level of anxiety.

"How gallant of you, Lord Spencer," she rejoined with a blinding smile. "It has been some time since I've enjoyed the company of a brazen rake."

The warm appreciation in his brother's eyes made Gerard grit his teeth. "I take it as my personal duty to fill that lack."

"And you shall do so admirably, I have no doubt."

His throat tight, Gerard cleared it, drawing their attention to him. Somehow he managed a smile that sparked a hot flicker in Pel's eyes. Words were caught and held on his tongue, squelched before they could be freed. He was desperate to say things that would make her stay—anything and everything, so he would not have to spend the evening alone. The night before had been hell while she was gone. The air in their rooms was scented of her skin, making it more obvious how cold and lonely the house was without her vibrant presence.

He sighed in resignation and held out his hand, every muscle hardening when her gloved fingertips pressed lightly into his palm. He escorted her to the door, draped her in her cloak, and returned to his study window to watch his carriage carry her away.

She belonged to him, as surely as his entailed estates.

Nothing and no one could take her away. But he had no wish to keep her by force. He wished to earn her regard, just as he had earned the respect of his tenants. Pride in ownership worked both ways, and until he'd worked side by side with his tenants on his many holdings—until he'd worn their clothes, attended their celebrations, and eaten at their tables—they'd had none for him, an errant lord who paid them no mind and felt no loyalty.

His methods had been extreme by any measure, and every time he moved his attentions to a new estate, he had to begin the process of building trust and respect anew. But it had been healing for him. A chance for him to find a home, a place to belong, things he'd never had before.

Now he knew it had been training for this. This was his true home. And if he could find a way to share it with Isabel, in every way, if he could cool his ardor enough and rein in the base needs that clawed at him, perhaps contentment with her could be his.

It was a goal worth striving for.

"She has thrown you over, has she, Lord Hargreaves?" asked a girlish voice beside him.

John turned his head away from the sight of Isabel across the ballroom, and bowed to the lovely brunette who spoke to him. "Lady Stanhope, a pleasure."

"Grayson has ruined your cozy little arrangement," she purred, her eyes leaving his to find Pel. "Look how zealously Lord Spencer guards her side. You know as well as I that he would not be here if Grayson had not ordered him to be. Makes one wonder why he is not here to see to the matter himself."

"I have no wish to discuss Lord Grayson," he said tightly. Unable to help himself, he stared at his former mistress. He still could not collect how everything could change so drastically in so short a time. Yes, he had noted Pel's increasing restlessness, but their friendship had been strong and the sex as satisfying as always.

"Even if discussing him could return Lady Grayson's attentions to you?"

His head whipped toward her. Dressed in blood red satin, Stanhope's widow was hard to miss, even amongst the crowd. He had noted her several times over the course of the evening, especially since she seemed to be spending a great deal of her time studying him. "What are you saying?"

Lady Stanhope's rouged mouth curved in a portentous smile. "I want Grayson. You want his wife. It would be to both of our benefits to work together."

"I've no notion of what you are talking about." But he was intrigued. And it showed.

"That's fine, darling," she drawled. "You can leave all the notions to me."

"Lady Stanhope—"

"We are allies. Call me Barbara."

The determined tilt of her chin and eyes as hard as the jade they resembled told John she knew what she was about. He glanced at Pel again and caught her staring back at him with her full bottom lip worried between her teeth. His pride smarted.

Barbara's hand slipped around his arm. "Let's walk, and I shall tell you what I have planned . . ."

Chapter 10

Sitting at her boudoir desk, Isabel addressed the last of her dinner invitations with a flourish that belied the apprehension she felt. Grayson had never been the type of man who would brush off such machinations. He was devious and lacked the morals that restrained most, and while he admired similar cunning in others, he did not feel as charitable to those who would try their trickery on him.

Fully cognizant of the fact that she was, in effect, poking a sleeping lion with a stick, she hesitated a moment, staring at the tidy stack of cream-colored missives at her elbow.

"Would you like these sent out immediately?" her secretary asked, hovering nearby.

She hesitated a moment, and then shook her head. "Not just yet. You may go for now."

Rising from her seat at the escritoire, Isabel knew she was only prolonging the inevitable by failing to set in motion her search for a mistress for Gray, but she needed a bit more inner strength to manage the task. The tension and heated awareness between them was anathema to her mental health.

She'd slept fitfully the night before. Her body, while sore, craved the feel of his. If only she knew what had caused their relationship to alter so drastically, perhaps she could find a way to change it back.

As Gray had requested earlier, she moved over to the adjoining door to speak with him, her stomach fluttering at the mere thought of seeing him. She had barely cracked the portal open when the sound of angry voices stilled her.

"What concerns me is the talk, Gray. Since I avoid those types of preening social events, I had no notion of how bad it is. It is truly dreadful."

"What is said about me is no concern of yours," Gray rejoined tightly.

"Damned if it isn't!" Spencer cried. "I am a Faulkner, too. You chastise me for running wild, and yet Pel has a far worse reputation. They wonder if you have the wherewithal to bring her to heel. They whisper about why you left, that perhaps your recalcitrant wife is too much for you. That you are not man enough to—"

"I suggest you say no more." Gray's interjection was fraught with menace.

"Turning a deaf ear does nothing to correct the damage. She was in the retiring room for no more than a few minutes, and in that time I overheard things that made my blood run cold. Mother is right. You should petition Parliament to be rid of her. You quite easily have two witnesses to her adultery. Hundreds, in fact."

"You tread on thin ice, brother."

"I will not tolerate the disparagement of our name, and I am aghast that you would do so!"

"Spencer." Gray's voice dropped in warning. "Do not do anything idiotic."

"I will do what is necessary. She is a mistress, Grayson. Not a wife."

There was a loud grunt, and the wall beside her shook violently. Isabel covered her mouth to stifle a cry.

"Say another unkind word about Pel," Gray bit out, "and I

will not restrain myself. I will not tolerate any slander of my wife."

"Bloody hell," Spencer gasped. His surprised voice was so close to the gap in the door she was certain she would be discovered. "You attacked me! What has happened to you? You have changed."

Stumbling footsteps told her that Gray had pushed his brother away.

"You say I have changed. Why? Because I choose to honor my promises and commitments? That is maturity."

"She does not afford a like respect to you."

The low growl from Grayson frightened Isabel. "Get out. I cannot be near you now."

"We are well met, then, for I cannot bear to be near you either."

Angry-sounding footfalls preceded the slamming of the hallway door.

Her heart racing madly, Isabel slumped against the wall and felt ill. She was well aware of the talk, which had started when they wed and grew worse as they lived separate lives. Gray's title held enough power that no one would dare cut her, and she had considered the gossip the price she must pay for her decisions and the freedom she desired. Gray had seemed immune, and so she had assumed he did not care. Now she knew he did care. A great deal. To learn that she had hurt Gray was so painful she could barely catch her breath.

Unsure of what to do or what to say to minimize the damage she had caused, Isabel stood motionless until she heard Gray's weary sigh. That soft sound touched her deeply, melting something that had long been frozen. She gripped the knob, pulled the door open . . .

. . . and was arrested by the sight that greeted her.

Gray was clad in only trousers, a new garment by the look of it, which reminded her of the tailor's earlier call. He stood by the bed, his hand on the carved post, his back and beautifully curved buttocks hard with tension.

"Grayson," she called quietly, her blood hot from the mere sight of him.

He straightened, but did not face her. "Yes, Pel?"

"You wished to speak with me?"

"I apologize. Now is not a good time."

She took a deep breath, and stepped further into the room. "It is I who owes you an apology."

He turned to face her then, causing her to reach for a nearby chair and grip the back of it. The sight of his bare torso stole her wits.

"You overheard," he said flatly.

"It was not my intent."

"We are not discussing this now." His jaw tightened. "I am not fit company at the moment."

Shaking her head, Isabel pushed away from her support and moved forward. "Tell me how I can help you."

"You won't like my answer, so I suggest you leave. Now."

Heaving out her breath, she fought back the urge to cast up her accounts. "How could we have erred so greatly?" she asked, almost to herself.

Veering off course, she walked toward the other side of the room. "Ignorance, I suppose. And arrogance. To think that we could live as we pleased and expect Society to accept us."

"Go away, Isabel."

"I refuse to come between you and your family, Gray."

"My family be damned!" he retorted. "As you will be, if you stay here any longer."

"Don't growl at me." She shot him a narrowed glance. "You once shared your problems with me. Now that *I* am the problem, I think that habit is even more important. And cease looking at me like that. . . . What are you doing?"

"I warned you," he said grimly. Moving so quickly she had no time to evade him, Gray caught her about the waist with his hands and carried her to the bathing chamber. His skin was hot, his grip too tight. He set her down, shoved her inside, and slammed the door shut between them.

"Gray!" she shouted through the portal.

"I am feeling violent, and your scent is making me lust-ful. Persisting with your inane prattle will see you tossed on your back and your mouth put to much better uses."

Isabel blinked in shock. His rudeness was meant to drive her away, to scare her, and it very nearly succeeded. She'd never had a man speak to her so crudely and in such anger. It did odd things to her insides, making her quiver and her breath shorten.

Standing with her hand pressed against the door, she listened for sounds of him. She had no notion of what she should do, but walking away when he was so inflamed seemed cow-ardly. And yet . . . She was no fool. She knew men far better than women, and the best thing to do with a surly man was stay out of his way. She was well aware of what would hap-pen should she choose to enter his rooms again. "Grayson?"

He did not reply.

There was nothing she could do for him, nothing that could change the facts or make him feel better beyond the temporary release of orgasm. But perhaps that was what he needed after hearing the disparagement of his virility. Per-haps it was what she needed, to forget for a short time that both of her marriages had failed. The first time, she had been young and naïve. But this time she had known better. How foolish to have thought Gray would not mature with age, which he appeared to have done by taking responsibility for Lord Spencer. Which left her wondering if perhaps Pelham also would have changed, had he been given the time.

"I can hear you thinking through the door," Gray said wryly, his voice directly opposite the barrier.

"Are you still angry?"

"Of course, but not with you."

"I *am* sorry, Grayson."

"For what?" he asked in a low tone. "Marrying me?"

She swallowed hard, the word "no" trapped in her throat because she refused to give it voice.

"Isabel?"

Sighing, she moved away. He was right. Now was not the time to discuss this, not when she couldn't think clearly. She hated the door between them. It blocked his scent and his touch and the hunger in his eyes—things she should not want. Why could she not be more practical about her wedded state, like the rest of her family? Why did her emotions have to become so tangled up and ruin everything?

"Just so we are clear," he said gruffly. "I am not sorry, and out of all the things said to me in the last hour, hearing you say we have done something wrong disturbs me the most."

Her steps faltered. How could he not regret the marriage that caused him such grief? If this was not enough to lessen his determination to have a true conjugal relationship, nothing would be.

Anger filled her at the sudden softening she felt toward him. She should not be melting over him. Her mother would not melt. Neither would Rhys. They would enjoy the great sex until they were sated and be done with it. Her chin lifted. That was what she should do also, if she were practical about such matters.

She left the bathing chamber, and walked slowly into her boudoir. The fact was, she could be practical about her affairs because the rules were set from the beginning and the end was anticipated. There was no ownership, such as she had felt for Pelham and was beginning to feel for Gray.

Drat the man! They had been friends. Then he had returned as a stranger, and took the place of her spouse.

A husband was a possession. A lover was not.

Her stomach flipped.

She is a mistress, Grayson. Not a wife.

Lord Spencer's angry words were, quite simply, the solution.

Yanking on the bellpull, Isabel waited impatiently for her abigail to come up and then, with the servant's help, she undressed. Completely. And unpinned her hair. Then she squared her shoulders and quickly crossed the distance back to Gray's room. She threw the door open, saw her husband reaching for a shirt that lay on the bed, and with a running start, jumped onto his back.

"What in—"

Caught off balance, he tumbled face-first into the bed. Isabel hung on. Reaching behind him, Gray flipped her onto the counterpane with a deep growl.

"Finally, you come to your senses," he muttered, before lowering his head and sucking a nipple into his mouth.

"Oh," she cried, startled by the feel of drenched heat. Heavens, the man recovered quickly! "Wait."

He grunted and went on suckling.

"I have rules!"

Heated blue eyes met hers, and he released her nipple with a loud pop. "You. Naked. Whenever I want you. Wherever I want you. Those are the only 'rules.'"

"Yes." She nodded, and he stilled, his large body turning hard as stone. "We will draft an agreement, and—"

"We have a written agreement, madam—a marriage certificate."

"No. I will be your mistress and you will be my lover. The arrangement will be clear and on paper, since I cannot trust you to keep to your end of bargains."

"Just for curiosity's sake," he began, pushing up from the bed to stand over her. His hands went to the placket of his trousers. "Are you deranged?"

She pushed up onto her elbows, her mouth watering as he shoved his garments to the floor and was suddenly, gloriously naked and impressively aroused.

He pounced on her with little finesse. "Your mental malady will not dampen my ardor, so you needn't worry about that. You can spout all the gibberish you like while I ride you. I will not mind a bit."

"Gray, really."

Catching her knee, he shoved her thighs wide and settled

his lean hips between them. "A wife is cherished and treated with a gentle hand. A mistress is a convenient cunt to rut in. Are you certain you wish to alter your status in our bedroom?"

It was then she realized he was still angry, his jaw clenched dangerously. The heavy heat of his erection was like lightning striking her skin. Gooseflesh spread over her body, and her breasts swelled painfully. "You don't frighten me."

His body was so hard and hot to the touch, it burned her. "You do not heed warnings very well," he murmured in a low tone, and before she could process it, he'd thrust his cock into her. Not quite creamy for him and still a bit sore, she cried out and arched upward, the entry both painful and unexpected.

His hand fisted in the length of her hair, keeping her head back and her throat exposed. It also kept her helpless and rigidly in place as he began to fuck her with fierce, powerful lunges.

"When we are through with each other," she gasped, her determination unwavering, "we will separate. I will return to my old residence. We will be friends, and you can regain face."

He rammed into her, striking so deep she lost her breath.

"You can have only me," she managed a moment later, moisture flooding her sex as he took what he wanted and excited her by doing so. "Slide between another woman's sheets and you void our arrangement."

Gray lowered his head and sucked hard on her neck. He grunted with every deep plunge of his cock, his heavy balls slapping against her with each downward stroke. The result of having her head held back was her breasts thrusting upward, and the coarse hairs on his chest scraped across her nipples. She whimpered at the feeling, her wits slipping rapidly.

She should not feel so good. Her position was uncomfortable, his touch bruising, his mouth and teeth hurtful against her tender throat. His hips pummeled hers, his shaft a thick intrusion that pumped through swollen tissues . . . And yet the absolute certainty in his touch, the complete lack of hesitation, his supreme arrogance in using *her* body for *his* pleasure was nearly rapturous.

"Yes . . ." As her body shivered on the verge of climax, she moaned a low plaintive sound. She clawed at his sides, dug her heels in his ass, and gave as good as she received.

"Isabel," he growled, his mouth pressed to her ear. "Brazen enough to tackle a man naked, but so swiftly mastered by a hard cock."

It would not be like it was before! "My rules," she reminded, then she sank her teeth into his chest.

"Damn your rules." Gray yanked out of her, his free hand gripping his cock and pumping, guttural sounds accompanying the spurting of his cum across her belly. It was base and raw, very different from his lovemaking of just a day before, and it left her writhing in an agony of lust.

"Selfish bastard."

Tossing his leg over her hips, he rolled and came over her, straddling her. His beautiful mouth was hard, his face flushed and eyes glazed. "A man is not required to pleasure his mistress."

"So you accept the arrangement," she bit out, her teeth clenched together. She was in control, regardless of how he might wish it otherwise.

As his hands began to rub his seed into her skin, his smile was cold and tight. "If you have a wish to make a devil's bargain, so be it." He caught her nipples between damp fingertips and rolled them.

Isabel slapped at him. "Enough!"

"I should allow you to leave, all angry and hot and wet. Maybe then you would feel a little of what I do."

"Spare me," she scoffed. "You had your pleasure."

He hummed a soft chastising sound. "Do you truly believe I could be sated while you are not?"

"Do I misunderstand the semen on my stomach?"

Gray leaned back to give her an unhindered view of the hard length of his cock. The sight of it was nearly too much for her overheated body. Even his arrogant smile did nothing to dampen her desire. He was built for a woman's pleasure, and he damn well knew it.

"I believe we have already established your stamina, Grayson."

His gaze narrowed, which aroused her suspicions. She could see his mind at work. Considering something devious, no doubt. "Any man kneeling over your creamy cunt would be ready to rut in it."

"How poetic," she murmured dryly. "Be still my heart."

"I save my poetry for my wife." He slid downward, his smile wicked enough to make her tense in apprehension. "If it were she in my bed, I would not leave her so distressed."

"I am not distressed."

He licked the edge of skin that prefaced the damp curls of her sex. She gasped.

"Of course not," he said, grinning. "Mistresses do not expect orgasms."

"I always have."

Ignoring her, he dipped his head and swiped his tongue through the lips of her sex. Her hips arched involuntarily. "I would tell my wife how I love the taste of her and the feel of her petal soft skin. How the scent of our combined lust arouses me further, and keeps me hard despite the many times I come on her."

She watched his strong hands with their neatly trimmed nails and unfashionable calluses press her legs open wider. The sight of his dark skin against her paler flesh was erotic, as was the lock of dark hair that fell over his brow and tickled her inner thighs.

"I would tell her how much I love the color of her hair here, the rich chocolate with glints of fire. It is like a beacon that lures me to her, promising untold delights and hours of pleasure." Gray pressed a kiss against her clitoris, and when she keened softly, he suckled, stroking his tongue leisurely back and forth across it.

Releasing the counterpane she held so tightly, she reached for him, her fingertips sliding through the thick silk of his hair to caress the sweat-dampened roots. He made that noise she adored, a cross between an arrogant grunt and a groan of encouragement, and then he rewarded her with faster licks.

Draping her legs over his shoulders, she tugged him closer, lifting her hips to swivel against his expert mouth. Any moment she expected him to stop, to tease her cruelly by leaving her wanting. Desperate to come, she begged, "Please . . . Gray . . ."

He mumbled reassurance, his large hands gentling her as he brought her to orgasm with the gentle fucking of his tongue. She froze, every muscle and sinew locked with the pleasure that unfurled slowly and increased in intensity until she shivered uncontrollably.

"I love that," he murmured, shrugging carefully out from under her and crawling up the length of her body. "Almost as much as I love this." He surged into her spasming depths with a growl.

"Oh my God!" She could not open her eyes, even to look at him, something she enjoyed so much she often stared. She was drunk on him—the smell of him, the feel of him.

The sight of him would ruin her.

"Yes," he hissed, sinking deep, his cock as hard as stone and hot enough to melt her. Curling his arms beneath her shoulders, Gray embraced her from head to toe. His mouth to her ear he whispered, "I would tell my wife how she feels to me, so hot and drenched, like dipping my cock into warm honey."

She felt the tight roping of his abdomen flex against her belly as he withdrew in a slow, torturous glide and then pumped back inside.

"I would love her body the way a husband should, with care for her comfort and an eye toward her pleasure."

Her hands caressed the curve of his spine, cupping his steely buttocks. She moaned as they clenched on a perfect stroke. "Keep doing that," she whispered, her head falling to the side.

"This?" He withdrew, and then, circling his hips, screwed back into her.

"Mmmm . . . A little harder."

The next pump of his hips struck deep. Delicious.

"You are a demanding mistress." As his mouth followed the curve of her cheekbone, he chuckled.

"I know what I want."

"Yes." His hand stroked her side, cupped her hip, and angled her perfectly for his measured thrusts. "Me."

"Gray." Her arms tightened, her body awash in lustful longing.

"Say my name," he urged hoarsely, his cock shafting her cunt in long, rhythmic plunges.

Isabel forced her heavy eyelids to open, and met his gaze. The request was not frivolous. His handsome features were open, boyish, stripped of their usual arrogant assurance. A mistress would not use his name. Neither would most wives. The intimacy was telling. And with his body riding hers with unfailing skill, devastating.

"Say it." Now it was a command.

"Gerard," she cried, as he made her come in a white hot flare of heat.

And he held her, and made love to her, and crooned praise to her.

Just as a husband would.

Chapter 11

"What have I done?"

Although he heard Pel's whisper, Gerard remained still with his eyes closed, feigning sleep. Her head rested on his bicep and the soft curve of her ass pressed against his hip. The air around them was redolent of sex and exotic flowers, and he felt like he was in heaven.

But obviously, his wife did not.

She heaved a forlorn sigh, and pressed her lips to his skin. The urge to roll and embrace her tightly was nearly overwhelming, but he resisted it. Somehow, he needed to puzzle her out. There was a key to her, if only he could find it.

To bargain with him for his fidelity . . . That was what she had done. He was flattered and touched, but decidedly curious as to her motives. Why not simply ask him to be true to her? Why go to such lengths—threatening to leave him—to accomplish her aim?

Constancy toward one woman was unknown to him. His needs were sometimes violent as they had been today, and while some women served such a purpose, others, such as his wife, were made for lovemaking. Opening his eyes was not required to know that Isabel's body was bruised by his ardor. If he subjected her to such treatment often she would grow to fear him, and that was something he could not bear.

But for now, she was his and promised to his bed. That would bide him some time to do a bit of research. He needed to learn more about her, so he could understand her. With understanding would come the ability to keep her happy. Or so he hoped.

Gerard waited until Pel was asleep before leaving the bed. Despite how he wished to linger, it was time to find Spencer and attempt to explain. Perhaps Spencer would understand, perhaps he would not, but Gerard could not allow the situation between them to remain as it was for a moment longer.

He blew out his breath. A temper was something he was still becoming accustomed to. Prior to four years ago, he had never felt deeply enough about anything to become angry over it.

Walking past the full-length mirror, Gerard paused, having caught a glimpse of himself as he passed by. He turned, and stared at his reflection, noting the bite mark on his chest. Swiveling at the hips, he perused his back and the scratches that laced either side of his spine. Just above his buttocks, two round shadows hinted at bruises to come, marks left by his wife's heels as she spurred him on.

"I'll be damned," he breathed, his eyes wide. He looked nigh as bad as Pel. No passive lover was she. He was well met.

Something wondrous tingled in his chest, and then burst forth as a low chuckle.

"You are an odd creature," came the sleep-husky voice behind him. "Laughing is not the first thing I think of doing when I see you naked."

Heat rushed over his skin. He moved back toward the bed, and as he did so, he could not help but notice the marks of his teeth on her neck. His blood heated and rushed at the sight. He was a primitive beast, but at least he knew it. "What *is* the first thing, then?"

Pel pushed herself up to a seated position. Disheveled and flushed, she looked ravished and it was an air of satiation that would linger around her throughout the evening, an unspoken claim.

"I think your ass is divine, and I wish to bite it."

"*Bite* it?" He blinked. "My ass?"

"Yes." She tucked the sheet beneath her arms, her face devoid of the humor that would have revealed she was teasing.

"Why on earth would you wish to do such a thing?"

"Because it looks taut and firm. Like a peach." Licking her lips, she arched a challenging brow. "I wish to see if it's as hard when clenched between my teeth."

His hands moved without volition to cover his rear. "You're serious."

"Quite."

"Quite." Gerard studied his wife with a narrowed glance. It never occurred to him that Isabel might also have some . . . *quirks* in the bedroom. Since she had indulged his anomalous cravings, he supposed it was only fair that he indulge hers, even if his flesh did tighten warily at the thought.

Her amber eyes darkened and heated, a sensual invitation to dally, and he could not refuse. Not when her capitulation was so fresh. He had wanted this, wanted her willing, and if that meant allowing her to bite his ass, he would bear it. It would only take a moment. Then he would dress and speak to Spencer.

"Odd, this," he muttered, lying facedown beside her.

"I did not suggest this very moment," she said dryly. "Or even that I wished to make the thought a reality. I simply answered your question."

He heaved out a relieved breath. "Thank God." But when he moved to leave the bed, she dropped the sheet and bared her breasts. Groaning, he asked, "How in hell is a man expected to go about his business when you tempt him so?"

"He isn't." Wiggling her courtesan's body out from under

his sheets, she stunned him with her beauty so that he lost the sense to move as she crawled over him. "Or are you comfortable only when you are the biter?"

Isabel straddled his back in reverse—her feet by his hands, her hips at his shoulders, her breasts at the small of his back. The lush feel of her curves and the seductive heat of her sleep-warmed body made him hard again.

And he had thought himself spent for a while.

Encircling her ankles with an apprehensive grip, Gerard waited. Then he felt her hands, so tiny and soft, stroking along the curve of his buttocks before squeezing gently. That he could not see her actions only increased the surprising eroticism of the act. Ridiculous though it was, the thought of her admiring another man in such a manner unnerved him.

"Have you always had this fascination?"

"No. You have a singular ass."

He waited for more, but she said nothing further. Instead she began to hum a soft appreciative sound, and his cock grew so hard it hurt to be prone. The tips of her fingers kneaded his flesh, rubbing and pressing in a way that made every hair on his body stand at attention. Gooseflesh dotted his skin. Closing his eyes, he buried his face in the bed.

A soft touch followed the crease where his buttocks met his thighs. Then he felt the heat of her breath gust across his skin. He tensed all over—starting at his rear and then spreading outward. The wait was endless.

And then she kissed him.

First one cheek, and then the other. Soft, open-mouthed kisses. He felt her nipples grow stiff against his back, and took some comfort knowing he was not alone in this. Whatever *this* was.

Then his wife bit him, ever so gently, and his toes curled.

His bloody toes curled!

"Christ, Isabel," he said hoarsely, his hips moving restlessly, pressing his aching cock into the bed. He knew for a certainty that no other woman could bite his ass and actually arouse him unbearably while doing so. He was positive that if another female were to take Pel's place he would be laughing now. But this was no laughing matter. This was torture of the most sensual kind.

Something hot and wet slid across his skin, and he jerked. "Did you *lick* me?"

"Shhh," she murmured. "Relax. I won't hurt you."

"You are killing me!"

"Should I cease?"

Gerard grit his teeth and considered. Then said, "Only if you wish to stop. Otherwise, no. However, I feel I should remind you that my body is yours to take whenever you desire."

"I desire it now."

He grinned at the steel that laced her bedroom voice. "Then by all means."

Time passed and he lost track of it, lost in the sultry scent of his wife and the masculine satisfaction derived from being so thoroughly admired. Eventually, she moved away from his rear and moved onto his legs. When she reached his feet, he laughed at her soft ticklish touch. When she reached his shoulders and her hair drifted over his back, he sighed.

One morning, not too long ago, he had sat on the short stone wall that surrounded one of his terraces and tried to remember what it felt like to smile with true contentment. What a godsend it was to have found that here, in his home. With Pel.

Then Isabel urged him to roll over, straddled his hips, and took him inside her, slowly. She was burning hot and drenched, and he watched, shaking, as his cock was engulfed inch by throbbing inch between the flushed, glistening lips of her sex.

"Oh God . . ." she breathed, her thighs trembling, her eyes heavy-lidded and locked with his. The soft whimper turned into rapid pants. That she enjoyed his cock to the extreme was not only obvious, but more than enough to make his balls crawl into his body.

"I won't last," he warned, his hands tugging her downward impatiently. He'd taken her several times now, but never had she taken him, and she was a mature woman with a comfortable understanding of her own desires. From the moment they had been introduced, he'd admired her poise and confidence. Now he found it both mesmerizing and satisfying to share the control of their bedsport with her. "I am ready to blow."

"But you won't."

And he didn't. Fear for her held him back, because she was his wife—his to please, his to enjoy, his to protect. He would not lose her like he lost Em.

His. She was his.

Now he need only convince her of that.

When Gerard finally found the strength of will to leave his bed, he went directly to Spencer's rooms, but did not find him there. A cursory search of the house turned up nothing. It was then he discovered his brother had departed soon after their row. To say he was worried would be an understatement. He had no notion of what Spencer had overheard the night before or who had spoken the words that so angered him.

I will not tolerate the disparagement of our name . . . I will do what is necessary.

Growling, Gerard went to his office and penned two quick notes. One waited for Isabel, while the other was dispatched immediately. He had planned to escort his wife to whatever events she had agreed to attend, and he'd looked forward to both her company and the chance to dispel the rumors that plagued them. Now he was forced to scour clubs, brothels, and taverns to be certain Spencer did not land firmly into a puddle of trouble, as their mother claimed was his wont to do.

Damn and blast, he thought, as he waited for his horse to be saddled and brought around. An entire afternoon of physical exertion had made him somewhat jellied in the legs and should the need come for fisticuffs, he was certain he would not be at his best. Because of this, he prayed Spencer was not pursuing a fight, but simply drinking or whoring. And of those two choices, Gerard preferred the latter. Sated, perhaps, his brother would be more amenable to listening to reason.

Vaulting into the saddle, he urged his mount away from the house that was now a home and wondered how many more decisions of his past would hurt those he cared for.

"What are you doing here, Rhys?" Isabel asked as she entered the parlor. Try as she might, she could not hide the irritated note in her voice. To wake up without Gray was bad enough; to read his curt and vague missive only compounded her disgruntlement.

> *I must see to Spencer.*
> > *Yours,*
> > *Grayson*

She knew how men related to one another—they argued, and then made up over ale and women. Well acquainted with her husband's stamina, she could not put the indulgence past him.

Her brother rose from his seat on the blue velvet settee and sketched a quick bow. Dashingly dressed in evening black, he was a remarkable sight. "I am at your service, madam," he intoned in a comical imitation of an upper servant.

"My service?" She frowned. "Whatever am I supposed to need you for?"

"Grayson sent for me. He wrote that he was unable to accompany you this evening and suggested I might like to. For if I did, surely I would be too weary to meet him in the rings at Remington's in the morning. And in his gratitude for my escort, he would excuse me. Indefinitely."

Her eyes widened. "He threatened you?"

"I warned you he would give me a thrashing for taking you away from him yesterday."

"Ridiculous," she muttered.

"I agree," he said dryly. "However, fortuituously I had plans to attend the Hammond ball regardless, as Lady Margaret Crenshaw will be there."

"Another victim on your list? Have you, at the very least, spoken to this one before?"

Rhys shot her a dark glance. "Yes, I have, and she was very pleasant. So, if you are ready . . . ?"

Although she had dressed for an evening out, she'd actually considered remaining at home to wait for Gray. But that would be foolish. He obviously wished her to go, since he went to such lengths to see her escorted. She was not a young girl any longer, nor naïve. It should not bother her one whit that Grayson had spent hours finding pleasure in her body, only to leave her behind for the evening. A mistress would find nothing untoward, she told herself.

And she continued to remind herself of that fact as the course of the evening progressed. But when she caught a glimpse of a familiar face in the crowded Hammond ballroom, the knowledge was discarded. Mistress or not, a knot formed in her belly, only to be quickly replaced by a cold flare of anger.

"Lord Spencer Faulkner is here," Rhys noted casually, as the young man entered the ballroom just a few feet away from where they stood along the edge of the dance floor.

"So he is." But Grayson was not. So he had lied to her. Why was she surprised?

She studied her brother-in-law carefully, noting both the

similarities to her husband and the differences. Unlike her close resemblance to Rhys, Gray and Lord Spencer had only a passing physical familiarity, which gave her a small glimpse of what their father must have looked like.

As if he felt her perusal, Spencer turned his head and met her gaze. For one brief, unguarded heartbeat she saw something decidedly unpleasant, and then it was shielded with studious impassivity.

"Well, well," Rhys murmured. "I believe we have finally met a man who is truly immune to your charms."

"You saw that?"

"Unfortunately, yes." His gaze raked the throng before them. "I can only hope that you and I were the only ones who—Good God!"

"What?" Alarmed by his shock, Isabel rose to her toes and looked around. *Was it Gray?* Her heart raced. "What is it?"

Rhys thrust his champagne at her with such haste the sloshing liquid nearly overwhelmed the flute, which would have ruined her satin gown. "Excuse me." And then he was off, leaving Isabel blinking after him.

Rhys followed the trim form that weaved easily through the guests. Almost as if she were a wraith, she went by unnoticed, an unremarkable woman wearing an unremarkable dress. But Rhys was arrested. He knew that dark hair. He had dreamt of that voice.

She left the ballroom, and moved swiftly down the hall. He followed. When she exited the manse through a study door, he gave up any effort to hide his pursuit and he caught the knob just as it swung away from him. Her small, piquant face tilted up to his, the wide eyes blinking.

"Lord Trenton."

He stepped out onto the terrace, and shut out the sounds of the ball with a click of the latch. Sketching a short bow, he caught up her gloved hand and kissed the back of it. "Lady Mystery."

She laughed, and his grip tightened. Her head angled to the side in what looked to be puzzlement. "You find me attractive, don't you? But you cannot reason why. Quite frankly, I am equally puzzled."

A soft chuckle escaped him. "Will you allow me to investigate a little?" He bent slowly, giving her time to pull away before he brushed his lips across hers. The soft touch affected him strangely, as did her scent, which was so soft it was a mere hint in the cool night air. "I think a few experiments might be in order."

"Oh my," she breathed. Her free hand moved to shelter her stomach. "That just gave me a little flutter right here."

Something warm expanded in his chest, and dropped to settle between his legs. She was not his type of female at all. Mousy. A bluestocking. Certainly he found her discourse refreshing in its frankness, but why he wished to toss up her skirts was a matter he could not reconcile. She was too slender for his tastes, and lacked the full womanly curves he appreciated. Still, he could not deny that he wanted her, and he wanted to know her secrets. "Why are you out here?"

"Because I prefer here to there."

"Walk with me, then," he murmured, tucking her hand in the crook of his elbow and leading her away.

"Will you flirt shamelessly with me?" she asked as she fell into step beside him. They found a winding garden path and strolled. The way was unlit so they progressed slowly.

"Of course. I will also discover your name before we part."

"You sound so certain of that."

He smiled down into her moonlit eyes. "I have my ways."

She harrumphed skeptically. "You shall have fun matching wits with me."

"I've no doubt your brain is formidable, but that is not the part of you I would use my wiles on."

She gave a chastising push to his shoulder with her free hand. "You are wicked to speak thusly to a woman of my inexperience. You are making me light-headed."

Rhys winced, slightly chagrined. "Sorry."

"No, you're not." Her hand brushed across where she had touched him a moment before and his blood heated, his step faltered. How could the brush of a gloved hand over the material of his coat and sleeve arouse him?

"Is this sort of bantering the way men speak to women they feel an intimacy with? Lady Grayson laughs often at things that are said to her by men I find to be quite dull."

Coming to an abrupt halt, Rhys glared down at her.

"I meant no offense!" she said quickly. "In fact, Lady Grayson is a woman I find to be multifaceted in only the most flattering sense."

Studying her carefully, he concluded she was sincere and began walking again. "Yes, once you become friends with a member of the opposite sex and you are comfortable with them, your conversation can become intimate."

"Sexually intimate?"

"Oftentimes, yes."

"Even though the end goal is not sexual, merely for temporary amusement?"

"You are a curious kitten." His smile was indulgent. To think that such a mundane act as flirtation could become exciting when seen through her eyes. He wished he could sit for hours with her and answer all of her questions.

"I'm afraid I lack the knowledge required to banter in the manner to which you are accustomed. So I hope you forgive me when I just ask you outright to kiss me."

He stumbled, scattering the gravel on the path. "I beg your pardon?"

"You heard me, my lord." Her chin lifted. "I would very much like you to kiss me."

"Why?"

"Because no one else ever will."

"Why not? You underestimate yourself."

Her smile was impish and filled him with delight. "I estimate myself just fine."

"Then certainly you know that another man will kiss you." Even as he said it, Rhys realized how deeply the thought disturbed him. Her lips were soft as rose petals and sweetly plump. They had cushioned his when he kissed her, and he found them to be the prettiest lips he'd ever seen. The image in his mind of another man sampling them made his fists clench.

"Another man may like to, but he won't." She stepped forward, and rose to her tiptoes, offering her mouth to him. "Because I will not allow him to."

Against his will, Rhys caught her to him. She was slender as a reed, her curves slight, but she fit to him. He held still for a moment, absorbing that fact.

"We fit," she breathed, her eyes wide. "Is that usual?"

He swallowed hard and shook his head, lifting one hand to cup her cheek. "I've no notion what to do with you," he admitted.

"Just kiss me."

Rhys bent his head, hovering only a hair's breadth away. "Tell me your name."

"Abby."

He licked her lower lip. "I want to see you again, Abby."

"So we can hide in gardens and be scandalous?"

What could he say? He knew nothing about her, but her attire, her age, and the fact that she ran about unescorted told him of her lack of consequence. It was time to marry, and she was not a woman he could court.

Her smile was knowing. "Just kiss me and say good-bye, Lord Trenton. Be content that you have given me the fantasy of a handsome, dashing suitor."

Words failed him, so he kissed her, deeply and with feeling. She melted into him, became breathless, gave a soft whimper that stole his wits. He wanted to take liberties with her. Strip her bare, share with her all the things he knew, see the sexual act as she would, with wonder.

So when she left him in the garden, the farewell he should have spoken would not come. And later, when he returned to the manse with a sham exterior of normalcy, he realized she had not said it either.

Chapter 12

"How interesting that she should arrive without Grayson," Barbara murmured, her hand tucked lightly over Hargreaves' arm. Turning her head, she perused the throng again.

"Perhaps he intends to join her later," the earl replied, with far more nonchalance than she would like. Should he suddenly decide he no longer wanted Isabel Grayson, she would be alone in her attempts to lure Grayson back to her bed.

She released him and stepped back. "Trenton has left her side. Now would be the time to approach her."

"No." He shot her an arch look. "Now is *not* the time. Think of the talk that would ensue."

"Gossip is our aim," she argued.

"Grayson is not a man to be toyed with."

"I agree, but neither are you."

Hargreaves stared across the ballroom, his narrowed gaze arrested by his former love.

"Look how morose she is," Barbara goaded. "Perhaps her decision is one she already regrets. But you will never know if you don't speak with her."

It was this last thought that garnered the results she wanted.

With a muttered oath, Hargreaves moved away, his broad shoulders squared in determination.

She smiled and turned in the opposite direction, seeking and then finding the young Lord Spencer. Feigning an attempt to move past him, Barbara brushed her breasts along his forearm and when he turned to her with wide eyes, she blushed.

"I do apologize, my lord." She looked up at him through her lashes.

He offered an indulgent smile. "No apologies necessary," he said smoothly, catching up her proffered hand. He moved to step out of her way, but she held tight. He arched a brow. "My lady?"

"I would like to reach the drink tables, but the crush is rather daunting. And I am so very parched."

His half smile was knowing. "I would be honored to offer my services."

"How gallant of you to come to my aid," she said, falling into step beside him. She studied him furtively. He was quite handsome, though in not the same way as his older sibling. Grayson had a dangerous edge that could not be ignored, despite his outward appearance of insouciance. Lord Spencer's nonchalance, however, was not a façade.

"I endeavor to make myself useful to beautiful women as often as possible."

"How fortunate for Lady Grayson to have two such dashing Faulkner men at her beck and call."

His arm stiffened beneath her gloved touch and she could not hold back her smile. Something was amiss in the Grayson household, a circumstance that could only work to her advantage. She would have to ply the youngest Faulkner with her wiles to discover what the issue was, but that was a prospect she found most appealing.

With a quick glance over her shoulder to be certain Hargreaves had gone to Isabel Grayson, Barbara wiggled her shoulders in anticipation and determined to enjoy the rest of Lord Spencer's evening.

"Isabel."

John halted a discreet distance away. His gaze raked her from head to toe, taking in the pearls weaved through her auburn tresses and her lovely dark green gown, the deep color of which set off her creamy porcelain skin to perfection. Her three-strand choker of pearls did an admirable job of attempting to hide the faint bruising around her neck, but he took note of it nevertheless. "Are you well?"

Her smile was both fond and sad. "As well as can be expected." She canted her body toward him. "I feel dreadful, John. You are a good man who deserved to be treated better than I have treated you."

"Do you miss me?" he dared to ask.

"I do." Her amber gaze met his directly. "Though perhaps not in the way that you might miss me."

His mouth curved. As always, he admired her candor. She was a woman who spoke without artifice. "Where is Grayson this evening?"

Her chin lifted slightly. "I will not discuss my husband with you."

"Are we no longer friends, then, Pel?"

"We certainly will not be if your aim is to pry into my marriage," she snapped. And then she blushed, her gaze dropping.

He opened his mouth to apologize, then stopped. Isabel's ill-humor had grown more and more frequent as their affair progressed. He now began to wonder if their relationship had been winding down prior to Grayson's return and he had simply been too dense to realize it.

Releasing a deep breath, he attempted to turn his thoughts inward in consideration of this possibility. However, a sudden disturbance and Pel's subsequent stiffness beside him drew his attention. He looked up and found the Marquess of

Grayson standing across the room. Grayson's gaze was first riveted on Isabel, then it moved to rest on him.

Chilled by that stare, John shivered. Then Grayson turned away.

"Your husband has arrived."

"Yes, yes. I know. Excuse me."

She had already traveled a short distance from him when he remembered Barbara's plan. "I will escort you to the terrace, if you like."

"Thank you," she replied with a nod that set her fiery curls in motion. He had always loved her hair. The combination of dark chocolate and reddish glints was striking.

The sight of it was almost enough to distract him from the icy blue gaze piercing between his shoulder blades.

Almost.

"Grayson!"

Gerard stared after his wife and tried to discern her disgruntlement. She was quite obviously put out by something he'd done, though he had no notion of what it could be. However, he was not surprised. Aside from his afternoon of wondrously satisfying bedsport, the rest of his day had been hellish.

He heaved a sigh and turned away. "Yes, Bartley?"

"It appears your brother was serious when he mentioned coming here. He arrived over an hour past and according to the footman stationed at the door, he has yet to depart."

Looking back over the crush, Gerard failed to see Spencer anywhere, but he watched as Isabel stepped onto a crowded outer terrace with Hargreaves. He wished he could speak with her, but he'd learned it was best to tackle one problem at a time, and Spencer was the graver issue at the moment. He trusted Pel. He could not say the same for his hotheaded brother.

"I shall start with the card room," he murmured, grateful

to have run into Bartley as the man was exiting Nonnie's Tavern. This ball was the last place he would have searched for Spencer.

"Is that not Hargreaves with Lady Grayson?" Bartley asked, scowling.

"Yes." Gerard turned away.

"Should you not say something to him?"

"What would I say? He is a good man and Isabel a sensible woman. Nothing untoward will happen."

"Well, even I know that," Bartley said with a laugh. "And how like you not to pay any mind. But if you are serious about courting your wife, I would suggest at least the pretense of jealousy."

Gerard shook his head. "Ridiculous. And I am certain Pel would say the same."

"Women are odd creatures, Gray. Perhaps there is something about the fairer sex I know that you do not," Bartley chortled.

"I doubt that." Gerard moved away to find the card room. "You say my brother was only slightly out of sorts?"

"So it seemed to me. However, he is certainly aware of my friendship with you. That might have sufficed to keep his mouth shut on the matter."

"One can only hope he showed such discretion all evening."

Bartley followed fast on his heels. "What will you do when you find him?"

Gerard came to a halt, easily absorbing the impact of Bartley against his back.

"What the devil?" Bartley mumbled.

Turning, Gerard said, "The search will progress far more swiftly if we part ways."

"Won't be near as fun."

"I am not here to have fun."

"How will I find you, if I manage to find him?"

"You will manage, clever chap that you are." Gerard continued on, leaving Bartley behind. The starch in his cravat was chafing, Pel was close and yet so far away, the upcoming confrontation with his brother weighed heavily . . . Altogether, his mood was not the most charitable.

And as his search lengthened, his mood only grew worse.

Isabel stepped onto the crowded balcony and attempted to ignore how Grayson's cut had wounded her. She thought it would be a difficult task, but as she spied a familiar head of graying hair, her thoughts were immediately directed elsewhere. She sighed. Releasing Hargreaves, she said, "We should part ways now."

Following her gaze, he nodded and quickly retreated, leaving her to make her approach to the Dowager Countess of Grayson. The older woman met her halfway and linked arms, leading her away from the other guests.

"Have you no shame?" the dowager whispered.

"Do you truly expect me to reply?" Isabel retorted. Four years and she still had not learned to tolerate the woman.

"How a woman of your breeding can show so little concern for the title she bears is beyond my collection. Grayson has always done his best to irritate me, but marriage to you is beyond the pale."

"Can you please find something new to harp about?" Shaking her head, Isabel pulled away. Now that they were no longer in sight of anyone, the pretense of familiarity could be dropped. The dowager's fervent desire to maintain the esteem of the Grayson name and lineage was understandable, but the manner in which she sought to achieve her aim was not one Isabel could champion.

"I will see him rid of you before I take my last breath."

"Good luck," Isabel muttered.

"I beg your pardon?" The dowager drew herself up.

"I have spoken to Grayson about separation many times since his return. He refuses."

"You have no wish to be married to him?" The dowager's

complete astonishment would have amused Isabel if she were less distressed over Gray's behavior since leaving her bed. To be set aside so easily . . . To be ignored so directly . . . To have trusted a man who lied to her . . .

It hurt, and she had promised herself that no man would ever hurt her again.

"No, I do not." She lifted her chin. "The reasons for our marriage seem foolish and ill-conceived now. I'm certain they always have been and we were both too obstinate to take note."

"Isabel." The dowager pursed her lips and fingered her weighty sapphire necklace with a narrowed, thoughtful glance. "You are serious?"

"Yes."

"Grayson insists that a petition for divorce will meet with failure. In any case, the scandal will be dreadful for all."

Tugging off one of her long gloves, Isabel reached out and fingered the petals of a nearby rose. So Gray had been considering severing their bond. She should have known.

How unfortunate for her that she was a woman who relished the companionship of others. She thrived on it. Perhaps if she did not, she would not feel such a need to be held and cared for, and she would not be in this position now. Many women abstained. She could not.

She sighed. The censure heaped on them for a divorce petition would be devastating, but how much more devastating would marriage to Grayson be? She'd nearly been destroyed by her last spouse and her attraction to the man Gray had become was just as powerful as what she had once felt for Pelham.

"What do you want me to say?" she asked bitterly. "That I am prepared for and accepting of a future as a woman divorced for adultery? I am not."

"But you are resolved, I can see it in the set of your shoulders. And I will help you."

Isabel turned at that. "You will *what*?"

"You heard me." A slight smile softened the dowager's harshly drawn mouth. "I am not sure *how* I will help you. I only know that I will, in whatever manner I can. Perhaps I will even see you well settled."

Suddenly, the events of the day were too much for Isabel. "Excuse me." She would find Rhys and ask him to escort her home. Faulkner scratches wounded her on all sides, and she wished for her room and a decanter of Madeira more than she wished for her next breath.

"I shall be in touch, Isabel," the dowager marchioness called after her.

"Lovely," she muttered, speeding up her steps. "I cannot wait."

Frustrated by his lack of success in finding Spencer, Gerard was about to do violence to someone, when he turned a corner and came to an abrupt halt, his way blocked by a woman backing out of a dark room.

She turned and jumped. "Good heavens," Lady Stanhope cried, her gloved hand sheltering her heart. "You frightened me, Grayson."

He studied her with an arched brow. Flushed and slightly disheveled, she was obviously fresh from some assignation. When the door opened again and Spencer stepped out with crumpled cravat, Gerard's other brow rose to match the first. "I have been looking for you for hours."

"You have?"

His brother was clearly far more relaxed than he had been earlier. Intimately familiar with Barbara's sexual appetite, Gerard was not surprised. He smiled. This was exactly how he had hoped to find Spencer.

"I would like to speak with you."

Spencer straightened his coat and shot a glance at Barbara, who hovered. "Tomorrow perhaps?"

Studying him carefully, Gerard asked, "What are your

plans for this evening?" He would not wait if his brother was still intent on some trouble.

Another pointed glance at Barbara settled Gerard's worries. If Spencer was fucking, he would not be fighting. "Breakfast in my study, then."

"Very well."

Lifting Barbara's bare hand to his lips, Spencer sketched an elegant bow and moved away, most likely to arrange their departure.

"I will be along in a moment, darling." Barbara's eyes remained locked on Gerard.

When they were alone, he said, "I am grateful for your association with Lord Spencer."

"Oh?" She made a moue. "A tiny flare of jealousy would be welcome, Grayson."

He snorted. "There is nothing between us to warrant jealousy, and there never has been."

Her hand came up to rest against his abdomen, her green eyes sparkling mischievously through her lashes. "There could be, if only you would warm my bed again. Although our liaison the other evening was lamentably short, it reminded me of how beautifully you and I suit each other."

"Ah, Lady Stanhope," Pel said tightly behind him. "Thank you for locating my husband for me."

Gerard did not have to turn around to know that his evening had, impossibly, taken a turn for the worse.

As the obviously rumpled countess moved away, Isabel stood silently, her fists clenched. Grayson eyed her warily, his powerful frame tense with expectation while she considered what she wanted to do. She had once fought hard for Pelham, and the effort had been draining and pointless. Husbands lied and strayed. Practical wives understood this.

With her heart encased in the icy shell she had learned to rely on, she simply turned her back to Gray with the intent to leave—the ball, his house, *him*. In her mind she was already packing, her brain quickly sorting through her belongings.

"Isabel."

That voice. She shivered. Why must he have that raspy bedroom voice that dripped lust and decadence?

Her steps did not falter, and when he caught her elbow to stay her egress, her thoughts shifted to her previous home and how all of her furniture would be sadly out of date.

Gray's gloved hand cupped her cheek. Forced her gaze to meet his. She registered blue eyes of a striking color and thought of her parlor settee, which was of a similar tone. She would have to throw it out.

"Christ," he muttered harshly. "Don't look at me like that."

Her gaze dropped to where his large hand gripped her forearm.

Before she realized it, he had pulled her into a dark room that reeked of sex and closed the door behind them. Her stomach roiled, and feeling the overwhelming urge to flee, she hurried across the moonlit space toward a room on the other side. It was a library where windowed doors led outside. There she paused and leaned her hands upon the back of a leather wingback chair, sucking in deep breaths of untainted air.

"Isabel." Gray's hands gripped her shoulders, moved down to tug her grip free of the chair back, and then linked his fingers with hers. His body was feverishly hot against her back. She began to sweat.

Green, perhaps? No, that wouldn't do. Gray's study was green. Lavender, then? A lavender settee would be a change. Or pink. No man would want to visit a pink parlor. Wouldn't that be lovely?

"Would you talk to me, please?" he coaxed. He was very good at coaxing. And wheedling and charming and fucking. A girl could lose her head over him if she lowered her guard.

"Tassels."

"What?"

He turned her to face him.

"Pink with gold tassels in the parlor," she said.

"Fine. Pink flatters my coloring."

"You will not be invited to my parlor."

His lips pursed, his frown deepened. "The hell I won't. You are not leaving me, Pel. What you overheard does not mean what you think."

"I do not think anything, my lord," she said evenly. "If you will excuse me . . ." She sidestepped.

He kissed her.

Like candle-warmed brandy the kiss hit her stomach first, then spread outward. Intoxicating. Making her thoughts and blood run sluggishly. Needing air, she took a deep breath through her nose and smelled Gray. Starched linen. Clean skin.

His embrace tightened, lifting her slightly until only the tips of her curled toes brushed against the Aubusson rug beneath them. Against her belly she felt his cock stir, but his mouth connected sweetly with hers, his tongue tasting and licking, not plunging. As the ice inside her melted under the heat of his ardor, she moaned. His lips were so beautiful, so soft against hers. The lips of an angel . . . with the skill and ability to deceive like the devil.

Clean skin.

Gray's mouth traveled along her cheekbone until he nuzzled against her ear.

"As impossible as it is, I want you again." He rounded the chair and sank into it, holding her in his lap as if she were a small child. "After this afternoon, my hunger should have settled down to a minor craving, yet at this moment it seems worse than before."

"I know what I heard," she whispered, refusing to believe what her nose suggested was the truth.

"My brother is brash," he continued, ignoring her. "And I wasted hours looking for him tonight. Still, despite the knowledge that he could be wounded, or could seriously wound someone else, it was the desire to be with you that created my unholy impatience."

"You have been with that woman intimately. Recently."

"I was relieved to learn he'd vented his earlier anger with a quick rut in the next room."

Isabel stilled. "Lord Spencer?"

"I was even more pleased to see him departing with Lady Stanhope to continue their activities in a more appropriate venue. His doing so frees the rest of my evening to seduce you."

"She wants you."

"So do you," he said smoothly. "I am an attractive man with an attractive purse and an attractive title." He pushed her gently away so he could meet her gaze. "I also have an attractive wife."

"Have you fucked her since you returned?"

"No." His mouth brushed across hers. "And I know you find that hard to believe."

Strangely, she didn't.

"If I were you, Pel, I am not certain I would believe a scoundrel like me either, especially with your past."

Her spine straightened. "My past does not signify." She'd had enough pity to last a lifetime, she did not require any more. Certainly she did not want any from Gray.

"Ah, but it does, as I am beginning to see." His face was stark in its perfection, his eyes narrowed and considering. The hard edges to his lips and mouth he'd shown when he first returned were back. Signs of a deep sadness.

"I am not a good man for you, Pel. I am not good at all. All men have faults, but I'm afraid I am nothing but faults. Still, I am yours and you must learn to bear with me, because I am selfish and refuse to let you go."

"Why?"

She held her breath, but it was his next words that made her dizzy.

"You heal me."

His eyes closed and he pressed his cheek to hers, the tender gesture startling her to the very marrow of her bones. The Marquess of Grayson was known for a great many things, but tenderness was not one of them. The fact that these displays were becoming more frequent in number terrified her. She could not be the salve that mended him for another woman.

"Perhaps I can heal you, too," he whispered against her mouth. "If you allow me to."

For a brief moment, she pressed her lips to his. Exhausted by the stresses of the day, she longed to curl into his chest and sleep for days. Instead, she wiggled off his lap and stood. "If healing means forgetting, I want no part of it."

He heaved out a breath as weary in sound as she felt.

"I have learned from my past mistakes, Gray, and I am glad to have learned." Her fingers twisted together restlessly. "Forgetting is not my aim. I *never* want to forget."

"Then teach me how to live with my mistakes, Pel." He stood.

She looked at him. Studied him.

"We should leave London," he said urgently. Coming to her, he caught up her hands.

"What?" Her eyes widened and she shivered. *Alone with Gray.*

"We cannot function together as a couple here."

"A couple?" Her head shook violently.

The door opened, startling them both. Gray pulled her to him with lightning speed, protecting her in an all-encompassing embrace.

Lord Hammond, the owner of the library in which they stood, blinked in the doorway. "I beg your pardon." He began to back out, and then stopped. "Lord Grayson? Is that you?"

"Yes," Gray drawled softly.

"With Lady Grayson?"

"Who else would I be consorting with in a darkened room?"

"Well . . . Ah . . ." Hammond cleared his throat. "No one else, of course."

The door began to swing closed again, and Gray took the opportunity to cup her breast. His mouth lowered toward hers, taking ruthless advantage of her inability to pull away.

"Er, Lord Grayson?" Hammond called out.

Gray sighed and raised his head. "Yes?"

"Lady Hammond has arranged a house party this weekend at our country estate near Brighton. She would be beyond pleased if you and Lady Grayson would attend. And I would relish the opportunity to reacquaint myself with you."

Isabel gasped as Gray's grip flexed rhythmically around her breast. Without the aid of candlelight or a fire, they could not be seen clearly. Still, the fact that another individual stood inches away from where she was being fondled so intimately made her heart race.

"How large is the party?"

"Not large I'm afraid. A dozen at last count, but Lady Hammond—"

"Sounds perfect," Gray interjected, his fingers tugging at her hardened nipple. "We accept your invitation."

"Truly?" Hammond's portly frame drew up to the limits of its inconsiderable height.

"Truly." Clutching her hand, Gray dragged her from the room, squeezing past the viscount, who was too surprised to move quickly enough.

Her emotions a morass, Isabel followed with only a slight drag.

Hammond followed quickly behind them. "Friday morning we set off. Is that acceptable?"

"It's *your* party, Hammond."

"Oh, yes . . . That's true. Friday, then."

With a deliberate flick of his wrist, Gray signaled a nearby footman to fetch cloak and carriage, and turned to another servant who hovered nearby. "Tell Lord Trenton I said his obligation has been met."

It was not lost on Isabel how easily her husband had managed to achieve his aim to spirit her away. She almost wished she could be angry about it, but she was too stunned.

Her husband had not lied or strayed.

But whether that was a blessing or a curse, she could not yet say.

Chapter 13

As the Grayson carriage pulled into the crowded drive of the Hammond residence, Isabel could not bite back her groan. One guest in particular filled her with dread.

Sitting across from her, Gray arched his brow in silent query.

Your mother, she mouthed, showing caution so as not to anger Lord Spencer, who shared a squab with her husband.

Gray pinched the bridge of his nose with a loud sigh.

Suddenly all the anticipation she'd had for the upcoming long weekend party fled. Stepping down from the carriage with Gray's assistance, she managed a smile and took inventory of the assembled guests. She shuddered when the Dowager Lady Grayson gifted her with a conspiratorial wink. There was no avoiding the fact that Isabel had liked the woman better when they had been at odds.

"Bella."

The relief she felt at the sound of the voice behind her was dizzying. Turning, she caught Rhys' outstretched hands like a lifeline thrown to a drowning woman. His smile was brilliant, his rich mahogany hair capped by a dashing hat.

"What are you doing here?" she asked, well aware that tame country parties were not his preference.

He shrugged. "I feel the need for a little respectable company."

Her eyes narrowed. "Are you ill?"

Laughing, he shook his head. "No, though I do believe I've caught a bit of melancholia. Something I'm certain a few days of fresh country air will do wonders to cure."

"Melancholia?" Tugging off her glove, Isabel pressed her wrist to his forehead.

Rhys rolled his eyes. "Since when does a bad mood cause fevers?"

"You have never been in a bad mood in your life."

"There is a first for everything."

A firm grip at her waist drew her attention.

"Grayson," her brother greeted, his gaze lifting above her head.

"Trenton," Gray returned. "I would not have expected to find you here."

"A temporary bout of insanity."

"Ah." Gray tugged her closer, a motion which had her gazing up at him with wide eyes. They'd had an unspoken accord to avoid touching each other in public, since it seemed to spark a flare of lust neither could control. "I appear to be suffering from the same ailment."

"Grayson. Isabel. Lovely to see you both here," the dowager said as she approached.

As Isabel opened her mouth to reply, Gray squeezed the upper swell of her buttock. She jumped, startling his mother. Reaching behind her, she swatted at his hand.

"Are you unwell?" the dowager asked, frowning in disapproval. "You should not have come if you are ill or out of sorts."

"She is perfectly healthy," Gray said smoothly. "As I can well attest."

Isabel stomped on his booted foot, although doing so caused no damage at all. *What was his intent?* She could not collect. To tease her so openly . . .

"Crudity is common," his mother reproved. "And beneath a man of your station."

"But, Mother, it is so enjoyable."

"Lord and Lady Grayson! How lovely of you to come."

Turning her head, Isabel found Lady Hammond descending the stairs from her front door. "We are delighted to be invited, of course," she replied.

"Now that you have arrived," the viscountess continued, "we can set off. What a lovely day to make the trip, don't you agree?"

"I do," she murmured, eager to return to their carriage.

"I shall ride with you, Grayson," the dowager said.

Isabel winced, suddenly finding the prospect of the day-long drive a torment.

Gray gave a soothing caress down the length of her spine, but the comfort it offered did not last. The rest of the morning and afternoon was spent in the tight confines of their traveling coach listening to his mother chastising them all for one transgression or another. She could only imagine the horror of living with a parent who found fault with everything, and she surreptitiously stroked Gray's thigh with the back of her hand in sympathy. He sat deathly silent the entire ride, coming to life only when they stopped to change horses and take luncheon.

It was with great relief that they arrived at the Hammonds' lovely country estate late in the day. As soon as the carriage rolled to a halt, Grayson leapt out and assisted her down. That was when she caught sight of Hargreaves, and realized why Grayson had been acting as possessive as he had. Even now, despite his outward appearance of boredom, she sensed his alertness in the proximity he kept to her and the slow sweep of his gaze across the drive.

"What a lovely estate," the dowager cried, bringing the pleased smile of the viscountess her way. It was indeed a praiseworthy property with its lovely golden brick exterior and profusion of colorful flowers and climbing vines.

A week here under other circumstances would be a joy. Considering the personages in attendance, including Lady Stanhope who was presently ogling Gray in a manner that riled Isabel, she doubted that would be the case in this instance. "We should have remained in London," she muttered.

"Shall we go?" Gray asked. "I have an estate not far from here."

She turned wide eyes to him. "Are you mad?" But she could see in the intensity of his blue eyes that he was quite willing to leave. While it seemed sometimes that no trace of the Grayson she once knew remained, flashes of the one she recalled occasionally appeared. He was more polished, more somber, but no less ruthless than he always had been. "No."

He sighed and offered his arm. "I knew you would say that. I hope you are amenable to spending a great deal of time in our rooms."

"We could have spent time in our rooms at home. Here it will be rude."

"You should have mentioned that earlier and saved us the trip."

"Don't foist the blame for this on me," she whispered, shivering slightly at the feel of his powerful forearm flexing beneath her fingertips. "This was entirely your doing."

"I wanted to travel away," he said dryly, his sidelong glance revealing his knowledge of his effect on her, "and spend some time with you and Spencer. I had no notion this would turn into a gathering of all the people we most wished to avoid."

"Isabel!"

Rhys' cry caught their attention. Walking backward with his gaze directed elsewhere, her brother nearly ran her over. Grayson, however, stepped in as a formidable buffer and saved her.

"Beg your pardon," her brother offered quickly, then he looked at her with a tangible excitement about him. "Do you know who that woman is over there?"

Looking around his tall frame, she saw a small group of women speaking with Lady Hammond. "Which one?"

"The brunette to the right of Lady Stanhope."

"Oh . . . Yes, I know her, although at the moment, her name eludes me."

"Abby?" he prompted. "Abigail?"

"Ah, yes! Abigail Stewart. Niece to Lord Hammond. His sister and her entrepreneurial American husband have passed on, leaving Miss Stewart orphaned, though quite wealthy I've been told."

"An heiress," Rhys said softly.

"Poor thing," Isabel said with a commiserating shake of her head. "She was hounded to death last season by every scapegrace and destitute man in England. I spoke with her briefly once. She is very bright. A bit rough around the edges, but charming."

"I never noticed her."

"Why would you? She hides herself well and she is not your type of female at all. Too smart for you," she teased.

"Yes . . . I'm certain that is true." He walked away frowning.

"I think you were correct," Gray said, his voice low and near enough to make her senses leap to attention. "I do believe he's ill. Perhaps we can follow his lead. You and I can feign poor constitutions and lie abed for a week. Together. Unclothed."

"You are incorrigible," she said, laughing.

With quiet efficiency, they and the other guests were settled in their rooms to freshen up before the evening meal. Gerard made certain that Isabel was well established and tended by her abigail, before excusing himself to meet with the other gentlemen below.

Despite the unfortunate choice of guests, he found some slight convenience in it. The odd menagerie created by the presence of his mother and Hargreaves allowed him to dispense with whatever remaining illusions they had about his marriage to Pel. His affairs were not to be interfered with. Foolish of them, really, to forget how few qualms he had. However, it was no great burden to remind them.

Entering the lower parlor, he took in the design of the room, noting the large windows framed with dark red, tasseled drapes, and the proliferation of burgundy leather chairs. A man's retreat. Just the type of setting he required to say what needed to be said.

He gave a curt nod to Spencer, refused the cheroot offered to him by Lord Hammond, and then strode across the Aubusson rug toward the window where Hargreaves stood studying the view outside. As he approached, Gerard examined the proud bearing and impeccable attire of the earl. This man had shared two private years with Pel and knew her far better than he himself did.

He remembered how she had been with Markham, lit like a candle with confidence and sparkling eyes. The contrast to the purely mercenary sexual regard with which she held him was striking and disturbing. The casual friendship they had once shared was now marred by tension. He missed the ease he'd once felt with her, and longed to bask in the kind of affectionate attentions she shared with others.

"Hargreaves," he murmured.

"Lord Grayson." The earl turned cool dark eyes on him. They were almost of a height, with Gerard having only a slight advantage. "Before you try to waylay attempts on my part to woo back Isabel, allow me to tell you I have no intentions in that regard."

"No?"

"No, but if she comes to me I will not turn her away."

"Despite the hazard such an action would place you in?" Gerard was a man of action, not empty threats. By the slight nod Hargreaves gave him, he could see the other man knew it.

"You cannot cage a woman like Isabel, Grayson. She values her freedom more than anything. I am certain it chafes her to realize she married you to be free, and yet finds herself trapped." His shoulders lifted in a shrug. "Besides, you will tire of her eventually or she of you, and this desire you have to claim her so primitively will fade."

"My *claim*," Gerard said dryly, "is not merely primitive. It is also legal and binding."

Hargreaves shook his head. "You have always wanted women who belong to someone else."

"In this case, the woman I want belongs to me."

"Does she? Truly? Odd you should discover that after five years of marital oblivion. I have seen you together since your return, as has everyone else. In truth, it appears you barely tolerate one another."

Gerard's mouth curved in a slow smile. "We definitely more than tolerate one another."

The earl's face flushed. "I do not have time to school you on women, Grayson, but suffice it to say that orgasms are not all a woman requires to be content. Isabel will not grow an attachment to you, she is incapable of it, and even if she were open to elevated feelings, an inconstant man such as yourself will never appeal. You are much like Pelham, you know. He, too, failed to see the prize that was his. I cannot count the number of times Isabel would tell me some humorous tale of your exploits and finish with, 'Just like Pelham used to do.'"

A blow to his gut could not have struck Gerard harder. Outwardly impassive, his insides knotted with apprehension. Markham had said the same. There could be no worse mark against him than to remind his wife of her late husband. If he could not, at the very least, prove himself better than Pelham, he would never win Isabel's affections.

But she had written him faithfully every week, and held on to that tenuous tie. Surely, there was some hope to be found in that?

Damn it! Why had he disregarded those letters?

"You say she is incapable of deep affections, and yet you think she may return to *you,* when she has never been known to revisit a paramour once finished with him?"

"Because we are friends. I know how she likes her tea, what her favorite books are . . ." Hargreaves straightened. "She was happy with me before you returned—"

"No. She was not. You know this as well as I." Isabel would not have been tempted away if Hargreaves had been what she wanted. She was not a fickle woman. But she *was* a woman who bore wounds, and Gerard was determined to heal them.

The earl's jaw tightened. "I think we understand each other. There is nothing left to be said. You are aware of my position. I am aware of yours."

Gerard tilted his head slightly in acknowledgment. "*Are* you aware? Be certain, Hargreaves. I am easily irritated and frankly, I will not have this conversation again. Next time I feel the urge to remind you of my marriage, I shall demonstrate the finer points of this discourse with the tip of my blade."

"Gentlemen, can I regale you with my tales of India?" Lord Hammond intruded, his gaze shifting nervously between them. "A fascinating country, I must say."

"Thank you, Hammond," Gerard said. "Perhaps over port this evening."

He withdrew and crossed the room to Spencer, who raised both brows as he approached.

"Only you, Gray, would be so brazen."

"Time is precious I've learned. I see no point in squandering it when directness works so well."

Spencer laughed. "I must admit, I was resigned to a week of lassitude. I am pleased to see there won't be a dull moment."

"Certainly not. I intend to keep you busy."

"Do you?"

Spencer's eyes lit up bright enough to compete with his

grin. Gerard realized again how much influence he had on his younger brother. He only hoped he made full and positive use of it.

"Yes. There is a Grayson property only an hour's ride from here. We will go there tomorrow."

"Smashing!"

Gerard smiled. "Now, if you will excuse me . . ."

"Can't stay away from her for long, can you?" Spencer shook his head. "You are more randy than I will ever be, I think. Much as it pains me to admit that."

"You assume when we are alone we only stay abed."

Spencer snorted. "Are you saying that is not the case?"

"I refuse to say anything at all."

Sinking deeper into her cooling bathwater, Isabel knew she should finish, but could not seem to manage the strength to do so. Despite how often she serviced him, Grayson's sexual appetite for her had not abated at all. Sleep was a luxury she snatched when she could.

She almost wished she could complain, but she was too sated to make the effort. It was difficult to muster true irritation when the man ensured she had a few orgasms for every one of his. And he had quite a lot.

He had begun to use French letters, no longer capable of withdrawing before he came. The lessening of sensation for him meant that he could fuck longer, a circumstance she had appreciated previously with the lovers she saw only once or twice a week. With her amorous husband it was very nearly too much. He enjoyed her writhing and begging for mercy beneath him, continuing the sensual torment until she could do nothing but whimper in pleasure and take what he gave her.

The man was an animal, nipping with his teeth, bruising with his hands, and she loved every moment of it. Grayson's passion was real, not practiced like Pelham's had been.

Isabel sighed. Against her will, memories of the last house party she'd attended with her late husband filled her mind, bringing with them the all too familiar roiling in her stomach. He had been in top philandering form then, dallying with other women in alcoves and slipping from his room at night. The entire fortnight had been hell, the time spent wondering which of the women drinking tea with her had serviced her husband the night before. By the time they left, she was fairly certain all the attractive ones had.

From that occasion onward, she'd denied Pelham her bed, which he had the temerity to protest until he realized she would cause him bodily injury if he insisted. Eventually, they had ceased to travel together at all.

The adjoining door opened and Gray's delicious voice dismissed her abigail. His footfalls as he approached were as sure and confident as always. There was a rhythm to them, a cadence, the sound of dominance. Grayson took for granted that every time he entered a room he owned it.

"You're chilled," he noted, his voice coming so close to her ear she knew he must be crouching beside her. "Let me assist you out."

Opening her eyes, she saw his outstretched hand, saw his face so close to hers, so intent on her. The way he examined her always took her off guard. Of course, she often found herself staring at him in the same manner.

As was happening more often, the sudden flare of possessiveness the sight of him aroused was painful and piercing. He was a man any woman would beg to claim as her own private property, but she, the only woman who had the right to do so, could not. Would not.

He had removed his clothes and now wore only a thick silk robe. Before she could stop herself, Isabel touched his shoulder and watched the blue of his eyes turn to icy fire. A touch, a smile, a lick of her lips—all could stoke his ardor in the space of one breath.

"I'm weary," she warned.

"You start it, Pel. Every damn time." As he stood, he pulled her up with him and then held a towel out for her.

"I do not!"

As he wrapped her, he kissed the tender spot where her shoulder met her throat—a gentle press of his lips to her flesh, not the heated open-mouthed kisses she had grown used to. "Yes, you do. On purpose. You want me panting for you."

"Your 'panting' is inconvenient."

"I have come to realize you like it inconvenient. You like me hard and aching for you in public, and in private. You like me mindless with lust until I would fuck you anywhere, in front of anyone, at any time."

She snorted, but shivered at his tone and the feel of his breath gusting across her damp skin.

Was it true? Was her aim to provoke him?

"You are always mindless with lust, Gray. You always have been."

"No. Lustful, yes. Mindless with it, never. Sometimes, I actually think I could take you in public, Isabel, the craving is so provoking. Deny me now, and I may bend you over the dinner table and provide the evening's entertainment." He nibbled her earlobe.

She laughed. "There is no hope for you. You are a beast."

He growled playfully and nuzzled against her. "You know how to tame me."

"Do I?" Turning in his arms, she faced him with a smile and brushed one fingertip across the bare skin revealed by the part in his dressing robe.

"Yes. You do." Gray caught her hand and thrust it lower, between the parting of his robe at his thighs so that she felt how hard he was.

"It is nearly ridiculous how quickly you rouse," she chastised with a shake of her head.

And he was so base about it, so blatant. Yes, she was seduced by him, but he was not a seducer. Perhaps his outrageous handsomeness had made the need for coaxing unnecessary.

Or perhaps it was the size of the cock that throbbed against her palm. That would accomplish the task for him nicely.

He flexed inside her clasp and smiled with wicked arrogance.

She smiled back, admitting to herself that she quite liked primitive. No games, no insincerity, no guessing.

"You don't *feel* tamed." She moved in a way that caused the towel about her to puddle on the floor. Stroking the heated length of his shaft, she licked her lips.

"Witch." He stepped forward, pushing her back, catching her hips when she stumbled in surprise. "You enslave me with sex."

"Not true." He rarely allowed her the lead, preferring to remain in control.

"I came in here with the express purpose of taking a nap. You instigated everything I must now do to you to slake my craving enough to catch some sleep."

The backs of her thighs hit the high bed, and he lifted and tossed her upon the turned-down mattress. Then he shed his robe and crawled over her.

Staring up at him, she found herself smitten with his smile, with the gleam in his eyes, with the dark silky hair that fell over his brow. How different he was from the brooding, gloomy man who had stood in her drawing room so recently. *Had she wrought this change? Did she hold that much sway over him?*

Her eyes drifted lower.

"That look," he said dryly, "is the reason we spend so much time in this position."

"What look?" Isabel batted her lashes mischievously, enjoying the renewed teasing banter she'd missed. There always seemed to be so much tension between them. Its absence was a pleasure.

Gray dipped his head and licked the tip of her nose, then pressed his mouth to hers. "It says, *Fuck me, Gerard. Spread my thighs, mount me, make me hoarse and limp from plea-sure.*"

"Good heavens," she purred. "It's a wonder I manage a word in edgewise with such chatty eyes."

"Hmmm . . ." His voice lowered to the tone she recognized as the immediate herald to troublemaking. "I certainly cannot manage speech when you look at me like that. Drives me insane."

"Perhaps you shouldn't look at me, then," she suggested, her hands coming up to stroke his lean hips.

"You would never allow me to ignore you, Pel. You foster my infatuation at every turn."

Infatuation. She shivered. *Could he care for her? Did she want him to?* "Why would I do such a thing?"

"Because you don't want my attention to wander." He kissed her before she could digest what he said.

Isabel lay still, her mouth ravished by a kiss that curled her toes, Gray's tongue licking across hers, gliding under it, drinking from her as if she were some delicacy. All the while in her mind, she considered what he had said. *Was she attempting to bind him to her with sexual extortion?*

When Gray lifted his head, his breathing was as disturbed as hers. "You do not afford me even half a moment to think of another woman." His eyelids lowered, shuttering his thoughts. "You take me to your bed at every opportunity. You exhaust me—"

"Ha. Your appetite is inexhaustible." But the rejoinder that was meant to be dismissing, was instead shaky and inflected with a question. *Had she gone from wanting him to stray, to wanting to keep him all to herself?*

In one graceful, fluid movement, he rolled and brought her over him. "I require as much sleep as any other human." He pressed his fingers over her mouth to silence a coming protest. "I am not so young as to forgo sleep altogether, so discard any attempt to use that excuse again. You are not too old for me. I am not too young for you."

Catching his wrist, she tugged his hand away. "You could always sleep apart from me."

"Don't be daft. You mistake my observation for a complaint, which it is not." Gray stroked the curve of her spine, applying pressure so that her breasts connected more fully to his chest. "Perhaps once or twice it has crossed my mind that I should manage my cock, instead of allowing it to lead me. But then I remember the feel of your cunt in orgasm, the way it clutches me, the way you arch up and cry out my name. And I tell my brain to cease prattling and leave me alone."

Dropping her forehead to his chest, Isabel laughed.

He tucked her into his side. "If you require a physical display of my affections at this moment, I am more than prepared to oblige you. We can't have you worried about waning interest and all that. Whatever you need, Pel, to make it possible to believe in me, I will do it. I suppose I should have stated that bluntly earlier so there would be no doubt. I am not Pelham."

The look in his eyes was fond, with banked lust—the look of a man who was just as content to hold her as he was to ride her.

Her throat tightened, her eyes stung.

"Where did you find these sudden insights into my behavior?" she asked softly. The Grayson she'd married had never looked far enough beyond himself to see such things.

"I told you, you have my undivided attention." His fingers plunged into her hair, loosening and then pulling out the pins that held it up, before tossing them to the floor. "There is no other person I would wish to be with more than you, female or otherwise. You make me laugh, you always have. You never allow me to become too full of myself. You see all of my faults and find most of them charming. I've no need of any other companions. In fact, you and I will remain in our rooms this evening."

"Now who's daft? Everyone will think we are up here having sex if we skip dinner."

"And they will not be wrong," he murmured, his lips to her forehead. "We are honeymooners, they should expect nothing less from us."

Honeymoon. Just that one word brought back the dreams she'd once had of a passionate, monogamous marriage. How hopeful she had been then. How naïve. She should be too old to experience that kind of eager anticipation for the future.

Should be. But was finding the opposite was true.

"But we shall also take our meal together up here," he continued, "and play chess. I will tell you of my—"

"You hate chess," she reminded, pulling back to look at him.

"Actually, I have learned to enjoy it. And I am quite good. Be prepared to suffer defeat."

Isabel stared up at him. So many times, she felt as if a stranger had returned to her. A man who looked very much like the man she married, but wasn't. *How much had he changed?* He was so mercurial. Even now he seemed different from the man who had left her room just an hour before.

"Who are you?" she breathed, her hand reaching up to touch his face, to trace the arch of his brow. So much the same. So very different.

His smile faded. "I am your husband, Isabel."

"No, you are not." She pressed him back, sliding over him again. The texture of his hard body was so wonderful to her—the hard ridges and planes, the dusting of hair over his sun-darkened skin.

"How can you say that?" he asked, his voice turning husky as she moved upon him. "You stood next to me at the altar. You said the vows, and heard mine."

Lowering her head, she took his mouth in a lush kiss, suddenly wanting him. Not because she was physically unable to resist the temptation he presented, but because she saw something in him she had failed to see before—commitment. He was committed to her, to learning about her and understanding her. The knowledge made her shiver, made her sink into his embrace, made her relish the feel of his strong arms encircling her back.

He turned his head, evading her questing mouth. Panting, he said, "Don't do this."

"Do what?" She caressed the length of his torso, cupped his hip, shifted so she could reach between his legs.

"Don't tell me I am not your husband and then silence me with sex. We will have this out, Pel. No more of this nonsense about mistresses and the like."

She stroked his cock with a firm, sure hand. If anything proved that Gray had changed it was his resistance to lovemaking while seeking a deeper connection. Despite every bit of her brain that said her life experiences were correct in their dismissal of lasting marital affection, some tiny voice inside her urged her to believe otherwise.

He caught her wrist and bucked with a curse, taking the advantage. Looming over her, he pinned her arms to the bed. His face above her was hard as stone, his eyes glittering with the determination that was mirrored by his tense jaw.

"You've no wish to fuck me?" she asked innocently.

Growling, he said, "There is a heart and mind attached to the cock you enjoy so well. Altogether they form a man—your spouse. You cannot fragment the whole and take only the pieces you want."

His declaration shook her, then decided her. Pelham . . . the Grayson she once knew . . . Neither would ever say such a thing. Whoever this man was above her, she desired to know him. To discover him, and the woman she felt like when she was with him.

"You are not the husband I said my vows to." She saw him prepared to protest, and rushed ahead. "I did not want him, Gerard. You know that."

The sound of his name sent a visible ripple through the length of his frame. His gaze narrowed. "What are you saying?"

She arched beneath him, stretching, enticing. Spreading her thighs, she welcomed him. Opened to him. "I want you."

"Isabel . . . ?" He pressed his damp forehead to hers, his hips settled against hers, his heavy cock finding her slick for him through no physical manipulation on his part. "Christ, you will be the death of me."

Her head fell to the side as he entered her slowly. So slowly. Bare skin to bare skin. She had missed the feel of him this way, without a barrier between them.

The difference between this and their usual coupling was marked. When he'd first returned, he had been gentle, but the strain of that control had been obvious. Now, as he rocked deeper and deeper into her eager body, she knew he moved leisurely because this moment was one he wished to lengthen.

His mouth to her ear, he whispered, "Who do you want?"

Her voice came slurred with pleasure. *"You . . ."*

Chapter 14

There were a thousand excuses for why Rhys was standing in the Hammond garden late in the evening. There was only one true reason. And she was presently moving toward him with a shy smile.

"I was hoping I would find you out here," Abby said, holding out her bare hands.

He bit the tip of his gloved finger and yanked off his glove, so that when he caught her hands he could feel them. The simple, chaste contact flared heat across his skin, and he did the last thing a gentleman would do—he pulled her closer.

"Oh my," she breathed, eyes wide. "I do enjoy it when you act the scoundrel."

"I will do much more than act," he warned, "if you continue to seek me out."

"I thought it was *you* seeking *me* out."

"You should stay away, Abby. I seem to have lost my senses where you are concerned."

"And I am a woman who desperately enjoys, perhaps even needs, having a handsome man lose his senses over her. It never happens to me, you know."

His conscience losing the battle, Rhys lifted his hand,

cupped her nape and fitted his mouth to hers. She was so slight, so slender, but she lifted to her tiptoes and kissed him back with such sweet ardor that she nearly knocked him off his feet. The soft scent of her perfume mixed with the scents of evening flowers, and he longed to bask in it, roll around a bed in it.

She had dressed differently tonight, in beautiful golden silk that hugged her body perfectly. Understanding how hounded she was by fortune hunters, he appreciated her need to fade into the woodwork with ill-fitting, unattractive garments and hide in dark gardens.

Lifting his head, he murmured, "You are aware of where these meetings are leading?"

She nodded, her chest rising and falling against his with panting breaths.

"Are you also aware of where this can*not* lead? There are limits imposed by my station. I should accept them grace-fully and walk away, but I am weak—"

She silenced him with her fingers over his lips, her pi-quant face lit with a dazzling grin. "I do love that you have no wish at all to marry me. To me, that is not a weakness, but a strength."

Rhys blinked. "Beg your pardon?"

"There is no doubt in my mind that you want *me*, and not my money. It is quite remarkable really."

"Is it?" he choked out, his cock as hard as a poker. Why the devil this woman had such an effect on him he could not collect.

"Quite. Men who look like you never find anything at all appealing about women who look like me."

"Fools, the lot of them." The conviction in his voice was genuine.

Abby leaned her cheek against his chest with a soft laugh. "Of course. Why men like Lord Grayson are so taken with women who look like Lady Grayson when I am around is an absolute mystery."

He stiffened, shocked at the undeniable flare of jealousy he felt. "You are attracted to Grayson?"

"What?" She pulled back. "I find him attractive, certainly. I doubt there is a woman alive who wouldn't. But I am not attracted to him personally, no."

"Oh . . ." He cleared his throat.

"How will you begin my ravishment?"

"Little one." He shook his head, but could not restrain his indulgent smile. Brushing the back of his hand along the curve of her cheekbone, he admired the way the moon was reflected in her eyes. "Understand, I mean to have more than a few kisses and some improper fondling. I will bare your skin, spread your thighs, steal what should be a gift for your husband."

"That sounds wicked," she breathed, gazing up at him raptly.

"It will be. But I assure you, you will enjoy every moment."

He, however, will probably wallow in guilt for the rest of his life, but he wanted her desperately enough to make that future torment worthwhile.

He pressed his lips very softly to hers, his hand at her waist slipping to cup what felt to be a fine derriere. "Are you certain this is what you want?"

"Yes. I have no doubts. I am seven and twenty. I have met hundreds of gentlemen over the course of my life and none of them have affected me as you have. What if no man ever will but you? I will regret forever that I did not enjoy what I could of your attentions."

His heart clenched painfully. "Losing your virginity to a cad such as myself will make your wedding night very awkward."

"No, it will not," she assured him confidently. "If I do marry, it will be with a man who is smitten enough with me to skip dinner like Lord Grayson has done for Lady Grayson."

"What Grayson feels is not 'smitten,' love," he said dryly.

Abby waved a careless hand. "Whatever name you give to it, he grants no significance to anything in her past. My future spouse will feel the same about me."

"You sound so certain."

"I am. You see, he would have to love me desperately to win my hand, and a little matter of a torn piece of flesh would not matter to him. In fact, I intend to tell any future spouse of mine all about you, and—"

"Good God!"

"Well, not literally," she hastened to say. Her gaze turned dreamy, her smile fond. "I would simply tell him of the man who made my stomach flutter and my heart race when he smiled. How wonderful that man was to me, what happiness he brought me after the death of my parents left my life a misery. And he will understand, Lord Trenton, because when you love someone that is what you do. You understand."

"What a dreamer you are," he scoffed in an attempt to hide how deeply her words touched him.

"Am I?" Frowning, she pulled away. "I suppose you are correct. My mother warned me once that affairs are practical endeavors, not the stuff of romance."

Rhys arched a brow, then linked their fingers and pulled her toward a nearby bench. "Your mother said that?"

"She said it was foolish of women to think that affairs were grand passions and marriages a duty. She said it should be the opposite. Affairs should be nothing more than a satiation of needs. Marriages should be lifelong commitments to deep-seated desires. My mother was a forward-thinking woman. After all, she *did* marry an American."

"Ah yes, that's true." Sitting, he pulled Abby into his lap. She weighed nearly nothing and he tucked her close, resting his chin on her head. "So she is the one responsible for filling your head with all that love nonsense."

"It's not nonsense," she chided. "My parents were mad for each other and very, very happy. The smiles on their faces when they were together again after an absence . . . The glow they had when they shared a smile over the dining table . . . Wonderful."

Licking the exposed column of her throat, he reached her ear and whispered. "I can show you wonderful, Abby."

"Oh my." She shivered. "I swear my stomach just turned a flip."

He loved how he affected her, how open and innocent she was in her responses. She was so pure of character. Not because she was naïve—she saw the workings of the world clearly—but because the less admirable facets of mankind did not disillusion her. Yes, she had been hunted by disreputable gentlemen, but she saw that for what it was—the stupidity and greed of a few men. The rest of the world was given the benefit of her doubt.

It was that quality of hopefulness which he found so irresistible. He would most likely be damned to perdition for taking her, but he could do nothing else. The thought of never having her, never experiencing her joy in passion was unbearable.

"What wing of the manse are you in?" he murmured, wanting to lie with her *now*.

"Let me come to you."

"Why?"

"Because you are the more experienced and jaded of the two of us."

"What does that have to do with anything?" *Would the woman ever cease confounding his wits?*

"You have this scent about you, my lord. Your cologne and soap and starch. It is quite delicious and when your skin heats up, the smell sometimes makes me feel as if I could swoon. I can only imagine how much more pronounced the effect will be after the physical exertions of lovemaking. I doubt I would be able to sleep a wink with that scent all over my bed linens. For you, however, the odor of sex would be nothing of note. Therefore, *I* should smell up *your* sheets, rather than you smell up mine."

"I see." Before he knew what he was doing, he had her bent over the cool stone bench and he was kneeling over her, taking her mouth with a need he had not felt since . . . since . . . *blasted!* Who in hell cared when it had been. It was damn well happening now.

His hands cupped the slight curves of her breasts and squeezed, eliciting a moan from her that swelled upward and filled the area of the garden they occupied. Discovery was a very real hazard and yet he could not find the will to cease. He was drunk on *her* scent, her response, the way she arched upward into his embrace and then shrank back, frightened.

"My very skin aches," she whispered, writhing.

"Hush, love," he soothed, his lips moving against hers.

"I—I feel so hot."

"Shhh, I will ease you." He stroked down the length of her side, trying to gentle what was quickly becoming a wild passion.

Her hands slipped between his coat and waistcoat, clawing at his back. The scratching made his cock throb and he paid her in kind by scraping the tips of his short nails across her hardened nipples. With one hand gloved and the other not, he knew the dual sensations would madden her.

"Christ almighty," she gasped. Then she grabbed his ass and yanked their hips together.

His breath hissed between his teeth. She cried out.

"Abby. We must find a room."

She turned her face into his throat, her lips moving feverishly across the sweat-dampened skin. "Take me here."

"Don't tempt me," he muttered, certain he was only minutes away from doing just that. If anyone were to stumble upon them now, there would be no way to explain. He was crouched over her like an obvious lecher. She was the innocent, who hadn't the wherewithal to deny a seasoned rake's advances.

How had they ended up like this? A stolen moment or two of her company, and he was about to break his one cardinal rule: no deflowering virgins. What fun was there in that? No quick rut, this. There would be blood, tears. He would have to seduce her properly, take his time, delay his own gratification. . . .

"My lord, please!"

Hell and damnation. It sounded like heaven.

"Abigail." He meant to hurry her off so they could meet naked—er, properly. But he was having the hardest time removing his fingers from around her nipples. Yes, her breasts were small, but her nipples were not. He couldn't wait to—

Her lovely gown tore as he yanked the shoulder down and bared her breast. She cried out again as he lowered his mouth and suckled her. Such long, delicious nipples. They rolled over his tongue like berries and were just as sweet.

"Please, oh please, my lord." She arched upward into his mouth and he almost came, that silken undulation an unbearable tease to his near-to-bursting cock.

It was only the sound of approaching laughter that saved her from ruination on a garden bench.

"Bloody hell." He moved swiftly, pulling her up and straightening her bodice. The nipple he had been sucking poked wantonly through the silk and he rubbed his thumb over it, unable to help himself.

"Don't stop!" she protested loudly, forcing him to cover her mouth with his hand.

"Someone is coming, love." He waited until she nodded her understanding. "Do you know where my room is?" She nodded again. "I will be there shortly. Don't dally. I will hunt you down if you do."

Her eyes widened. Then she nodded emphatically.

"Go."

Rhys watched her take a side path toward the manse and disappear from sight. Then he ducked behind a nearby vine-covered arbor and waited. It wouldn't do for both of them to return to the house too closely to each other. Even if neither or only one were seen, it was best to be overly cautious.

"But to petition Parliament, Celeste?" came Lady Hammond's voice from a nearby intersecting lane. "Think of the scandal!"

"I have thought of nothing but that for nearly five years," retorted the dowager Lady Grayson. "I have never been so mortified as I was when they did not attend dinner this evening. Which was an excellent repast, I must say."

"Thank you." There was a long pause, then, "Grayson seems quite taken with his wife."

"In only the most superficial sense, Iphiginia. Besides, she has no wish to be married. Not only has she proven that over the last four years, she has also said as much to me."

"She did not!"

Blinking, Rhys thought exactly the same thing. Isabel would never say such a thing to Grayson's mother.

"She did," the dowager replied. "She and I have agreed to assist each other."

"You jest!"

Good God! Rhys growled low in his throat. Bella would not be pleased when he saw her again. Damned if he wouldn't be pulling her out of another scrape.

Waiting until the women moved further along, he then left his hiding spot and moved surreptitiously through the garden toward the manse, where sinful pleasures awaited him.

Abby paused a moment at Trenton's doorway, wondering if one was supposed to knock before an assignation, or if she now had the right to just walk in unannounced. She was still debating this when the door flew open and she was yanked inside.

"What the devil took you so long?" Trenton complained, turning the lock and scowling down at her adorably.

Her stomach performed its little somersault again.

He was dressed in a burgundy silk robe, which revealed dark curling hair on his chest and hair-dusted calves that betrayed his nakedness beneath. With his arms akimbo, he was missing only the tapping foot to be a perfect picture of impatience.

Over her.

Her stomach flipped again.

How beautiful he was. What perfection! She sighed audibly. He was, of course, a bit hyperopic to miss her lack of physical charms, but she would not complain about that.

He reached for her and she sidestepped quickly. "Wait!"

"For what?" His scowl deepened.

"I—I have something to show you."

"If it's not you naked and writhing," he grumbled, "I am not interested."

She laughed.

She had watched him during dinner, noting his ready charm and droll discourse. The females seated on either side of him had been captivated, but she had felt his regard return to her often.

"Grant me a moment." She arched a brow when he opened his mouth to protest. "This is *my* deflowering. Once we reach the bed, I will cede command of this affair to you. Until then, however, I would like the preliminaries to be under my control."

Trenton's lips twitched and his eyes sparkled with a heat that made her shiver with anticipation. If his behavior in the garden was any indication, he was going to devour her. "As you wish, love."

Moving behind the privacy screen, she began to undress. This was not at all how she had imagined losing her virginity. There was no tender, patient husband waiting to treat her like fine porcelain. There was no ring on her finger or name attached to hers.

"What the devil are you doing?" he muttered, as if she were the most beautiful woman in the world and worthy of such avid interest.

He did have a way of looking at her that made her *feel* beautiful.

"I am almost done." She had dressed in the gown that was the simplest to remove without assistance, but it was still a chore. Finally, though, she was free and prepared. Taking a deep breath, Abby stepped out from behind the screen.

"About bloody . . ." His words faded into silence as he ceased pacing and turned to face her.

She shifted nervously under the sudden overwhelming heat of his gaze. "Hello."

"Abby." Just one word, but it was filled with awe and pleasure. "My God."

The fingers of her right hand fluttered nervously along the low neckline of her red gown. "My mother was blessed with a larger bosom, so I am afraid I cannot do the garment justice."

Trenton approached with his innate elegant grace, his cheekbones flushed, his lips slightly parted on rapid breaths. "If you did any more justice to that garment, I would be on my knees."

Blushing, she looked away, relishing the flutters she felt as he drew closer and then touched her gently. "Thank you."

"No, love," he murmured, his voice husky and deep, rippling down her spine. "*I* thank *you*. I cherish the gift you are giving to me."

With a finger beneath her chin, he angled her mouth and fitted his lips to hers. The kiss started softly, but quickly built until his mouth was slanting feverishly over hers, stealing her breath, making her dizzy. She quivered against him and was caught close to his hard body, lifted, and laid upon the bed.

Then he was everywhere. Stroking, kneading. His fingers tugging, pinching. His mouth wet and suckling. Nipping teeth. Hoarsely voiced words of encouragement and praise.

"Trenton!" she begged, certain she would die as her body

shuddered with longing he seemed determined to stoke, but not appease. For all his impatience earlier, he was not rushed now.

"Rhys," he corrected.

"Rhys . . ."

Unsure of what to do, what to say, she could only touch his shoulders, his beautiful hair, the straining and sweat-dampened length of his muscular back. What a work of art he was, his body able to arouse her just by sight. All men were not as blessed as he was and she knew she was beyond fortunate to share her bed with such an incomparable masculine creature.

"Tell me how to please you."

"If you pleased me any more, love, we would both regret it."

"How is that possible?"

"Trust me," he murmured before taking her mouth and sliding his hand up from the back of her knee to her hip. Before she could protest his fingers were parting the lips of her sex.

He groaned as his touch slipped through the slickness that gathered there. "You're dripping."

"I—I'm sorry." She felt herself blush to the roots of her hair.

"Dear God, do not be sorry." Rhys came over her, nudging her thighs wider. "It's perfect. You are perfect."

She wasn't. Not nearly. But the reverent way he touched her told her that for the moment at least, he truly thought she was.

Because of this, she bit her lip and held back her sobs as the broad head of his cock breached her, then pierced her and stretched her unmercifully. Despite her resolve to be a lover he would enjoy, she struggled.

Rhys pinned her hips, held her in place, slid inexorably into her. " . . . Hush . . . a little more . . . I know it hurts . . ."

And then something inside her made way for him and he was seated fully, a thick throbbing presence.

His palms cupped her cheeks, his thumbs brushed away her tears, his mouth worshipped hers. "Little one. Forgive me the pain."

"Rhys." She clung to him, grateful for him, knowing the trust she had in him was a rare, precious gift. Why this man, this stranger, should affect her the way he did, Abby could not collect. She was simply glad to have him for the little time he would be hers.

He held her, soothed her with praise. How soft she felt, how perfectly she fit him, how touched he was by the moment. She doubted a husband could have appreciated her more.

When she calmed, Rhys began to move, a torturously slow glide of his rock hard flesh from her swollen sex and then a sleek return. What pain there was faded and pleasure blossomed, unfurling like a flower so that she did not realize how she arched up to meet his downward thrusts until he spoke.

"Just like that," he growled, his skin dripping sweat. "Move with me."

Following his urgently voiced commands, she wrapped his pumping hips with her legs and felt him slide impossibly deeper. Now every perfect stroke struck a place inside her that made her toes curl, made her writhe and claw at his back.

"Thank God," he grunted when she dissolved into blissful release with a startled gasp.

Then he shuddered brutally and flooded her with liquid heat. Clutching her so tightly it was hard to breathe, he gasped, *"Abby!"*

She held him to her heart and smiled a woman's smile.

No, it was not at all how she had dreamed of losing her virginity.

It was so much better.

Rhys woke to a softly muttered curse and opened his eyes. Turning his head, he could barely discern Abby hopping on one foot while holding the other.

"What the devil are you doing stumbling about in the dark?" he whispered. "Come back to bed."

"I should go." With the poor light provided by the banked fire, he noted that she was dressed as she had been when he'd opened the door to her.

"No, you should not. Come here." He pulled the counterpane and linens back invitingly.

"I shall fall asleep again and never make it back to my room."

"I will wake you," he promised, already missing her slight body against his.

"It's simply not practical for me to fall asleep again, only to be woken up in a few hours to move to my room where I shall fall asleep again and be woken up again by my abigail."

"Love." He sighed. "Why be practical alone when we can be impractical together?"

He barely made out the shaking of her head. "My lord—"

"Rhys."

"Rhys."

Ah, that was better. That softly dreamy quality that entered her voice when she said his name.

"I want to hold you a little longer, Abby," he coaxed, patting the bed beside him.

"I must go." She moved to the door and Rhys lay stunned, feeling bereft and put out by her ease in leaving him when he so desperately wished she would stay.

"Abby."

She paused. "Yes?"

"I want you." His voice was sleep-husky, which he hoped hid the tightness of his throat. "Can I have you again?"

The pause that stretched out made him grind his teeth. Finally she replied in a tone one would use to accept an invitation to tea. "I would like that."

Then she was gone, as any sensible light-o-love would go. Without a lingering kiss or longing touch.

And Rhys, a man who had always been sensible about his affairs, found himself insensibly piqued.

"This is not at all what I envisioned when you asked me to accompany you," Spencer grunted, hefting a boulder into place.

Gerard smiled and stepped back to note the progress they were making on the low stone wall. His intention had not been to labor, but when they'd come across a large number of his tenants working on the endeavor, he appreciated the opportunity. Hard work and aching muscles had taught him a great deal about looking inward for satisfaction and relishing the simple things, like a job well done. It was a lesson he was determined to pass on to his brother.

"Long after you and I are gone, Spence, this wall will remain. You are a part of something lasting. If you consider your past, can you think of anything else you have done that leaves a mark on this world?"

Straightening, his brother frowned. With their shirtsleeves rolled up, and dusty, scuffed hessians, they looked very little like the peer and family they were. "Please don't tell me you have become philosophical as well. 'Tis bad enough you are doting on your own wife."

"I suppose doting on someone else's wife would be better?" Gerard said dryly.

"Damned if it wouldn't be. That way, when you have had your fill, she becomes another man's teary puddle and not your own."

"What faith you have in me, little brother, considering my wife's ability to bring men to tears."

"Ah yes, messy, that. I don't envy you." He wiped the sweat off his forehead with the back of his hand and then burst into a grin. "However, when Pel's crushed you beneath her heel like an annoying bug, I will be at the ready to help you recover. A little wine, a little women, and you shall be good as new."

Shaking his head, Gerard looked away with a laugh and found his attention caught by a scuffle between two young men just a short distance down the grassy hill. Concerned, he left his spot.

"No need to worry, my lord," came a gruff voice beside him. He turned to find the largest of the men standing at his side. "'Tis only my boy Billy and his friend."

Gerard returned his attention to the scene and found the boys racing each other off the hill to the flat land below. "Ah, I remember days like that in my youth."

"I think we all do, my lord. See the young girl sitting on the fence?"

Following the pointing finger, Gerard's heart stilled at the sight of the pretty blonde who laughed at the two boys running toward her. Silvery hair caught the sunlight, competing in brilliance with her smile.

She was lovely.

And very much like Emily in appearance.

"The two of them 'ave been competing for her affections for years. She 'as 'erself a soft spot for my boy, but in truth, I 'ope she's wise enough to pick the other."

Gerard tore his riveted gaze away from the young beauty, and arched both brows. "Why?"

"Because Billy only *thinks* 'e fancies 'er. 'E's got to compete with everyone, be better than everyone, and even though 'e knows she's not the one for 'im, 'e just cannot bear to lose 'er adoration. 'Tis purely selfish. But the other boy, 'e really loves 'er. 'E's always 'elping 'er with 'er chores, walking with 'er to the village. Caring for 'er."

"I see." And Gerard did, in a way he never had before.

Emily.

He had not thought of her at all on his Grand Tour. Not once. Too busy whoring to think of the adoring girl back home. Only upon his return and discovery of her marriage did he make any effort. Had he been like Billy? Simply jealous of attentions he hadn't appreciated until they were given to another?

You have always wanted women who belong to someone else.

Dear God.

Gerard turned, moved to the finished portion of the low wall, and sat, his gaze sightless as he looked inside instead of outward.

Women. He suddenly thought of them all, all the ones who had crossed his path.

Was it only competition with Hargreaves that had driven him to want Pel so desperately?

Warmth built in his chest and spread outward as he thought of his wife. *I want you.* The way those words had made him feel had nothing to do with Hargreaves. It had nothing to do with anyone but Isabel. And now that a mirror had been set before him, he realized that she was the only woman who had ever made him feel that way.

"Are we done?"

Raising his gaze, he found Spencer standing before him. "Not nearly."

Flooded with guilt for what he had done to Emily, Gerard set to work, doing what he had done for four long years—exorcised his demons by exhausting them.

"Lady Grayson."

Lifting her gaze from the book before her, Isabel saw John approaching where she sat on the rear Hammond terrace and offered him a gentle smile. Nearby to the right, Rhys sat with Miss Abigail and the Hammonds. To the left, the Earl and Countess of Ansell were enjoying afternoon tea with Lady Stanhope.

"Good afternoon, my lord," she greeted in return, admiring his trim form dressed in dark gray, and his sparkling eyes.

"May I join you?"

"Please do." Despite the things left unspoken between them, she was grateful for his company. Especially after sharing tea with the dowager, who had thankfully just departed.

Closing her novel, she set it aside and gestured to a servant for more refreshments.

"How are you, Isabel?" he asked with a searching glance, once he settled in the seat across from her.

"I am well, John," she assured him. "Very well. How are you?"

"I, too, am well."

She glanced around, then lowered her voice. "Please tell me truthfully. Have I hurt you?"

His smile was so genuine it soothed her immeasurably. "My pride smarts, yes. But truthfully, we were slowly approaching the end of our association, were we not? I was oblivious to it, as I have been oblivious to most things since Lady Hargreaves passed on."

Her heart welled with tenderness. Having lost a love once, she knew partly how it felt. It must have been much worse for John, since he had been loved in return.

"My time with you meant a great deal to me, John. Despite the horridly abrupt way our liaison ended, you do know that, don't you?"

Leaning into the backrest, he held her earnest gaze and said, "I do know that, Isabel, and your feelings for me made it much easier to see the purpose of our liaison and give it the closure it deserves. You and I came together for solace, the both of us wounded by our marriages—me, by the death of my beloved wife, and you, by the death of your not-so-loved husband. No strings, no demands, no goals . . . just companionship. How could I ever resent you for moving forward when something deeper came into your life?"

"Thank you," she said fervently, taking in every aspect of his handsome features with renewed affection. "For everything."

"In truth, I envy you. When Grayson came to me, I—"

"What?" She blinked in surprise. "What do you mean 'he came' to you?"

John laughed. "So, he didn't tell you. My respect for him has increased two-fold."

"What did he say?" she asked, nearly overrun with curiosity.

"What he said is not important. It is the passion with which he said it that I envied. I want that, too, and I think I am finally ready for it, thanks in no small part to you."

She wished she could reach out and squeeze his hand, which rested casually on the table, but she could not. Instead, she urged, "Promise me that we shall always be friends."

"Isabel." His voice held a smile. And a thread of steel. "Nothing on this earth could prevent me from being your friend."

"Truly?" She arched a brow. "What if I play matchmaker? I have a friend . . ."

John gave a mock shudder. "Now, that might do it."

As soon as Gerard and Spencer returned to the Hammond manse, they went straight to their rooms to bathe away the odors, sweat, and grime of the day.

Gerard longed to go to Isabel and had to fight the powerful urge to do so. He needed to talk with her, and share his discovery. He wanted to find comfort in her and soothe her fears with the knowledge that she was above all women to him. Most of all, he suspected she always would be and he wanted her to know that.

But then he wished to hold her, too, and he needed to be clean to do that.

So he sank into a hot bath, rested his head against the lip, and dismissed Edward.

When the door opened long moments later, he smiled, but

kept his eyes closed. "Good evening, vixen. Did you miss me?"

A throaty murmur of assent made his smile broaden.

Isabel drew closer and his blood quickened with anticipation. Languid from exhaustion and the warmth of the bath, it took him precious moments to register the scent of a foreign perfume as she bent over him, then the re-opening of the door . . .

What in—

. . . just before an equally foreign hand thrust into the water and wrapped around his cock.

He jerked in surprise, sloshing water over the rim of the tub as he opened his eyes and met Barbara's startled gaze. He'd noted the inviting glances she sent his way, but he had thought her wise enough to heed his returning scowl and warning at the Hammond's ball in town. Apparently not.

He caught her wrist just as her gaze lifted and then filled with abject horror.

"If you wish to keep that hand," came Pel's voice from the adjoining doorway. "I strongly suggest you remove it from my husband's bath."

Dripping with ice, the words chilled him despite the warmth of the water he sat in.

Bloody everlasting hell!

Chapter 15

Why does my wife have such an unfortunate way of finding me in the most compromising positions?

Baring his teeth, Gerard growled at his intruder, who stumbled back in fright. Rising from the water, he caught up the towel that had been draped over a chair by his valet and watched Pel stalk Barbara out of the room.

Isabel shouted down the hallway after Barbara's retreating figure. "I am not done with you, madam!"

Squaring his shoulders, Gerard waited for his lioness to turn and face him. When she did, he flinched at her thundercloud expression. She stared at him a moment with unreadable amber eyes, her hair loose and flowing about her torso, her lush body covered in a dressing gown. Then she turned away, moving quickly to her room.

"Isabel."

He fumbled for his robe and followed her, holding his hand out to prevent the rapidly closing door from smacking him in the face. Once inside, he studied her warily as he dressed, watched her pacing, wondered how to begin the conversation. Finally, he said, "I did not instigate nor participate in that advance."

She shot a sidelong glance at him, but did not still her pacing.

"I think you want to believe me," he murmured. She was not hurling invectives at him, or objects for that matter.

"It is not that simple."

Walking toward her, he caught her shoulders, forcing her to still. It was then he felt her labored breathing, which caused his heart to race desperately. "It *is* that simple." He shook her slightly. "Look at me. See *me*!"

Isabel's gaze lifted and bore that same dazed, unfocused film he had seen at the Hammond's ball.

Cupping her cheeks with his hands, he tilted her face up. "Isabel, my love." He pressed his cheek to hers and breathed deeply, inhaling her scent. "I am not Pelham. Perhaps, before . . . when I was younger . . ."

She clutched his robe in clenched fists.

He sighed. "I am no longer that man, and I have never been Pelham. I have never lied to you, never hidden anything from you. From the moment we met, I have opened myself to you like I have with no other. You have seen me at my worst." Turning his head, he kissed her cold lips, licking the seam, coaxing them softly to open. "Can you not find it in your heart to see me at my best?"

"Gerard . . ." she breathed, her tongue brushing tentatively along his, making him groan.

"Yes." He pulled her closer, taking ruthless advantage of that tiny show of weakness. "Trust me, Pel. I have so much I wish to entrust in you. So much to share. Please, give me— give *us*—that chance."

"I am afraid," she admitted, baring what he had known, but was waiting for her to say.

"How strong you are to reveal that," he praised, "and how lucky I am to be the man you share your fears with."

She tugged at the loose belt of his robe, undid her own, and pressed her bare skin to his. No barriers between them. Her cheek to his chest, he knew she listened to his heart, heard its steady beat. He reached beneath her dressing gown and stroked the length of her spine.

"I don't know how to do this, Gray."

"Neither do I. But surely, using our combined experience with the opposite gender, we can manage. I was always able to tell when a paramour was tiring of me. Surely—"

"You lie. No woman has ever lost interest in you."

"No *sane* woman," he corrected. "Did you see no warning signs with Pelham? Or did he just wake up one morning without his brain?"

Isabel rubbed her face in his chest and laughed. It was a shaky sound, but true mirth, nevertheless. "There were signs, yes."

"So we shall make another bargain, you and I. You tell me the moment you see what appears to be a sign, and I promise to reassure you in a way that leaves no doubt."

She pulled back and looked up him, her mouth lush and wide, her eyes fringed with chocolate-colored lashes. He stared, enraptured by her features, which were nowhere near refined or delicate. Isabel was a raving, brazen beauty.

"God, you are so lovely," he murmured. "It hurts sometimes to look at you."

Her creamy skin flushed, that telltale touch of color speaking volumes. Pel was a woman of the world if ever there was one, but he could make her blush like a schoolgirl.

"Do you think your plan will work?" she asked.

"What? Talking to each other? Never allowing doubts to fester?" He sighed dramatically. "Too much work perhaps? I guess we will simply have to stay abed and fuck like rabbits."

"Gerard!"

"Oh, Pel." Lifting her, Gerard spun in a circle. "I am mad for you. Can you not see that? As much as you worry about holding my interest, I worry about holding yours."

Isabel wrapped her slender arms around his neck and pressed a kiss to his cheek. "I am mad for you, as well."

"Yes," he said, laughing. "I know."

"Conceited rake."

"Ah, but I am *your* conceited rake, which is just how you want me. No, don't pull away. Let's make love, and then talk."

She shook her head. "We cannot skip dinner again."

"You dressed to seduce me, and now that your curves are pressed to my skin, you withdraw? What torture is this?"

"Considering how no provocation is required to lure you to sex, that was not my intent. I am undressed in this fashion because I napped." Her mouth curved in that wicked smile he adored. "And dreamt of you."

"Well, now I am here. Use me as you wish. I beg of you."

"As if you are deprived." She stepped back, and he made a great show of struggling to release her.

Growling, he muttered, "I wish I could say coming here was an error, but I think not."

"I think not either." She shot him a seductive glance over her shoulder. "And . . . good things come to those who wait."

"Do tell me more," he purred, following her.

"I shall tell you while you help me dress. But first things first, you keep that woman away from you, Grayson. If I find you with her again, I will definitely take that as a sign."

"Never fear, vixen," he murmured, wrapping his arms about her waist as she paused in front of the armoire. "I believe your point was well and truly made."

She laced her fingers with his at her abdomen. "Hmmmph. We shall see about that."

"I thought she intended to scratch my eyes out!"

Spencer shook his head and looked across the Hammond lower parlor to where Isabel stood off to the side, speaking with Lady Ansell. "What the devil were you thinking?"

Barbara wrinkled her nose. "When I exited my rooms and saw Grayson entering his, I assumed Pel was still below with the other guests."

"It was daft of you, however you look at it." He caught the eye of his brother, whose glowering look spoke volumes. *Rein her in,* it said.

"I know," she said morosely.

"And really, you know, I've tried to tell you—one Faulkner cock is as good as another."

"Yes, I suppose that's true."

"Have you learned your lesson? Stay away from Grayson."

"Yes. Yes. Will you promise to save me from her wrath?"

"Perhaps . . ."

She understood. "I will make my excuses in a moment." Barbara moved away.

Anticipating a night of carnal gratification, Spencer watched her sashay away with a smile.

"Did I hear Lady Stanhope correctly?" bit out a voice from behind him.

"Mother." He rolled his eyes. "You really must stop eavesdropping."

"Why did you warn her away from Grayson? Let her have him."

"Apparently, Lady Grayson took exception to that idea, to the point where Lady Stanhope fears for her person."

"What?"

"And Lord Hargreaves has gracefully withdrawn from the field. The newly reunited Graysons no longer have any impediments to marital bliss."

Glaring across the room, she muttered, "That woman agreed to cast him aside. I should have known she was lying."

"Even if she had not been, Gray is so taken with her, I doubt anything would keep him away. Look how he devours her with his gaze. And truth be told, I spoke with him a great deal today and she makes him happy. Perhaps you should concede this particular battle."

"I will not!" she retorted brusquely, brushing her dark gray skirts with gloved hands. "I will not live forever and before I take my dying breath I wish to see Grayson with a suitable heir."

"Ah . . ." He shrugged. "Well, perhaps it will be that which decides events in your favor. Pel has never struck me, or anyone else for that matter, as the maternal type. Had she longed for children, she would have increased long ago. Now her age is advanced and likely prohibitive to conception."

"Spencer!" His mother caught his arm and turned bright eyes to meet his. "You are a genius! That is exactly it."

"What? Which part?"

But his mother had already moved away, her slight shoulders straightened with a determination that made him glad to be exempt from its direction. He did, however, feel bad for his brother and so he moved to Gray's side as Lord Ansell left it.

"Sorry," Spencer murmured.

"Why did you bring her with you?" Gray asked, misunderstanding the apology.

"I told you. I was certain this trip would be a bore of heinous proportions. You cannot expect that I would be celibate in addition to that. I would offer to exhaust her from her meddling, but I ache all over, damn it. My arse, legs, arms. Some good I shall be to her, though I am determined to make my best effort."

Laughing, his brother clapped him on the back and said, "Well, her 'meddling' may have been fortuitous."

"*Now* I am certain you want a trip to Bedlam. No man possessed of all his mental faculties would say that being caught by his wife with his cock in another woman's hands was fortuitous."

Grayson smiled, and Spencer grumbled, "Well, out with it, man. You must explain, so that I may use a like circumstance to my advantage."

"I would not recommend a like circumstance to anyone. However, in this particular case it allowed me the opportunity to set my wife's greatest fear at ease."

"And that is?"

"For only I to know, brother," Gray said cryptically.

"My dear guests, your attention please!" Lady Hammond called out, tinkling a few keys on the pianoforte for greater effect.

Gerard looked at their hostess and then allowed his gaze to drift to Pel, just as hers moved to meet his. Her wide smile filled him with contentment. An hour or two more, and they could be alone.

"As a bit of training for tomorrow's scavenger hunt, Hammond and I have hidden two items somewhere in the manse—a gold pocket watch and an ivory comb. Unless the door is locked, or it is one of your bedchambers, any room is a possible hiding place. Please, if you find an item, make it known. I have a treat in store when the hunt is over."

Moving to his wife, Gerard was preparing to take her arm when she arched a wicked brow and stepped back. "If you hunt me instead, my lord, we will enjoy ourselves more than we would the watch or comb."

Instantly, Gray's blood both quickened and heated. "Minx," he whispered so as not to be overheard. "Put me off before dinner and then make me chase you for it afterwards."

The curve of her lush mouth deepened. "Ah, but I am *your* minx, which is just how you want me."

The low growl that escaped him could not have been contained if he'd tried. Everything primitive in him responded to her verbal acquiescence to his ownership. The desire to toss her over his shoulder and find the nearest bed was both embarrassing and arousing. The sudden darkening of her eyes told him that she understood what beast she'd stirred and welcomed it. Welcomed him. How was it possible that he had found a wife both genteelly raised and a tigress in bed?

His smile was feral.

She winked and turned on her slippered heel, strolling

out of the room with the other guests, her hips moving with an exaggerated swing.

He gave her a few moments head start, and then he pursued her in earnest.

Isabel followed Gray surreptitiously, avoiding both his gaze and the other guests. She should have allowed him to catch her half an hour ago, but she so enjoyed watching his sultry stride and flexing ass. Lord, her husband had the most beautiful ass. And that walk. It was the walk of a man absolutely certain he would be fucking shortly. It was languid and loose-limbed. Irresistible.

He was coming back around again and this time she would draw him in, her blood as hot as she was certain his must be. Focused as she was on Grayson, she failed to register the form behind her until a hand was clamped over her mouth and she was dragged back into hiding.

Only when Rhys spoke and she knew her abductor did she cease her startled struggling, her heart still racing. He released her and she rounded on him.

"What the devil are you doing?" she whispered crossly.

"I was about to ask the same of you," Rhys retorted. "I overheard the dowager Lady Grayson telling Lady Hammond about your pact."

Isabel winced. *How had she forgotten about that?* "Dear God."

"Exactly." He glowered down at her, every inch the chastising older brother. "Bad enough you would even speak aloud of leaving Grayson, but to say it to his mother who is now spreading the tale. What were you thinking?"

"I was not thinking," she admitted. "I was distressed and spoke rashly."

"You chose to marry him. You must now live with that choice as all women of your station do. Can you not find a way to coexist?"

She nodded rapidly. "Yes, I think we can. We have agreed to make the attempt."

"Oh, Bella." Rhys sighed and shook his head, his disappointment tangible, flooding her with guilt. "Did you not learn to be practical with Pelham? Carnal craving is not love or even the prelude to it. Why must you be so set on romance?"

"I am not," she argued, looking away.

"Hmmm . . ." He caught her chin and dragged her gaze back to his. "You lie, but you are a grown woman and I cannot make your decisions for you. We shall just leave it at that. But I worry over you. You are too sensitive, I think."

"We cannot all have hearts of steel," she grumbled.

"Gold." His smile faded as he expressed his concern. "The dowager is not a woman to take lightly. She is determined, although I do not know why. You are a duke's daughter and a fine pairing for any peer. If you make a true match with Grayson, I cannot see the objection."

"No one makes her happy, Rhys."

"Well, she will find her path damned uncomfortable if she thinks to tangle with our pater, and he *will* intercede, Bella."

Isabel sighed. As if their pasts and personal issues were not dilemma enough, she and Grayson had external combatants as well. "I shall speak to her. For all the good it will do."

"Good."

"There you are," Gray purred behind her, the moment before his hands cupped her waist. "Trenton. Do you not have a watch to hunt?"

Rhys sketched a slight bow. "I believe I do." His parting glance at Isabel spoke volumes, and she gave a slight nod before he turned about and moved down the gallery.

"Why do I feel as if the mood for play is lost?" Gray asked when they were alone.

"It is not."

"Then why are you so tense, Pel?"

"You could correct that." She turned in his arms.

"If I knew the cause," he murmured. "I'm certain I could."

"I wish to be alone with you."

Nodding, he led her toward their wing, but when she heard voices approaching, Isabel pulled him into the nearest room. "Lock the door."

With the drapes closed, the room they entered was so dark she could not see, which was just what she wanted at the moment. She heard the lock click into place.

"Gerard." Turning, she surged into him, her hands slipping beneath his jacket to embrace his lean waist.

Caught off guard, Gray stumbled backward until he hit the door. "Christ, Isabel."

She lifted to her tiptoes and buried her face in his neck. *How she loved the feel of him!*

"What is it?" he asked gruffly, his arms coming around her.

"Is this all we have? This craving?"

"What the devil are you talking about?"

She licked along his throat, consumed by a fever for him in her blood. She had never surrendered to him. Not completely. Perhaps it was that last bit of resistance which goaded his pursuit. If so, she needed to know that now. Before it was too late.

Cupping his ass, Isabel rubbed her body against his.

He shuddered. "Pel. Do not provoke me thusly here. Let's go to our room."

"You seemed game for the chase earlier." She kneaded along his spine through the thin satin back of his waistcoat. All the while she pressed into him, her breasts to his chest, her belly to the rigid length of his cock.

The darkness was freedom. All there was in her world at the moment was the large body she desired, the smell of Gray, the deliciously raspy voice, warmth. Heat. Need.

"You were playful then. I anticipated a bit of fondling, stolen kisses." He gasped as she stroked him through his trousers, but he did not stop her. "Now you are . . . you are . . . Bloody hell, I've no notion what you are, but it requires our bed, my cock, and uninterrupted hours."

"What if I cannot wait?" she breathed, squeezing the thick head of his shaft through her glove and his broadcloth.

"You would have me take you here?" His voice was thick with lust. "What if someone should come? We've no idea what room we are in."

Her fingers worked at the placket of his trousers. "Someplace unused, since there is no fire in the grate." She hummed her pleasure as he sprang free, hard and straining. "I am offering you the opportunity to take me in a public arena, as you said you were quite capable of doing."

He caught her wrist, but undeterred, her other hand reached around and squeezed his ass. Enflamed, he growled before twisting swiftly so that she was against the door. "As you wish."

As his hands delved beneath her skirts, he bit hard at her shoulder.

Her head drifted to the side as he parted her and stroked her clitoris. She widened her stance shamelessly and reveled in his expertise. He had once spent hours fucking her with his fingers and his tongue, determined to know every nuance of her body's ability to orgasm.

"What has possessed you? What did Trenton say to you?" His long fingers slipped inside her, stroking skillfully. Wetness spread across her flesh at the point where his bared cock thrust impatiently against her. "Jesus, Pel. You are soaked."

"And you are dripping semen down my leg." She shivered with the first stirrings of release, every part of her aching for more than just this. "Take me. Please. I want you."

As she had hoped, it was the last words that moved him. He cupped the back of her thighs and lifted her effortlessly. Isabel reached between them and guided him to her, moaning in near delirium as he lowered her onto his jutting cock.

Gray leaned forward, his chest moving against hers in

harsh, uneven breaths. She held him, breathed him in, absorbed the feel of his weight against her, his thickness inside her.

Did you not learn to be practical with Pelham?

"Is this all that we have?"

"Isabel." He nuzzled against her throat, his open mouth hot and wet against her. A hard shudder coursed through his frame when she tightened around him. "I pray this is all we have, for I cannot survive any more than this."

Pressing her cheek to his, she moaned softly as he moved. Withdrawing. Sliding back inside. Slowly. Savoring.

"More." It was not a request she made.

He paused, tensing.

"Damn you," Gray muttered finally, his fingers digging painfully into her flesh. "Can I ever pump deep enough? Can I ever fuck you enough? Sate you enough? Will I ever be *enough*?"

Bending his knees, he increased his pace, thrusting high and hard and deep, until she felt him in her throat. Startled by his sudden vehemence, she could say nothing.

"Is this all we have, you ask? Yes!" He rammed her into the door, bruising her spine, pinning her there. Making her cry out softly with pleasure and pain, unmoving except for the heated length throbbing inside her. She writhed and scratched at him, on the edge. She clung to his shoulders, his hips, trying to move, but there was no way. "You and I and no one else, Isabel. If it drives me into the grave, I will find a way to be what you need."

In her heart, warmth unfurled. Gray was not like Pelham. He was open and honest. His passion was real and truly heartfelt.

Perhaps she was not practical when it came to marriage, but with her husband she had no need to be. "I want to be what you need, as well. Desperately." She made the admission without fear.

"You are." He pressed his sweat-dampened face against hers. "For God's sake, you are everything."

"Gerard." Her fingers tangled in his silky hair. "Please."

He moved, building a steady rhythm and maintaining it. She allowed him the lead, becoming limp except for the inner muscles she tightened around his pumping cock. He grunted at every tight squeeze. She moaned with every deep plunge. There was no race to the finish, only a giving, one to the other, using their knowledge to ensure the greatest pleasure.

When he set his mouth to her ear and panted, "Christ! I cannot . . . Pel! I cannot stop! I'm going to come . . .", she gasped, "Yes! Yes . . ."

His hands at her thighs spread her wide, he thrust to the hilt and groaned, a tortured sound so loud she heard him over the roaring of blood in her ears. His orgasm was violent, his powerful body shaking, his cock jerking, his chest heaving as he gave her what she'd once spurned. Filled with him, overflowing with the essence of him, she held tight and came around him in a breathless, burning release.

"Isabel. My God, Isabel." He crushed her to him. "I'm sorry. Let me make you happy. Let me try."

"Gerard . . ." She pressed kisses across his face. "*This* is enough."

Chapter 16

As he left Bella behind, Rhys was so lost in thought he failed to look ahead. Turning the corner, he ran into a hastily moving body and had to reach out swiftly to prevent her fall.

"Lady Hammond! My apologies."

"Lord Trenton," she replied, straightening her skirts and touching a hand to her golden curls, which showed a faint trace of gray. When she looked up at him with a bright smile, he was startled, considering how he had very nearly run her over. "I apologize, as well. I was not minding my path in my haste to ensure my guests' enjoyment."

"Everyone is having a fine time of it."

"I am so relieved! I must thank you for the attention you paid to Hammond's niece this evening. The poor dear is so beleaguered by destitutes. I am certain discourse with a non–marital-minded man was refreshing. She was in as fine a mood as I have ever seen, which pleases me greatly. I appreciate your forbearance in speaking with her for such a length of time."

He held back a grunt. The image of him as a benign figure who had no sincere interest in Abby irked him in a way he could not understand. He longed to retort and refute, to say she was unique and desirable for more than her purse. But why he wished to defend her so fiercely eluded him. Perhaps it was guilt.

"No thanks are necessary," he assured her with practiced smoothness.

"Are you enjoying the scavenger hunt?"

"I was, yes. Now though, I will bow out and leave the rest of the guests to the glory."

"Is anything amiss?" she asked, the concerned hostess.

"Not at all. I am simply very good at such pursuits, and it would not be very sporting of me to win tonight, when I have every intention of winning tomorrow." He winked.

She laughed. "Very well. Good eventide to you, my lord. We shall see you over breakfast."

They parted ways and Rhys took the shortest route to his rooms. Once he'd undressed, he dismissed his valet for the evening and settled before the fire with a decanter and glass. Shortly, he was in his cups and somewhat eased of his regret over Abby, at least until the door opened.

"Go away," he muttered, making no effort to cover his legs, which were bared by the part in his robe.

"Rhys?"

Ah, his angel.

"Go away, Abby. I am not in any condition to receive you."

"You look perfectly conditioned to me," she said softly, coming over and circling the chair until she stood between him and the fire.

Divested of her underskirts for ease in undressing, he could see the outline of her lithe legs through her gown. He grew hard, a condition he was unable to hide, dressed as he was.

She cleared her throat, her gaze riveted.

Feeling the urge to shock her, Rhys yanked aside one edge of his robe and bared his upthrust cock. "Now that you have seen what you came here to see, you can go."

Abby sat in the chair across from him, her back ramrod

straight, her gaze curious and capped with a studious frown. She was so damned adorable, he had to look away.

"I did not come here to simply gaze at what I want and not have it," she said primly. "A sillier concept I've never heard of."

"I have something sillier for you," he retorted gruffly, shifting his half empty glass to create prisms from the firelight. "You working so industriously toward an unwanted pregnancy."

"Is that the impetus behind this mood you are having?"

"My 'mood' is called 'guilt,' Abigail, and since I've not felt that particular emotion before, I am not comfortable with it."

She was silent for long moments. Long enough for him to drain his drink and refill it. "You regret what happened between us?"

He did not look at her. "Yes."

A lie, for he could never regret the time he had spent with her, but it was best if she did not know that.

"I see," she said softly. Then she stood and came toward him. She paused beside his chair. "I am sorry you regret it, Lord Trenton. Know that I never will."

It was the wavering undercurrent in her voice that made him move lightning quick to capture her wrist. When he forced himself to look at her, he saw tears, which cut him so deeply he dropped the glass in his other hand, the thud of its impact drowned by the roaring of blood in his ears. The feel of her, just that slight, fragile piece of her, set off memories of touching other parts. Impossibly, he began to sweat.

She tried to pull herself free, but he held fast, rising to his feet, gripping the back of her neck roughly. "See how I hurt you? How I can do nothing but hurt you?"

"It was heaven," she cried, swiping furiously at her tears. "The things you did . . . the way you felt . . . the way *I* felt!"

Abby struggled, but he maintained his grip. She glared at him through her weeping, her cheeks flushed, her lips red and parted. "I see my mother was correct. Affairs are physical release, nothing more. I suppose sex must feel this way for everyone. *With* anyone! Why else would so many indulge?"

"Cease!" he barked, his heart racing as he saw the path of her logic.

Her voice rose. "Why else would the experience mean so little to you? Stupid of me to think you and I are unique. I am so easily replaceable for similar intimacy. I conclude that any other man could provide a like orgasmic event for me!"

"Damn you. No other man."

"To hell with you, my lord!" she cried, glorious with indignant fury. "I am no great beauty, but I am certain there are men who could make love to me without regret."

"Let me assure you," he bit out, "any other man who touches you will regret it immensely."

"Oh." As she blinked up at him, her free hand fluttered to her throat. "Oh my. Are you being possessive?"

"I am never possessive."

"You threaten any man who might touch me. What do you call that?" She shivered. "Never mind. I love it, whatever you call it."

"Abby," he growled, furious at the tightening he felt in his gut. *Would she forever drive him insane?*

"That growl . . ." Her eyes widened, then softened. "Your roguish tendencies turn my insides to jelly, did you know that?"

"I did not growl!" Against his will, his arm drew into his body, pulling her with it.

"Yes, you did. What are you doing?" she gasped when he licked the very edge of her lips. "You intend to ravish me, do you not?"

His half-drunken brain was inundated with the warmth of her slender body, the soft scent of her, and the voice he loved. Her cries in orgasm were enough to make his cock weep with joy. It was leaking even now, he was so aroused, and she had done nothing to make him feel this way. It was simply *her*. Something indefinable about her.

"No," he murmured in her ear. "I intend to *fuck* you."

"Rhys!"

When he released her wrist and reached for her breast, he was not surprised to find her nipple hard against his palm. Those long, delicious nipples. He pulled her to the floor.

"What? Here?" Her shock would have made him laugh, if he weren't concentrating so fiercely on yanking her skirts out of the way. "On the *rug*? What about the bed?"

"Next time."

Finding her slick and hot, Rhys began to work his cock into her with a groan of surrender. Abby whimpered softly.

"Will you regret this, too?" she asked, squirming beneath him.

He knew she was sore, could feel how swollen her tissues were, but could not desist. Watching her as he forced her body to take him, he nearly drowned in those blue eyes with their golden flecks. "Never," he vowed.

"You lied earlier." Her smile was brilliant and watery with renewed tears. "I have never been so happy to have been lied to."

He had never been so happy either.

Which was a torment worse than hell itself.

Unwilling to leave Isabel after her apparent upset the night before, Gerard found himself walking several feet behind her as the Hammond party left their horses with grooms and walked to a location prepared for an alfresco picnic. Dressed in flowered muslin with a large satin bow at the back and a wide-brimmed straw hat upon her upswept auburn tresses, his wife looked both elegant and young. The latter effect was enhanced by her sparkling eyes and wide smile.

That he was responsible for her look of contentment was astonishing to him. Prior to four years ago, he had never pleased anyone but himself, and he'd never in his life made a woman happy outside of sexual intercourse. He had no notion how he'd managed the deed. He knew only that he would continue to keep her so blissful if it killed him.

To wake to Isabel pressing kisses to his chest with laugher in her eyes was beyond heavenly. To feel her turn to him, snuggle with him, reach for him when she grew cold . . . It was a type of intimacy he hadn't known existed, and he had found it with his wife, the most beautiful and wonderful woman in the world. He deserved it less than anyone, but he had it. And he would cherish it. Spilling his seed inside her had been a foolhardy lapse, one he would not repeat. He could not risk impregnating her.

Glancing aside, he studied Trenton and said, "You still look morose. The country air not working its wonders on you?"

"No," Trenton grumbled, frowning. "My ailment cannot be cured by fresh air or anything else."

"What kind of ailment is that?"

"The female kind."

Laughing, Gerard said, "I hope to be slowly developing a cure for that myself. Unfortunately, I doubt it would help you if I do."

"Once Isabel discovers a dalliance on your part," Trenton warned ominously, "the saints above will not be able to cure you."

Gerard came to an abrupt halt and waited for Trenton to face him. The rest of the party continued on until they were quite alone. "Is that what you told my wife last night? That I would stray?"

"No." Trenton stepped closer. "I merely told her to be practical."

"Isabel is one of the most pragmatic women I know."

"Then you do not know her well."

"Beg your pardon?"

Trenton smiled wryly and shook his head. "Isabel is a romantic, Grayson. She always has been."

"Are we talking about *my wife*? The woman who discards men who become too attached to her?"

"Lovers and spouses are two very different things, would you not agree? She will become attached to you if you continue on your present course. And women can be positively demonic when their affections are rebuffed."

"Attached to me?" Gerard asked softly as wonder filled him. If this morning's playful affection was any indication of what Pel was like when attached, he wanted more of it. All of it. Today was the best day of his life. What if all of his days could be like this one? "I've no intention of rebuffing her. I want her, Trenton. I intend to keep her happy."

"To the exclusion of all others? Nothing less will content her. For some unknown reason, she has odd delusions of love and fidelity in marriage. She certainly did not learn that in our family. From faery tales, perhaps, but not from a firm grounding in reality."

"No others," Gerard said, distracted. He looked ahead, wishing he could see his wife from this vantage. As if she felt his silent demand for the sight of her, she appeared and waved, causing him to take an involuntary step toward her.

"You are champing at the bit," Trenton observed.

"How should I win her heart?" Gerard asked. "With wine and roses? What do women consider romantic?"

Wildflowers picked as afterthoughts and off-the-top-of-his-head poems had lured Em, but his goals were different now, more important. He could not leave this to chance. Everything for Isabel had to be perfect.

"You are asking *me*?" Trenton's eyes widened. "How the devil would I know? I've never in my life wanted a woman to fall in love with me. Damned inconvenient when they do."

Gerard frowned. Pel would know and he longed to ask her, just as he had always turned to her for advice and her opinions. But in this instance, he was quite definitely on his own. "I will puzzle it out."

"I am glad you appreciate her, Grayson. I often wondered

what Pelham was looking for outside of wedlock when he had Isabel so smitten within it. He was a god to her in the beginning."

"He was an idiot. I am no god to Pel. She is well aware of all my shortcomings. If she can see past them, it will be a miracle." He began walking and Trenton fell into step beside him.

"I would think that to love a person in spite of their faults, rather than because you cannot see those faults, would be the deeper of the two attachments."

Considering that thought a moment, Gerard broke out in a grin. Which faded as they rounded a large tree and he saw Hargreaves speaking with Isabel. She laughed at something said to her, and the earl's returning look was both open and fond. They stood together with an obvious familiarity.

Inside him, something twisted and churned. His fists clenched. Then she saw him, and excused herself, moving toward him swiftly.

"What delayed you?" she asked, taking his arm with blatant ownership.

The writhing thing inside him quieted and he exhaled audibly. He wished he were alone with her, talking with her as they had last night when they'd returned to their rooms. Lying in bed with Pel curled to his side and their fingers linked over his chest, he had told her about Emily. Told her about what he had discovered about himself, and listened to her assurances and voice of reason.

"You are not a bad man," she had said. "Merely one who was young and in need of adoration after living with a mother who could do nothing but chastise you."

"You make it sound so simple."

"You are complicated, Gerard, but that does not mean it is not something simple that goads you."

"Such as?"

"Such as saying farewell to Emily."

Puzzled, he asked, "How am I to do that?"

She rose to hover above him, her eyes glowing with the reflection of the firelight. "In your heart. In person. In any way at all."

He shook his head.

"You should. Perhaps during a long walk. Or you could write her a letter."

"Visit her grave?"

"Yes." Her smile took his breath away. "Whatever you need to do to say good-bye and set aside your guilt."

"Will you go with me?"

"If you wish me to, of course I will."

In the space of an hour, she changed his self-loathing to self-awareness and acceptance. She made everything seem right, made every challenge bearable, made the completion of difficult tasks seem possible. He longed to provide the same for her, to be as valuable a partner to her as she was to him.

"And you?" he asked. "Will you allow me to help you make peace with Pelham?"

She lowered her cheek to his chest, her hair spilling over his shoulder and arm. "Anger at his memory has strengthened me for so long," she said softly.

"Strengthened *you*, Pel? Or your barriers?"

Her sigh blew hot across his skin. "Why do you pry at me?"

"You said this was enough, but it isn't. I want all of you. I am not inclined to share parts of you with any man—dead or living."

Her breathing stilled until he almost shook her in alarm. Then she gasped and clung to him, her legs tightening around his, her hands clutching his shoulders. He embraced her just as fiercely in return.

"You can hurt me," she whispered. "Do you understand that?"

"But I will not," he vowed, his lips to her hair. "Eventually, you will come to believe that."

After a time, they drifted into sleep, the deepest slumber

Gerard had known in many years, because he was no longer trudging through his day waiting for it to end. He had something to look forward to upon waking.

"Isabel," he said now, leading her a short distance away from the other guests. Ways to win her deeper affections sifted through his brain. "I should like very much to take you to my estate tomorrow."

She glanced aside at him from beneath her hat, the jaunty angle revealing the curve of her lips and not much more. "Gerard, you may take me anywhere."

The double entendre was not lost on him. It was a beautiful day, his marriage was on the mend, he had romance on his mind and in his heart. Nothing could steal his contentment. He was about to reply, his heart light at Pel's teasing banter . . .

"*Grayson.*"

The crossly voiced intrusion could not have come at a worse time.

Heaving out a disappointed breath, he turned reluctantly to face his mother. "Yes?"

"You cannot continue to avoid the other guests. You must attend this afternoon's treasure hunt."

"Certainly."

"And supper this evening."

"Of course."

"And the ride scheduled for tomorrow."

"My apologies, madam, but I cannot oblige you there," he said smoothly, finding her overbearing tendencies lacking their usual irritating effect. Even his mother could not ruin his day. "I have the time reserved for Lady Grayson."

"Have you no shame?" the dowager snapped.

"Scarcely any, no. I thought you knew that."

Isabel bit off a laugh and looked away quickly. He somehow managed to keep his face impassive.

"What is so important that you would abandon your hosts again?"

"We travel to Waverly Court tomorrow."

"Oh." His mother frowned at him a moment, an expression so common to her countenance that lines permanently etched its passing. "I should like to go. I've not been there in many years."

Gerard was silent a moment, remembering suddenly that his parents had spent some time in residence there. "You are welcome to join us."

The smile she bestowed on him startled, the transformation of her features was so unnerving. But it disappeared as quickly as it came. "Now come join the rest of the party, Grayson, and behave yourself as is appropriate to your station."

Watching his mother walk away, he shook his head. "I hope you can disregard her gloom."

"I can with you at my side," Isabel replied offhand, as if she were not saying something that completely rocked him to the core.

He took a brief moment to catch his bearings, and then allowed his grin to break free.

No doubt about it. Nothing could ruin his day.

"Lady Hammond would have to pair us together," Rhys muttered, moving rapidly up the wooded path.

"The thought of hunting treasure with you made me giddy," she teased. "I am dreadfully sorry if you do not feel the same about being with me."

The side glance he shot at her was so hot, her skin felt burned. "No. I would not call what I feel 'giddy.'"

The dead leaves along the trail crunched beneath every heavy step of his hessians. Dressed in dark green, he was stunningly handsome. Once again, she marveled that such a bold, masculine creature would find anything arousing about her, but it was clear the marquess did. And was very upset by that fact.

"If I had any say in the matter," he grumbled, "I would pull you into that clearing over there and lick you from head to toe."

Staring straight ahead, Abby had no idea what a woman was supposed to say in reply to such a statement. So she looked at the paper in her unsteady grip and said, "We need a smooth stone. There is a river around the bend up there."

"That dress you are wearing is distracting."

"Distracting?" It was one of her most flattering, a soft pink muslin with burgundy satin ribbon edging the low-cut bodice. She had selected it just for him, even though she hadn't the bosom to make it truly fetching.

"I know with a quick tug, your nipples will pop free and I can suck on them."

Her empty hand sheltered her racing heart. "Oh my. You are being very naughty."

He snorted. "Not as naughty as I would like to be. Pinning you to a tree and lifting your skirts would do nicely."

"Lifting my—" She stumbled to a halt as every cell in her body responded to the picture his words evoked. "It is the middle of the day."

Rhys, lost in his own thoughts, took several steps forward before realizing she remained behind. He turned to face her, his rich hair glinting in the filtered light of the overhead canopy. "Are your nipples different in the sunlight? Is your scent altered? Your skin less soft? Your cunt less tight and wet?"

She shook her head rapidly, unable to speak.

His gaze bore intensely into hers. "I have to depart in the morning, Abby. I cannot remain here and debauch you further. That I am trusted to be alone with you is like trusting the wolf to guard the lamb. It's perverse."

Try as she might to keep her mother's advice firmly in her mind, she could not do it. Her heart ached. She could only hope her exterior did not betray her.

"I understand," she said tonelessly, all her previous enjoyment in the day gone.

Why did this man appeal to her so deeply?

She had lain in her bed after leaving him and pondered that question for hours. In the end, she decided it was a combination of many things, some external, like his attractiveness and charm. And others internal, like his tendency to find new joy in her discoveries about how men and women related with one another. With him, she did not feel gauche. She was desirable, witty, and wise. Rhys thought it was "wonderful" that she enjoyed puzzling out scientific equations. He had even kissed the ink stains on her fingers as if they were a thing of beauty.

He was known for his ennui and jaded views, but Rhys was only dormant, not dead. She longed to be the catalyst that revived him, but she knew his sense of duty to his title would never allow her to be.

It would be best if he left.

"It would be best if you left."

He stared at her for a long moment, unmoving, so when he lunged at her and grabbed her roughly, she was caught completely unawares. His hands in her hair, he kissed her with unrestrained passion, his thrusting tongue stealing her breath and her wits.

"You make me forget myself," he said harshly against her bruised lips. "To see you dismiss me so summarily drives me insane."

"*Something* has obviously driven you insane," snapped a familiar female voice.

Rhys groaned. "Bloody hell."

"Leave it to you, Trenton," drawled Lady Grayson, "to ruin my day."

Chapter 17

"I've no notion what to say to you, Rhys," Isabel scolded, glaring up the narrow path at her brother.

Gray leaned over and murmured, "I will see Hammond's niece back to the manse so that you may speak with Trenton in private."

"Thank you." Her eyes met his for a moment and she squeezed his hand in gratitude. She watched as he collected the obviously flustered girl and led her away. Then she rounded on Rhys. "Have you lost your mind?"

"Yes. God, yes." His countenance was gloomy as he kicked at a tree root that rose slightly above the dirt.

"I know you were out of sorts when we left London, but to use that child as salve for your—"

"That 'child' is the same age as your husband," he pointed out dryly, making her gasp in horror.

"Ooohhh . . ." She chewed her lower lip and began to pace.

Lately, she often forgot about the age difference in her marriage. After she'd first wed Grayson, the gossips had salivated over her superior years, but she managed to ignore them. Now, however, she was most definitely entertaining a younger man in her bed.

But she could not think of that now.

"Do not dare make that comparison." Her chin lifted. "Grayson is far more experienced in such matters, whereas it is quite obvious that Miss Abigail is not."

"It was almost effective in distracting you," he muttered.

"Ha!" She shook her head and then said more somberly, "Please tell me that you have not taken her to your bed, Rhys."

His shoulders drooped.

"Dear God." Isabel paused her pacing and stared at her brother as if he were a stranger. The Rhys she knew would have no interest in an innocent bluestocking. "How long has this been progressing?"

"I first made her acquaintance at that blasted breakfast you forced me to attend." He growled. "This is all *your* doing."

She blinked. Weeks. Not merely the last couple of days. "I am attempting to understand. Not to sympathize, mind you," she added hastily. "But simply to comprehend it. I cannot."

"Do not ask me to enlighten you. All I know is that I cannot be within a few feet of her without my brain ceasing to function. I become some boorish rutting beast."

"Over *Abigail Stewart*?"

The glare he shot her spoke volumes. "Yes, over Abigail. Damn it, why can no one see her worth? Her beauty?"

Wide-eyed, she studied him in detail, noting the flush at the crest of his cheekbones and the brightness of his eyes. "Are you in love with her?"

His look of astonishment would have been comical if she weren't so disturbed. "I am in lust with her. I admire her. I enjoy talking with her. Is that love?" He shook his head. "I will be Sandforth eventually and must consider the dukedom before considering my own desires."

"Then what were you doing with her alone in the garden? This path is well-trodden. Any one of the other guests could have happened upon you. What of Hammond? What would you have said to him in return for abusing his hospitality and trust this way if he had been the one to discover you embracing?"

"Damnation, Bella! I do not know. What more can I say? I erred."

"You *erred*?" Isabel blew out her breath. "Is that why you came? To be with her?"

"I had no notion she would be here, I promise you that. I meant to distract myself from thoughts of her. Remember when we arrived? I had to ask you who she was."

"Are you expecting the girl to become your mistress?"

"No! Never," he said emphatically. "She is much like you—filled with dreams of romance and love in marriage. I've no wish to take that away from her."

"But you took the virginity meant for that great love?" She arched a brow. "Or was she not a virgin?"

"Yes! Of course she was. I am her only lover."

Isabel said nothing. The notes of pride and possession in his tone were clear to both of them.

Rhys groaned and rubbed the back of his neck. "I am departing in the morning. The best thing I can do at this point is stay away."

"You never heed my advice, but I will share it with you anyway. Consider your feelings for Miss Abigail carefully. Having known both happiness and despair in my marriages, I strongly recommend you find a spouse you enjoy spending time with."

"You would have an American as the Duchess of Sandforth?" he asked incredulously.

"Alter your thinking, Rhys. She is the granddaughter of an earl. And frankly, there must be something exceedingly extraordinary about her for you to lose your head as you have done. If you put your mind to it, I am certain you can help reveal that side of her to the world."

He shook his head. "Romantic nonsense, Bella."

"Certainly being practical in one's choices is wise when

the heart is not involved, but when it is, I think you should weigh those additional concerns carefully."

Frowning, he stared up the path in the direction Gray and Abigail had taken. "How furious was our pater when you selected Pelham?"

"Nowhere near as furious as he was when I wed Grayson, but he adapted." Stepping closer, Isabel set her hand on his shoulder. "I don't know if you will find comfort in this, or pain, but it was quite clear to me that she adores you."

He winced and held out his arm to her. "I don't know how I should feel about that either. Come. Let's return to the house. I must set my valet to packing."

A depressive air hung about the Hammond party in the parlor that evening. Rhys lacked his customary charm and quick wit, and retired early. Abigail put on a brave face, and to the casual eye, one would find nothing amiss, but Isabel could see the strain that tightened the other woman's mouth. Beside her on the settee, Lady Ansell was equally despondent, despite having won the treasure hunt earlier.

"Your necklace is a lovely piece," Isabel murmured, hoping to cheer the viscountess.

"Thank you."

They had known each other casually for years, though after her recent marriage to the viscount, Lady Ansell had spent a great deal of her time traveling abroad with her husband. Not quite pretty, the viscountess nevertheless was a handsome woman, tall and proud in bearing. It was clear to many that her match with Ansell was a love match, which gave the woman a sparkle to her eyes that more than made up for her lack of classical beauty. Tonight, however, that sparkle was missing.

Lady Ansell turned to face her, revealing a reddened nose and quivering lips. "Forgive my importunateness, but would you walk in the garden with me? If I go alone, Ansell will come and I cannot bear to be alone with him now."

Startled by the request, and concerned, Isabel nodded and rose to her feet. She shot a placating smile at Gray before exiting out the open glass-paned doors to the terrace and leaving him behind. Strolling along the lighted gravel paths with the statuesque blonde, Isabel maintained her silence, having learned long ago that sometimes it was best simply to be present, no discourse necessary.

Finally, the viscountess said, "I feel dreadful for poor Lady Hammond. She is certain that despite her careful planning, her party is a crashing bore. I have tried my best to enjoy myself, I truly have, but I am afraid no amount of festivities can enliven my mood."

"I will reassure her again," Isabel murmured.

"I'm certain she would appreciate it." Sighing, Lady Ansell said, "I miss wearing the glow you bear. I wonder if I will ever reclaim it for myself."

"I have found that contentment moves in cycles. Eventually, we rise above the depths. You will, too. I promise you."

"Can you promise me a child?"

Blinking, Isabel had no notion of what to say to that.

"I'm sorry, Lady Grayson. Forgive my curtness. I do truly appreciate your concern."

"Perhaps speaking your troubles aloud will help ease your mind?" she offered. "I will lend you my ear, and my discretion."

"I have regret. I do not think there is ease from that."

From her own experience, Isabel knew this was true.

"When I was younger," the viscountess said, "I was certain I would never find a spouse who would suit me. I was too eccentric, and eventually I became a spinster. Then I met Ansell, who loved to travel as much as my parents had. All of my originality appealed to him. We are quite evenly matched."

"Yes, you are," Isabel agreed.

A faint smile softened the other woman's palpable sadness. "If only we had found each other sooner, perhaps we could have conceived."

Icy fingers wrapped around Isabel's heart. "I am sorry." It was inadequate, but all she could manage.

"At nine and twenty, the physician says perhaps I have waited too long."

"Nine and twenty . . . ?" Isabel asked, swallowing hard.

A suppressed sob rent the still night air. "You are near my age; perhaps you understand."

All too well.

"Ansell assures me that even if he had known I was barren, he would still have wed me. But I have seen the way he looks at small children, the longing in his eyes. There comes a time when a man's need to produce issue is strong enough to be felt by others. My one duty as his viscountess was to bear his heir and I have failed him."

"No. You mustn't think that way." Isabel hugged her waist to ward off a sudden chill. All the joy she had once felt in the day slipped away from her. Could happiness be hers when the age for new beginnings belonged to women much younger than she was?

"This morning my courses started and Ansell was forced to leave our rooms to hide his dismay. He claimed he wished to ride in the early morning air, but in truth, he could not bear to look at me. I know it."

"He adores you."

"You can still find disappointment in those you adore," Lady Ansell argued.

Taking a deep breath, Isabel acknowledged that her time for childbearing was slipping rapidly through the hourglass. When she barred Pelham from her bed, she had ended what dreams she'd had of having a family of her own. She had mourned the loss deeply for many months, and then she'd found the strength to move past that dream.

Now, with her future filled with renewed possibilities, time was running away from her and circumstances forced her to wait even longer. Propriety and common sense dictated that she refrain from pregnancy until there could be no public doubt the child was Grayson's.

"Lady Grayson."

The deep, raspy voice of her husband behind her should have startled her, but it did not. Instead, she was assailed with a longing so intense it nearly brought her to her knees.

Turning, both she and Lady Ansell found their spouses and host rounding a corner flanked by yew hedges. With his hands held behind his back, Gray was the picture of coiled predatory grace. He had always carried his power with envious ease. Now, with his dangerous edge blunted by her ability to sate his desires, he was even more compelling. The sultriness of his stride and half-lidded eyes made her mouth water, as she knew they would most women. That he was hers, that she could keep him and bear children with him made tears well. It was simply too much after going so long without.

"My lords," she greeted hoarsely, remaining rooted to Lady Ansell's side by good manners and nothing else. Had she the choice, she would have moved into Gray's arms immediately.

"We have been sent to find you," Lord Hammond said with a tentative smile.

After a quick perusal of her companion reassured her of the viscountess' renewed composure, Isabel nodded and was grateful to return to the manse where concerns of babies and regrets could be momentarily set aside.

The sound of crunching gravel alerted Rhys to the approaching figure. If he'd had any doubt that he was making the right decision, it was dispelled when Abby came into view, bathed in moonlight. The racing of his heart and nearly overwhelming need to crush her to him proved Bella's words true—Abby was the person he wished to make his life's journey with.

"I went to your rooms," she said softly, as direct as always.

How he adored that about her! After a lifetime of saying what was expected and hearing equally worthless discourse in return it was a joy to spend time with a woman who had no social artifice at all.

"I suspected you would," he replied gruffly, backing up when she stepped forward. The color of her eyes was not visible in the near darkness, but he knew it as well as he knew the color of his own. He knew how they darkened when he filled her, and how they glistened when she laughed. He knew every ink stain on her fingers, and could tell her which ones hadn't been there the last time he saw her. "And I knew that if you did, I would take you to bed."

She nodded her understanding. "You are departing tomorrow."

"I must."

The determined finality in Rhys' tone pierced Abigail like a rapier thrust.

"I shall miss you," she said.

Though the words themselves were the truth, the casual tone she used to impart them was a lie. The thought of the endless days before her without Rhys' touch and his hunger, was devastating. Even having known it would end like this, she was still unprepared for the pain of separation.

"I will come back for you as soon as possible," he said softly.

Her heart stilled before leaping. "Beg your pardon?"

"I travel to visit my father tomorrow. I will explain the situation between you and me, and then I will return to London and court you as I should have done from the beginning."

The *situation*.

"Oh my." Abby walked slowly over to a nearby marble bench and sat, her gaze lowering to her twisting fingers. The moment Grayson's voice had interrupted their kiss, she had dreaded this result. What had been nothing but joy and love for her, was now a lifetime duty for Rhys. She could not allow him to make the sacrifice, especially considering how obviously he resented his craving for her.

She looked at him and managed a soft smile. "I thought we agreed to approach our affair pragmatically."

He frowned. "If you think I have done anything pragmatically since meeting you, you are daft."

"You know what I mean to convey."

"Things have changed," he argued gruffly.

"Not for me." She held out her hands to him, then caught the gesture and clasped them back together. Any sign of weakness and he would note it. "Surely Lord and Lady Grayson will afford you their discretion if you ask it of them."

"Of course." He crossed his arms. "What are you saying?"

"I don't want to be courted, Rhys."

He gaped at her. "Why the devil not?"

She affected a shrug. "We had an agreement. I am not inclined to alter the rules at this point."

"Alter the rules . . . ?"

"I enjoyed our time together immensely and I will always be grateful to you."

"Grateful?" Rhys parroted, staring at Abby in confounded wonder. He longed to go to her, to hold her and break through the wall that was suddenly between them, but it was too dangerous. Ravishment was a very real hazard.

"Yes, quite." Her smile was a thing of beauty that shattered him.

"Abby, I—"

"Please. Say no more." Rising to her feet, she approached him and rested her fingertips over his tense arm. Her touch burned through the velvet of his coat. "I will forever count you as a dear friend."

"A friend?" He blinked furiously as his eyes burned. Releasing his breath, Rhys soaked up the sight of her—the tightly coiled dark tresses, the high waist of her pale green gown, the gentle swell of her breasts above the scooped neckline. All his. Nothing, not even her outrageous dismissal, would ever convince him otherwise.

"Always. Will you promise me a dance when next we meet?"

Rhys swallowed hard. There were a hundred things he wished to say, questions to ask, assurances to give . . . but they were all dammed up behind the lump in his throat. Here he had been falling in love, while Abby had merely been falling into bed? He refused to believe that. No woman could melt for a man the way she did for him and not feel something deeper than friendship.

A harsh laugh erupted without thought. If that wasn't a perfect comeuppance for a seasoned rake, he had no notion what was.

"Farewell until then," Abby said, before turning and walking away with undue haste.

Crushed and confused, Rhys sank onto the bench still warm from her body heat and dropped his head in his hands.

A plan. He needed a plan. This could not be the end. Every labored breath protested the loss of his love. There was something he was missing, if only he could think well enough to discover it. He had been with enough women to know that Abby cared for him. If what she felt wasn't love, surely there was a way to make it turn into love. If Isabel could be swayed, so surely could Abigail.

Lost in the process of thinking while fighting abject despair, he failed to register his lack of privacy until Grayson stumbled out from behind a tree. Disheveled and sporting leaves in his hair, the Marquess of Grayson was an odd sight.

"What are you about?" Rhys muttered.

"Do you know that in the whole of this garden I cannot

find one red rose? There are pink roses and white roses, even an orange shade of rose, but no true red."

Running his hands through his hair, Rhys shook his head. "Is this part of your wooing of Isabel?"

"Who else would I be doing this for?" Grayson heaved out his breath. "Why could your sister not be the practical sort I thought she was?"

"I have discovered that practicality in women is exceedingly overappreciated."

"Oh?" Grayson arched a brow and dusted himself off as he moved closer. "I take it the situation between you and Miss Abigail is not proceeding satisfactorily?"

"Apparently, there is no situation," he said dryly. "I am a 'dear friend.'"

Grayson winced. "Good God."

Rhys rose to his feet. "So, considering the ruination of my own love life, if you reject my offer to help yours I would understand completely."

"I will take all the assistance I can get. I've no wish to spend the whole of my night gardening."

"And I've no wish to spend the whole of my night pining, so the distraction will be welcome."

Together, they moved deeper into the garden. Thirty minutes and several pricks of rose thorns later, Rhys grumbled, "This love business is dreadful."

Tangled in a climbing rose, Grayson growled, "Here, here."

Chapter 18

Standing in the doorway that separated his room from the adjoining sitting room, Gerard watched his wife glance at the small walnut clock on the mantel, tap her foot impatiently, and then mutter an oath under her breath.

"Such language from a lady," he drawled, relishing the warmth he felt at the knowledge that she missed him. "Puts me in the mood for sex."

She spun to face him and set her hands on her hips. "Everything puts you in the mood for sex."

"No," he argued, entering the room with a wicked smile. "Everything *about you* puts me in the mood."

She arched a brow. "Should I take your disheveled appearance and long absence as a sign? You look as if you've been tumbling a serving maid in the bushes."

Lowering his hand to rub the hard length of his cock, he said, "Here is a sign you can take. Proof that my interest is only for you." Then he pulled out the hand he had hidden behind his back, revealing a perfect red rosebud atop a very long stem. "But I think you will find this one more romantic."

Gerard watched Pel's eyes widen and knew that as far as roses went, the one he held aloft was a prime specimen. After all, nothing but the absolute best would do for his wife.

Her smile shook slightly, and her amber eyes glistened, making the itchy scratches on the backs of his hands pale to insignificance.

He knew that look. It was the smitten glance young debutantes had been giving him for years. That it now came from Isabel, his friend and the woman he lusted for so desperately, made everything he did not understand about courting come into clarity. Finesse may be something his primitive brand of claiming lacked, but he had always been able to be honest with Pel. "I want to woo you, win you, dazzle you."

"How is it that you can be so crude one moment and yet so appealing the next?" she asked with a shake of her head.

"There are moments when I am unappealing?" He clasped a hand over his heart. "How distressing."

"And impossibly, you look delectable with twigs in your hair," she murmured. "All that effort spent on me, and outside of bed, no less. A girl could swoon."

"Feel free, I'll catch you."

Her laugh made everything in the world right again. Just as it had done from the moment he met her.

"Do you know," he murmured, "that the sight of you—dressed or undressed, sleeping or waking—has always calmed me?"

She tugged the rose free of his grasp and lifted it to her nose. "'Calm' is not a word I would select to describe you."

"No? What would you choose, then?"

As she moved to add the rose to a nearby vase, he shrugged out of his coat. The knock that interrupted her reply surprised him. Then he listened to Isabel instruct the servant to bring hot water for his bath and he nodded to himself. His wife had always been one to anticipate a man's comfort.

"Stunning," she said when they were alone again. "Overwhelming. Determined. Relentless. Those descriptors suit you best."

Pausing before him, she slowly undid the carved buttons

of his waistcoat. "Brazen." Pel licked her lower lip. "Seductive. Definitely seductive."

"Married?" he suggested.

She lifted her gaze to meet his. "Yes. Definitely married." Running her hands up his chest and over the tops of his shoulders, she pushed the garment off of him.

"Enchanted," he said in a tone made husky by the effect of her perfume and attentions.

"What?"

"Enchanted would describe me perfectly." Thrusting his hands through her rich auburn tresses, he tugged her hard against him. "Captivated."

"Do you find any oddness in our sudden fascination with one another?" she asked in a tone that begged for reassurance.

"Is it so sudden? I cannot seem to remember a time when I did not think you were perfect for me."

"I have always thought you were perfection, but never did I think you were perfect *for me.*"

"Yes, you did, or you would not have wed me." He nuzzled his mouth against hers. "But you did not think I was perfect for loving, which I am."

"We really must work on building your self-confidence," she whispered.

Gerard twisted her head slightly to better fit their kiss and then licked across her lips. When her tongue flicked out to meet his, he hummed a soft chastising sound. "Allow me to kiss you. Just take it. Take me."

"Give me more then."

His smile curved against hers. A woman after his own heart. "I want to lick away every trace of any other kiss you have ever had." Cupping her nape in a hold that established his dominance, he followed the velvety softness of her upper lip with the tip of his tongue. "I want to give you your first kiss."

"Gerard," she whimpered, trembling.

"Do not be frightened."

"How can I help it? You are destroying me."

He nipped her plump lower lip with his teeth and then suckled it rhythmically, his eyes closing as the wanton taste of her inundated his senses. "I am rebuilding you, rebuilding *us*. I want to be the only man whose kiss you remember."

Sliding one hand down to the curve of her derriere, he urged her against him. With his arms filled with alluring softness, his nostrils filled with exotic flowers and aroused woman, his taste buds soaked in rich flavor, Gerard was left with no doubt that he loved Isabel more than anything. It was like nothing he had ever felt for anyone and it made him happy in a way nothing in his life ever had, or ever could. He tasted her tears and knew what she couldn't yet say.

He was about to say it for her when the scratching at the door parted them. It took far too long to have the bath prepared and the servants dismissed, but the resulting feel of Pel's fingers sifting soap through his hair and over his back was worth the wait. Then he noted the shaking of her hands and knew he had to distract her from her fears until he could take her to bed. There they'd never had any difficulty connecting intimately. With that in mind, he hurried the process.

"Would you like to discuss what lured you and Lady Ansell out to the garden earlier?" he asked, belting his robe before accepting the warmed brandy she offered him.

"Fresh air?" She took a seat in a nearby chair.

Gerard moved to the window. "You can simply tell me to mind my own affairs."

"Mind your own affairs," she retorted with laughter in her voice.

"Now I am intrigued."

"I knew you would be." He heard her sigh. "Apparently, conception is a problem for them, and it is causing a strain."

"Lady Ansell is barren?"

"Yes, her physician says the state is due to her advanced years."

He shook his head in sympathy. "Unfortunate for them that Ansell is an only child, so the burden rests entirely upon their shoulders." Taking a large swallow, he considered his own good fortune in having siblings. "You and I will never face that strain."

"I suppose not."

There was something in her tone that made his stomach clench in apprehension, but he hid the reaction by keeping his back to her and his tone casual. "Are you considering pregnancy?"

"Did you not say that you wished to build something lasting? What is more lasting than lineage?"

"Having two brothers negates that concern somewhat," he said carefully, fighting off the sudden tremor that moved him. The mere thought of Isabel increasing struck terror in him like he had never known. His hand shook so badly, the liquor in his glass sloshed precariously. He was only grateful that she could not see his upset from her vantage behind him.

Emily.

Her death and the death of their child had very nearly destroyed him, and he had not loved Em like he loved Isabel. If something were to happen to his wife, if he should lose her . . .

He squeezed his eyes shut and forced his grip to relax before he shattered the goblet.

"Does it negate your wish to have issue?" she asked behind him.

He heaved out his breath. *How in hell was he to respond to that?* He would give up everything to have a family with her. But he would not give *her* up. Though the possible result would be bliss, the risk innate in that possibility was agonizing even to contemplate.

"Is there a rush?" he asked finally, turning to meet her gaze to search for the strength of her resolve. She sat nearby, her back ramrod straight, her legs crossed primly, her gown draped loosely about her shoulders and slightly gaping between the breasts. The perfect dichotomy of impeccable breeding and carnal seduction. Perfect for him. Irreplaceable.

She shrugged, which relieved him immeasurably. She was making conversation, nothing more. "I was not implying a need for haste."

Waving his hand in deliberately careless fashion, Gerard affected a complete lack of concern and changed the subject. "I hope you enjoy Waverly Park. It is the closest of my residences to London and one of my favorites. Perhaps, if you agree, we can arrange to spend more time there."

"That would be wonderful," she agreed.

There was a distance fraught with tension between them, such as two fencers would experience while circling one another. He could not bear it.

"I would like to retire now," he murmured, studying her over the rim of his goblet. There was never any distance between them in bed.

A faint hint of a smile teased her mouth. "You suffer no weariness after tramping through hedges?"

"No." He moved toward her with obvious purpose.

Her eyes widened and the ephemeral curve of her lips turned into the come-hither grin of a siren. "How delicious."

"Would you like to nibble on me?" He set the glass on a tabletop as he passed it.

Isabel laughed as he caught her about the waist. "You do realize that I always know when you have an ulterior motive?" She followed the curve of his brows with her fingertips. "You have the devil in your eyes when you are attempting to distract me."

He kissed the tip of her nose. "Do you mind, vixen?"

"No. I would indeed love to nibble on you." Her expert fingertips deftly loosened and then parted his robe. "There is so much to tempt me. I cannot decide where to begin."

"Are you soliciting suggestions?"

Running her fingertips lightly down the center of his

chest, she tilted her head to the side as if pondering and said, "That is not necessary." His cock rose up. "I think it's plain which part of you is the most eager for my touch."

Every cell in his body, though tensed in expectation, sighed with satisfaction at her nearness. It always had. Being with Isabel made the world around him a better place, as maudlin as others would find that sentiment.

Her lips, so plump and hot, pressed against his neck, her tongue flicking out to taste his skin. "Ummm . . ." She hummed the pleasure she found with him, her hands sliding beneath his robe to caress his back. "Thank you for the rose. I have never had a rose picked by hand just for me."

"I would pick a hundred for you," he said gruffly, the memories of thorn pricks and muttered curses fading into obscurity. "A thousand."

"My darling. One is more than enough. It's perfection."

Everywhere she touched him heated and grew hard. No one else in his life had loved him like this. He felt it in her fingertips, in the brush of her breath across his flesh, in the way she trembled and grew aroused merely looking at him. Her tiny hands were everywhere, stroking, kneading. She loved the hard ridges of his muscles, despite how unfashionable they were.

She licked down his chest, taking tiny bites with her teeth, arousing him so fully that cum beaded up on the head of his cock and then slid down the upthrust length. As Pel dropped to her knees, she followed the glistening trail with her tongue, making him shudder and groan.

"Your mouth would ruin a saint," he growled, thrusting his fingers into her fiery tresses. Staring down at her, he watched as she gripped the base of his shaft and angled him down to her waiting mouth.

"What does it do to a man who is far from saintly?"

Before he could catch his breath to reply, she'd engulfed the straining tip in burning, liquid heat. His eyelids grew heavy, his breathing labored as she suckled him between those lush, ripe lips. He swelled in response to the steady, rhythmic pulls, sweat beading along his pores as the flush of pure lust swept across his flesh.

None of the women in his past who had serviced him in this manner could compete with his wife. For Isabel it was not a duty or a prelude to sex. For her it was a joy in and of itself, something she enjoyed as much as he. Something that heated her skin, soaked her sex, beaded her nipples. She moaned along with him, worshipped him with her tongue, fondled the hardened cheeks of his ass.

She loved him.

The skin of his cock was dry and stretched tight where he could not fit. The weight of his balls drew up, ready to spurt the gift of life he would never give her.

It was this last thought that urged him to finish in her eager mouth. Isabel loved it when he came in that fashion, loved to feel him quiver on unsteady legs and cry out her name. But she also loved it when he was hard and thick like this. Loved how deeply he could stroke inside her, and right now that was where he needed to be—connected with her. From now until death parted them, they would have only each other. She was all he needed. He hoped she felt the same about him.

"No more." Pushing her head away, he stepped back from temptation, his cock an angry red and jerking in frustration.

Isabel pouted her protest.

Gerard stepped backward, sinking onto the settee she had recently risen from, and gesturing impatiently for her to join him. Shrugging out of her dressing gown, she did just that, approaching him in a cloud of flame-touched tresses and seductively swaying hips. Then she climbed over him, straddling him, her hands on his shoulders, her full breasts swaying before his eyes.

Consumed with fever for her, he buried his face in the fragrant valley between her breasts, pulling the scent of her into his blood with deep desperate breaths.

"Gerard," she crooned, her fingers drifting into his damp hair and massaging the roots. "How I adore you."

Incapable of speech, he turned his head and ran his tongue across her nipple before closing his lips and suckling her, taking from her all the sustenance his soul needed. She gasped, a sound tinged with pain, and he cupped the warm undercurve and lifted, to make it more comfortable for her. Then he noted how heavy her breast was, and tender, if her sharp whimper was any indication.

He'd come in her!

The sudden flare of panic he felt nearly unmanned him. If not for Pel choosing that moment to sink her drenched cunt around his cock, he might have lost his erection altogether, which had never happened to him in his twenty-six years.

"Have I hurt you?" he managed, keeping his head lowered to hide his horror. *Surely it was too soon. . . . It couldn't be . . .*

Isabel hugged him closer and began to move, mewling softly as she stroked deep inside herself with the hard length of him. "My courses approach," she gasped. "It's nothing."

The relief that flooded him was so powerful, he had to remember to breathe, every muscle drained by the receding tide of terror. He held his wife's straining body to his, biting his lip to keep some semblance of control as she undulated against him in perfect rhythm. Their bodies fit perfectly, as did their personalities, their tastes, their likes and dislikes.

And she loved him. He knew that like he knew nothing else—with bone-deep clarity and assurance. For all that he was, with all of his faults and failings, she adored him anyway. She had given him joy when he had been certain there was no more joy to be had. If he lost her . . .

He would die.

"Isabel." His hands rested on either side of her spine, absorbing the feel of her slender muscles flexing with her exertions. Up and down, she worked their bodies with an understanding of what pleased him as only a woman who loved him would know. It made their joining more than sex, more than carnal gratification.

"Slide a little lower," she instructed, urging him to alter the cant of his hips. "Right there." Pel sank deep onto him, the slick lips of her cunt encircling the very root of his cock. "Ohhhh . . ."

She tightened around him deliciously, and lust singed its way up his spine, making him arch away from the damask embroidered settee back and into her. "Ah, Christ!"

"That's it," she praised, her nails biting into the flesh of his shoulder. "Enjoy the ride."

"Pel," he managed, gasping with fear. "I can't last."

He could not spill in her again. . . .

She rose and fell with such grace, her curvy body lithe and filled with quiet feminine strength. She was so tight, so hot and drenched, he knew he was losing his mind just as he had lost his heart.

"Come," he bit out, clutching her hips and thrusting madly into her. A silken fist. A burning glove. "Come, damn you!"

Gerard yanked her down as he ground upward, listening as she gave a thready cry, watching as her head fell back, feeling her clench tight around him and then milk his tortured cock with the same rhythmic suckling as he had felt in her mouth.

The moment she rested limp against his chest he withdrew, catching his cock in hand and pumping, spurting his seed outside of his wife.

Agonized, he pressed his cheek to her heart, listening to the rapid, passionate beat as he hid his tears in the exotic floral sweat that pooled between her breasts.

Chapter 19

For Isabel, the ride to Waverly was a lovely one, despite the presence of her mother-in-law. The pride with which Gray brought attention to and explained various landmarks was obvious. It deepened their growing bond to share this day and this place, to build these memories. She listened with rapt attentiveness as he spoke in his raspy voice, watching the light in his eyes and the animation of his features.

How different he was from the young, jaded man who had left her side so long ago. That man had died with Emily. The husband she had now was entirely her own and had never given his heart to another. And though he had not yet said it aloud, she suspected he loved her.

The knowledge made her day brighter, her mood lighter, her steps surer. Certainly with love between them, they could conquer any difficulties. True love meant accepting a person with all their faults. Isabel couldn't help but hope that Grayson would love her in spite of hers.

As the carriage rolled to a stop before the Waverly Park manse, Isabel drew herself up and prepared to meet the staff. Today the formality held new significance. In the past, she had not truly felt like Grayson's marchioness, and while she had no trouble assuming the authority of the station she was bred for, it had not previously given her the sense of satisfaction it gave her now.

Over the course of the next few hours, she toured the manse with the efficient housekeeper and took note of the deference paid to Gray's mother, who appeared to have no trouble praising the servants for a job well done, despite her difficulty in doing the same for her sons. Still, the dignified compliments the dowager paid to the staff for remembering certain tasks impeded the passing of the reins to Isabel.

When they were done, she and the dowager sat in the upstairs family parlor for tea. The room, though slightly dated in its décor, was lovely and soothing with shades of deep gold and pale yellow. They managed to hold a civilized conversation regarding the nuances unique to running that particular household. Briefly.

"Isabel," the dowager said, in a tone that made her tense. "Grayson seems determined to establish you in all ways as his marchioness."

Lifting her chin, Isabel replied, "I am equally determined to fulfill that role to the best of my abilities."

"Including discarding your lovers?"

"My private affairs are none of your concern. However, I will say that my marriage is solid."

"I see." The dowager gifted her with a smile that did not reach her eyes. "And Grayson is not disturbed by the prospect of lacking an heir from his own loins?"

Isabel paused with a piece of buttered scone lifted halfway to her mouth. "Beg your pardon?"

Gray's mother narrowed her pale blue eyes and studied her over the rim of her flowered teacup. "Grayson makes no objection to your refusal to bear him children?"

"I am curious as to why you believe I do not want children."

"Your years are advanced."

"I know my age," Isabel said curtly.

"You have never shown any desire to be a mother before."

"How would you know that? You have never expended any effort to ask me."

The dowager took her time returning her saucer and cup to the table before asking, "So you do wish to have children?"

"I believe most women have that desire. I am no exception."

"Well, that is good to hear," came the murmured, distracted reply.

Staring at the woman across from her, Isabel attempted to collect her aim. There was one, if only she could puzzle it out.

"Isabel." The sound of her favorite raspy voice soothed her immensely.

She turned with a bright smile to face Gray as he entered. His hair was windblown and his cheeks flushed, the handsomest man she had ever seen. She had always thought so. Now, looking at him with all the love she possessed, she was rendered breathless by the sight of him. "Yes, my lord?"

"The vicar's wife gave birth to their sixth child today." He held out both hands to her, and then pulled her to her feet. "A small crowd gathered with well-wishes. Instruments were brought out to provide music, others brought food. Now something of a celebration is happening in the village and I would dearly love to take you there."

"Yes, yes." Her excitement was sparked by his, her fingers tightening in response to his affectionate squeeze.

"May I come?" his mother asked, rising.

"I doubt it would be something you would enjoy," Gerard said, tearing his gaze away from Pel's radiant face. Then he shrugged. "But I have no objection."

"A moment to refresh, if you would, please," Isabel asked softly.

"Take all the time you need," he assured her. "I will have the landaulet brought around. It is a short distance, but neither of you are dressed for the walk."

Isabel left the room with her customary graceful glide. He began to follow her when his mother halted his egress.

"How will you know if the children she bears are truly yours?"

Gerard stilled, then turned slowly about. "What the devil are you talking about?"

"You don't honestly believe she will be faithful to you, do you? When she increases, the whole of Society will wonder who the father is."

He sighed. *Would his mother ever leave well enough alone?* "Since Isabel will never become pregnant, your distasteful scenario will never come to fruition."

"I beg your pardon?"

"You heard me clearly the first time. After what happened to Emily, how could you think I would ever go through that ordeal again? Michael or Spencer's eldest male issue will inherit. I will not risk Isabel when there is no dire need to."

She blinked, and then broke out in a broad grin. "I see."

"I hope you do." Shaking a finger at her, he narrowed his gaze and said, "Do not think to blame this on my wife as a shortcoming. *I* have made the decision."

His mother nodded with unusual docility. "I understand completely."

"Good." He turned away again and strode to the door. "We shall be departing shortly. If you want to come, be ready."

"Never fear, Grayson," she called after him. "I would not miss this for the world."

"Celebration" was an apt description for the merry crowd that filled the lawn before the vicar's small house and the church next to it. Beneath two large trees gathered a few dozen dancing and loudly conversing villagers, and one beaming vicar.

Isabel could not help but offer a wide smile to everyone

who approached their equipage in welcome. Grayson made a grand show of introducing her to the boisterous group, and she was greeted with great excitement.

For the next hour, she watched as Gray mingled. He spoke at length with the gentlemen he had labored alongside while building part of the stone wall, and deepened their regard with his ability to recall the names of their family members and neighbors. He lifted small children into the air, and reduced a group of smitten young girls to fits of giggles by complimenting their pretty hair ribbons.

All the while, Isabel basked in his charm from afar and fell so deeply in love, she ached all over with it. Her chest grew tight, and her heart clenched. The innocent infatuation she had felt for Pelham was nothing, *nothing* compared to the mature joy she found with Grayson.

"His father had the same charisma," the dowager said beside her. "My other sons do not display it in quite the same measure and I am afraid their wives will dilute the trait further. A pity it will not be passed down from Grayson, who has it in such abundance."

Shielded by her enjoyment of the day, Isabel shrugged off the usual irritation she felt with the dowager. "Who can foretell what traits a child will bear when it has yet to be conceived?"

"Since Grayson assured me back at the manse that he has no wish to beget issue off you, I think it's safe to say that he will not be passing along any traits at all."

Isabel glanced aside at her mother-in-law. With her once pretty features shielded by the brim of her hat, the dowager revealed no outward sign to the milling guests of the ugliness hidden beneath the façade. But that underlying rot was all Isabel could see.

"What are you talking about?" she snapped, turning to face her antagonist head-on. She could take poorly veiled barbs, but pure undiluted venom was too much.

"I offered my felicitations to Grayson on his decision to dedicate himself to preserving the title as he should." The dowager's chin lowered, shielding her eyes, but still revealing the smug curve to her thin lips. "He was quick to assure me that Emily is the only woman who would ever carry a child of his. He loved her, and she is irreplaceable."

Isabel's stomach roiled at the sudden remembrance of Gray's happiness over Em's condition. Thinking back, she found she couldn't recall a time since his return when Grayson had ever mentioned wanting to have children with *her*. Even last night, he had avoided the subject rather than address it, stressing that his brothers would see to the task of begetting an heir. "You lie."

"Why would I lie about something so easily disproved?" the dowager asked with mock innocence. "Truly, Isabel, you two are the most mismatched pair. Of course, if you can put aside any desire for children of your own and live with the knowledge that Grayson's heir will be the product of another woman, you may manage to rub along with some semblance of contentment."

Isabel's hands clenched into fists, and she fought the urge to hiss and scratch like a furious cat. Or cry. She couldn't decide which. But she knew either response would only give the dowager an advantage. So she managed a smile and a shrug. "I will take great pleasure in proving you wrong."

Moving a short distance away, she rounded the trunk of a large tree. There, safe from prying eyes, she fell back against the rough bark, heedless of the dirt and possible damage to her gown. Shaking, she laced her fingers together and took deep breaths. She could not appear less than fully composed.

Despite everything inside her that told her to have faith, to believe that she was good enough for Grayson, to trust that he cared for her and wanted her happiness, there was still the voice inside her that reminded her that Pelham had found her lacking.

"Isabel?"

As Grayson stepped beneath the shade of the tree, she met his concerned gaze. "Yes, my lord?"

"Are you well?" he asked, stepping closer. "You look pale."

She waved her hand carelessly. "Your mother is stirring the pot again. It's nothing. A moment and I will regain my composure."

The warning rumble in his throat soothed her, the sound of a man ready to defend his mate. "What did she say to you?"

"Lies, lies, and more lies. What recourse is left to her? You and I are no longer estranged, and we share the same bed, so the only thing she could wound me with was the topic of children."

Gray tensed visibly, something she noted with a flare of unease.

"What about children?" he asked gruffly.

"She claims you do not want any with me."

He stood unmoving for a long while and then winced. Her heart stopped, and then caught in her throat.

"Is it true?" Her hand lifted to her bosom. "Gerard?" she prodded when he did not answer.

Growling, he looked away. "I want to give you things, *all* things. I want to make you happy."

"But no children?"

His jaw tightened.

"Why?" she cried, her heart breaking.

Lifting his gaze to hers, he bit out, "I will not lose you. I *cannot* lose you. Risking you to childbirth is not an option."

Stumbling away, Isabel covered her mouth.

"For God's sake, don't look at me like that, Pel! We can be happy just the two of us."

"Can we? I remember the joy you felt when Emily was pregnant. I remember your exuberance." Shaking her head, she pressed her fingertips hard against her lower lip to still its quivering. "I wanted to give you that."

"Do you also remember my pain?" he asked, on the defensive. "What I feel for you is beyond anything I have ever felt for anyone. To lose you would destroy me."

"You think I am too old for you." Unable to bear the sight of his torment, which reflected her own, she stepped around him.

"This has nothing to do with age."

"Yes, it does."

Gray caught her arm as she walked by. "I promised you I would be enough, and I will be. I can make you happy."

"Release me," she said softly, meeting his gaze. "I need to be alone."

The blue of his eyes swirled with frustration, fear, and a tinge of anger. None of that affected her. She was numb, as she had learned long ago how to be when pierced with a mortal wound.

No children.

Pressing a hand over her aching chest, she tugged the arm that was still trapped in his grip.

"I cannot allow you to go like this, Pel."

"You have no choice," she said simply. "You will not hold me against my will in front of all these people."

"Then I shall go with you."

"I want to be alone," she reiterated.

Gerard stared at his wife's frigid shell and felt a gulf between them so wide he wondered if they could cross it. Panic made his heart race and his breathing shallow. "For Christ's sake, you never said anything about wanting children. You made me promise not to spill my seed in you!"

"That was before you made our temporary bargain into a permanent marriage!"

"How in hell was I to know that your feelings on the matter had changed?"

"Foolish me." Her eyes burned with amber fire. "I should have said, 'By the way, before I fall in love with you and want children, let me ask if you have any objections.'"

Before I fall in love with you . . .

At any other moment those words would have raised him to the heights. Now they cut him to the quick. "Isabel . . ." he breathed, tugging her closer. "I love you, too."

She shook her head, causing the artless curls at her nape to sway violently. "No." Her hand came up to ward him off. "That is the last thing I want to hear from you. I wanted to be a wife to you in all ways, I was willing to try, but you refuse me. We have nothing left now. *Nothing!*"

"What the devil are you talking about? We have each other."

"No, we do not," she said, with such finality his throat clenched tight as a fist, cutting off his air. "You took us beyond friendship and we cannot go back. And now . . ." She choked on a sob. "I cannot make love to you now, so we have no marriage either."

He froze, the beat of his heart faltering. *"What?"*

"I would resent you every time you sheathed yourself in a French letter or withdrew to spill your seed. To know that you will not allow me to carry your child—"

Catching her about the shoulders, Gerard attempted to shake some sense into his wife. Isabel retaliated with a booted kick to his shin, causing him to swear and release her in surprise. She raced swiftly back to the waiting landaulet, and he hurried after her as fast as decorum would allow. Just as Isabel clambered without assistance into the equipage, his mother stepped into his path.

"Witch!" he growled, grabbing her by the elbow and yanking her roughly aside. "When I depart today, I am leaving you here."

"Grayson!"

"You like this property, so refrain from looking so horrified." He loomed over her, making her cringe. "Save your horror for the day you see me again. I pray you never do, because it will mean that Isabel would not take me back. And if that happens, even God himself will not be able to spare you from my wrath."

He threw her aside and followed the fleeing landaulet on foot, but found his way repeatedly blocked by reveling villagers. When he finally arrived at the manse, Pel had already taken the traveling coach and departed.

Fighting a near crippling fear that he had damaged Isabel's love beyond repair, Gerard saddled a horse and gave chase.

Chapter 20

Rhys waited in the hallway of the wing that housed Abby's rooms. He paced nervously and tugged at his cravat, but never took his gaze away from her door. His coach waited out front, and the servants were loading his trunks. Time was growing short. He would be leaving soon, but refused to do so until he had spoken with Abigail.

He had been trying all morning, to no avail. He had attempted to take the seat next to her at breakfast, but she moved too quickly, picking a chair bracketed with guests on either side. A deliberate avoidance.

Blowing out an impatient breath, he heard the lock turn, then Abigail stepped out. He pounced.

"Abby." Striding toward her quickly, he noted the pleasure that lit her eyes, before she lowered her lids and shielded them.

Damned wench was playing at something, and he would get to the bottom of it, by God! Make him fall in love with her and then toss him aside, would she? He would see about that.

"Lord Trenton. How are you this—Oh my!"

Catching her elbow, he dragged her down the hall and into the servants' stairwell. He paused on the tiny landing and looked at her, noting the slight parting of her lips. Before she could protest, he drew her to him and kissed her, taking her mouth in near desperation, needing her response like he needed to breathe.

When she whimpered and surged into him, Rhys had to bite back the shout of triumph. She tasted like sweet cream and warm honey, a simple flavor that cleansed his jaded senses, and made the world fresh and new. He had to tear himself away, something he barely managed after spending a miserable, sleepless night without her.

"You will marry me," he said gruffly.

Abby sighed and kept her eyes closed. "Now, why did you have to ruin a perfect farewell with that nonsense?"

"It is not nonsense!"

"It is," she insisted, shaking her head as she looked at him. "I will not say yes. So please, cease."

"You want me," he said stubbornly, rubbing his thumb across her swollen bottom lip.

"For sex."

"That is enough." It wasn't, but if he had her beneath him whenever he wanted, perhaps he could reclaim the ability to think. Once he could think, he could plan to win her. Grayson was bumbling along that path. He could simply follow the trail of crushed greenery.

"It isn't," she argued gently.

"Have you any idea how many unions have no passion at all?"

"Yes." She set her hand over his heart. "But I do not believe that passion will be enough to bear the things others will say about you taking an American to wife."

"Curse them all," he grumbled. "We have more than passion, Abby. You and I rub along well. We enjoy each other's companionship even out of bed. And we both like gardens."

She smiled and his heart leapt. Then she dashed it to pieces. "I want love, and I won't settle for less."

Rhys swallowed hard. It was obvious she did not love him,

but to hear her say it aloud was painful in the extreme. "Love can grow."

Her lip quivered beneath his thumb. "I do not want to take the chance that it won't grow. I must feel it, Rhys, in order to be happy."

"Abigail," he breathed, pressing his cheek to hers. He could win her heart. If she would only give him the chance.

Unfortunately, before he could press further, a door opened on a lower floor and the sounds of two maids speaking to one another rose up to them.

"Farewell, my lord," Abby whispered, before rising to her toes and gifting him with a bittersweet kiss. "Save that dance for me."

Then she was gone, and the sudden emptiness in his arms was echoed in his heart.

Pulling into the drive before the Hammond estate, Isabel was relieved to see Rhys' black lacquered coach preparing for departure. After spending the last hour soaking her kerchief over the demise of her marriage and her broken dreams, she needed her brother's shoulder to cry on and advice on how to proceed.

"Rhys!" she cried, descending the steps with the help of a footman and running toward him.

He turned with a frown, one hand set at his waist, the other rubbing the back of his neck. He stood tall and proud, his mahogany hair capped with a hat, his long legs sheathed in trim, fitted trousers. To her aching heart, the sight of her brother offered comfort in and of itself.

"Bella? I thought you had left for the day. What has happened? You've been crying."

"I am riding with you back to London," she said hoarsely, her throat raw. "I can be ready within moments."

Looking over her head, he asked, "Where is Grayson?"

She shook her head violently in answer.

"Bella?"

"Please," she murmured, lowering her gaze because his compassion and concern threatened to instigate a torrent of tears. "You will turn me into a watering pot in front of the servants. I shall tell you everything, once I've refreshed myself and collected my abigail."

Rhys muttered an oath under his breath and tugged at his cravat. "Make haste," he growled, shooting an anxious glance at the front entrance. "Please believe that I don't mean to be harsh or uncaring, but truly ten minutes is all I can spare."

Nodding, Isabel hurried into the house. Everything she had with her could not be packed in ten minutes, so she splashed water on her face, took what she needed to be comfortable on the long drive, and left a note for Grayson to see to the rest of her belongings.

At any moment, she expected her husband to appear and the anxiousness of waiting made the cold knot in her belly tighten. She felt rushed, off-kilter, breathless. Her entire world was spinning without the steady core she thought she had discovered in Gray. She should have known she would be lacking in some way. This tightness in her chest that made her dizzy was her own fault. The reality had always been there—she was too old for Gray and he did not trust that her body could give him the children she knew he desired. If she were younger, she doubted he would have such fears about her health.

"Come along," she said to Mary, and they followed the footman, who carried her valise down the stairs to the front driveway.

Rhys waited out front, pacing restlessly. "Damned if you didn't take forever," he muttered, gesturing her abigail to the nearby servants' coach, before catching Isabel's arm and pulling her toward the waiting carriage. He pulled open the door and nearly thrust her inside.

Isabel had to scramble to stay on her feet and as she lifted her head within the confines of the coach, she understood her brother's need for haste. Above a gag, eyes of bright blue with golden flecks met hers.

"Dear heaven," she muttered, backing out quickly. She glanced around in search of a possible audience, then whispered furiously, "What are you doing with Miss Abigail in the coach trussed up like a dinner fowl?"

He heaved out his breath and then set his hands on his hips. "Blasted woman won't listen to reason."

"What?" Her arms' akimbo pose mimicked his. *"This* is reason? The future Duke of Sandforth kidnapping an unmarried girl?"

"What recourse do I have?" Holding out his hands to her, he asked, "Was I simply to walk away when she refused me?"

"So you will force the girl into marriage by compromising her? What basis is that for a lasting union?"

He winced again. "I love her, Bella. I cannot imagine going on with my life without her. Tell me what to do."

"Oh, Rhys," Isabel breathed, her tears beginning anew. "Do you not think that if I knew how to create love where none existed, I would have done so with Pelham?"

Perhaps it was a familial curse of some terrible sort.

She had wished desperately for Rhys to find a true loving partner. What was left of her heart was broken further to learn that he had fallen in love with a woman who did not return his affections.

Fierce kicking against the interior of the carriage drew their attention. When Rhys moved toward the door, Isabel stepped into his path. "Allow me. You have done quite enough, I think."

Raising her skirts, she used the small step to gain entry into the coach. She sat on the opposite squab, pulled off her gloves, and began to work on removing the gag that allowed only muffled protests to be heard over Rhys' constant muttering about *"impossible women."*

"Please do not scream when this comes off," she begged softly as she worked at the knot. "I realize you have been treated abominably by Lord Trenton, but he truly does care for you. He is simply misguided. He would not have—"

Abigail writhed frantically as the gag worked free. "My hands, my lady! Free my hands!"

"Yes, of course." Isabel swiped at the tears that wet Abigail's cheeks, then tugged at the soft cloth that wrapped around her wrists. The moment the tie loosened, Abigail worked her arms free and threw herself out the open door of the coach at Rhys. His tall frame absorbed the impact easily, though his hat was knocked away.

"Abby, please!" he begged as she pounded ineffectually at his shoulders. "I *must* have you. Yield to me! I will make you love me, I promise."

"I already love you, you idiot!" she sobbed.

He pulled back with wide eyes. "*What?* You said you only wanted— Damnation, you *lied* to me?"

"I'm sorry." Her feet dangled above the ground as he hugged her.

"What the devil is your objection to marrying me then?"

"You did not tell me you felt the same."

Setting her down, Rhys scrubbed a hand over his face and growled. "Why in the world would a man marry a woman who drives him insane if not for love?"

"I thought you only wished to marry me because we were caught kissing."

"Good God." His eyes closed, even as he reached for her again. "You will be the death of me."

"Say it again," she implored, her lips pressed to the line of his jaw.

"I love you madly."

Isabel looked away from the scene, a fresh kerchief pressed to her face. "Remove his bags," she said to the nearby footman, who hurried to do as she ordered. She settled into the seat, leaned her head back and closed her eyes, which didn't stop the tears from leaking out regardless.

Perhaps it was only she who was cursed.

"Bella."

Opening her eyes, she glanced at Rhys, whose torso filled the doorway.

"Stay," he said softly. "Talk to me."

"But it is so annoying when women start discussing their feelings," she replied with a watery smile.

"Don't make light. You should not be alone now."

"I want to be alone, Rhys. Staying here, pretending to be well when I am not, would be the worst form of torture."

"What in hell happened with you and Grayson? He was sincere in his wish to win your affections. I know he was."

"He succeeded." Leaning forward, she spoke urgently. "You took a risk for love, and it has paid you handsomely. Promise me you will always put your love above everything else, just as you did today. And never underestimate Miss Abigail."

Rhys scowled. "Please do not speak in riddles, Bella. I am a man. I lack comprehension of the female language."

She set her hand over his where it curled around the door frame. "I must go before Grayson arrives. We will talk more when you return to London with your fiancée."

It was that one-word reminder that caused him to nod and step back. He would stay and speak with the Hammonds. She would survive, as she always had.

"I will hold you to that, Bella," he warned.

"Of course." She offered him a wavering smile. "I am so happy for you. I do not approve of your methods," she amended hastily, "but I am glad that you have found the one woman for you. Please make my apologies for me. I did not have the time."

He nodded. "I love you."

"My, you are becoming proficient at saying that, aren't you?" Isabel sniffled and swiped at her eyes. "I love you, as well. Now let me go."

Rhys stepped back and shut the door. The coach lurched

into motion, leaving the setting of fleeting bliss behind, but taking the memories with it.

Isabel curled into the corner and cried.

Gerard rode his mount hard through the Hammond park gate. When he drew to a halt before the front steps, he threw himself down and tossed the reins to the startled groomsman. Disregarding any semblance of decorum, he ran up the stairs to his rooms.

Only to find his wife gone and a tersely worded note requesting that her belongings be sent to her. His response knotted his gut and stole his breath like a physical blow.

He realized then how wounded she was. He sank onto the nearest chair, Pel's missive crushed within his clenched fist. He was stunned, unable to comprehend what had happened to the happiness they'd enjoyed upon waking mere hours ago.

"What transpired?" asked a voice from the open doorway to the main gallery.

Glancing up, Gerard found Trenton leaning against the jamb. "I wish I knew." He sighed. "Were you aware that Isabel wanted children?"

Trenton pursed his lips a moment. "I do not recall ever discussing the topic with her, but it stands to reason that she would. She is romantically inclined. I cannot imagine a woman finding anything more romantic than a family."

"How could I have missed that?"

"I've no notion. Why is having a child a problem? Surely you want the same." Trenton pushed upright and entered, taking the wingback opposite.

"A woman I once cared for died in childbirth," Gerard murmured, staring down at the wedding band on his finger.

"Ah, yes. Lady Sinclair."

Gerard's gaze lifted with a scowl. "How in hell can Isabel

ask me to relive the experience? The mere thought of her increasing fills me with such terror I can hardly bear it. The reality would kill me."

"Ah, I see." Settling back into the chair, Trenton crossed one foot over the opposite knee and gave a thoughtful hum. "Forgive me for discussing something delicate, but I am not blind. Over the weeks since your return, I have seen bruises on Isabel. Occasional bite marks. Scratches. I would venture to say you are not a man who practices moderation in his appetites. And somewhere along the way, you found some confidence that she could withstand such depth of ardor."

"Damned if this isn't uncomfortable to discuss," Gerard muttered.

"But I am not wrong?" Trenton prodded. When Gerard gave a jerky nod, he said, "If memory serves me correctly, Lady Sinclair was of delicate stature. In fact, the difference between her and Bella is so extreme one cannot help but wonder how it is that you were so attracted to both."

"Different motivators behind the two attractions." Gerard stood and walked slowly about the room, searching out pockets of exotic floral scent in the air. Em had appealed to his pride. Pel appealed to his soul. "Very different."

"My point exactly."

Taking a deep breath, Gerard leaned against the mantel and closed his eyes. Isabel was a tigress. Em had been a kitten. The sunset to the sunrise. Opposites in every way.

"Women survive childbirth daily, Grayson. Women far less spirited than our Isabel."

This was true, there could be no denying it. But while his mind spoke reason, his heart knew only the unreasonableness of love.

"If I were to lose her," Gerard said, his tone anguished, "I do not know what would become of me."

"Seems to me, you are already well on your way to losing her. Would it not be better to take the risk and chance keeping her, than to do nothing and lose her for certain?"

The logic of that statement was undeniable. Gerard knew that if he did not bend in this, he would lose Pel. Her distress today had made that abundantly clear.

He heard Trenton rise and turned to face him. "Before you go, Trenton, may I beg the use of your carriage?"

"No need. Bella took mine."

"Why?" The dead weight of apprehension settled in Gerard's stomach. Had his fear caused Isabel to forsake everything that belonged to him?

"It was hitched and ready in the drive. No, don't ask. It is a long story, and you had best be off if you hope to make it back to London before sunrise."

"Lord and Lady Hammond?"

"Are blissfully unaware of any unpleasantness. With minor effort you can keep it that way."

Nodding his agreement, Gerard straightened and mentally began the preparations he needed to excuse himself and his wife from the party without arousing undue suspicions. "Thank you, Trenton," he said gruffly.

"Just fix what has gone awry. I want Bella happy. That is all the thanks I require."

Chapter 21

Gerard judged the distance to the second floor window of his London residence, leaned back, and took aim with a pebble. He waited until he heard the small but satisfying *tink*, before drawing his arm back and throwing another.

The sky was beginning to lighten, turning the dark charcoal gray to a pale pink. He was reminded of another morning, and another window. But the goal he sought was the same.

It took several hits before he achieved the desired result—the sash lifted and Pel thrust her sleep-mussed head out.

"What are you doing, Grayson?" she asked in that low, throaty tone he adored. "I warn you, I am not in the mood to recite Shakespeare."

"Thank God for that," he said with a hesitant laugh.

Apparently, she had vivid remembrances of that morning, too. There was hope in that.

With an audible sigh she settled into the window seat and arched a brow in silent query. No surprise to Isabel to find a man tossing things to win her attention. The whole of her adult life, men had been trying to gain entry to her bedroom.

Now, her body was promised to *his* bed, for the rest of her life. The pleasure the thought gave him spread rapidly through his body and warmed his blood. Then he chilled just as swiftly.

As the rising sun revealed her beloved face, he saw that her sherry-colored eyes were sad, and the tip of her nose was red. She had cried herself to sleep by the look of it, and it was entirely his fault.

"Isabel." His voice was a raw plea. "Let me in. It's cold out here."

Her wary expression turned to one even more guarded. Leaning farther out the window, her unbound tresses drifted over a shoulder bared by her loosely belted dressing gown. From the soft sway of her full breasts he knew she was naked beneath. The effect that knowledge had on him was as predictable as the sunrise. "Is there some reason you cannot enter?" she asked. "Last I queried, this was your home."

"Not the manse, Pel," he clarified. "Your heart."

She stilled.

"Please. Let me explain. Let me make things right between us. I *need* to make things right between us."

"Gerard," she breathed, so softly he barely heard his name drift down upon the chilly morning breeze.

"I love you desperately, Isabel. I cannot live without you."

Her hand came up and covered trembling lips. He stepped closer to the house, every cell in his body reaching out to her.

"I pledge my troth to you, my wife. Not for my needs, as I did before, but for yours. You have given me so much— friendship, laughter, acceptance. You have never judged me or chastised. When I did not know who I was, you cared for me anyway. When I make love to you, I am content and I wish for nothing else."

"Gerard."

His name, spoken in her broken voice, struck deeply. "Will you let me in?" he implored.

"Why?"

"I want to give all that I am to you. Including children, should we be so blessed."

She was silent for so long he grew dizzy from holding his breath. "I agree to talk. Nothing more."

His lungs burned. "If you still love me, we can manage the rest."

Her arm extended out to him. "Come up."

Turning on his heel, Gerard ran to the door and then up the stairs, the desperate need to be with his wife riding him hard. But when he entered their rooms, he drew up short. The sight that greeted him was *home*, despite the tension that crackled between him and Pel.

A fire lay banked in the marble-framed hearth, ivory satin tented the ceiling, and Isabel stood before the window, her lush curves draped in deep red silk. It was an excellent color for his wife, whose lush flamboyance needed a bold setting. And this room, where they had spent so many hours talking and laughing, was an excellent setting for a new beginning. Here, they would conquer the inner demons that strove to drive them apart.

"I've missed you," he said softly. "When you are not beside me, I feel very alone."

"I missed you, too," she admitted, swallowing hard. "But then, I wonder if I ever really had you. I think, perhaps, Emily still holds a part of you captive."

"As Pelham holds you captive?" He shrugged out of his great coat, and then his coat, taking his time because he noted how warily she watched him. Turning his head, his gaze met Pelham's in the portrait. "You and I both made poor choices for ourselves earlier in life, and we are both scarred by them."

"Yes, perhaps we are each ruined in our own way," she said wearily, moving to her favorite chaise.

"I refuse to believe that. There is a reason for everything." Gerard tossed his waistcoat across the back of a gilded chair and crouched before the fire, stoking it and throwing on more coal until heat began to fill the room. "I'm certain that had I not known Emily, I would not be able to appreciate you as I do. I would not have had the comparison required to recognize how perfect you are for me."

She snorted softly. "You only thought I was perfect when you assumed I had forsaken motherhood."

"And you," he continued, ignoring her. "I doubt you would find my uncontrollable passion for you to be so welcome had you not been wooed with calculated seduction by Pelham."

The silence that greeted him was rife with possibilities. He felt the spark of hope he'd tucked close to his heart expand into a blaze to match the one in the hearth before him.

He stood. "However, I think it is time to reduce this marriage of four into a more intimate union of two."

Turning to face her, he found her sitting upright on the chaise, her face pale and beautiful, her eyes welling with tears. Her fingers were laced so tightly together they were white, and he went to her, sat at her feet, and warmed her icy hands with his own.

"Look at me, Pel." When she met his gaze, he offered a smile. "Let's make another bargain, shall we?"

"A bargain?" One finely arched brow rose.

"Yes. I agree to start anew with you. In every way. I will not burden our love with guilt from the past."

"Every way?"

"Yes. Nothing held back, I swear it. In return, you will take down that portrait. You will agree to believe that you are perfection itself. That there is nothing—" His voice broke, forcing him to close his eyes and take a shuddering breath.

Parting the ends of her gown, Gerard nuzzled his cheek against the satin skin of her thigh and breathed in her scent, calming the emotion that overwhelmed him.

Her fingers drifted into his hair, stroking the roots, loving him silently.

"There is nothing I would change about you, Isabel," he whispered, drinking in the sight of the mature beauty and inner strength that made her who she was. Unique and priceless. "Most especially not your age. Only an experienced woman could manage a man as overbearing as I can be."

"Gerard." She slid down beside him, and pulled him to her breast. There, she held him to her heart. "I suppose I should expect that any time you throw stones at my window, it is a herald to how drastically my life is about to change."

"Yes, you should."

"Wicked rogue." Her lips curved against his forehead.

"Ah, but I am *your* wicked rogue."

"Yes." She laughed softly. "That's true. You are far different from the man I married, but your wickedness is one thing that, thankfully, did not change. You are just exactly the way I want you."

He moved, cradling her spine as he lowered her to the floor. "I want you, too."

Isabel gazed up at him, her hair a banner of fire, her skin as pale as ivory where it was revealed by the parted edges of her gown. His dark hand brushed aside the intruding material, revealing the full breasts and ripe curves he worshipped. He shoved his hand into his pocket and withdrew the ruby ring he had purchased for her. With shaking fingers, Gerard slipped it into place, kissing the stone before turning her hand and pressing his lips against her palm.

Heat swept across his skin like a hot breeze, nerve endings tingling to acute awareness, his mouth watering. Bending his head, he licked the softness of one nipple and then the other, parting his lips more fully and drawing her into his mouth. His eyes slid closed, his blood growing sluggish with desire and love, as he drank in her taste with long, deep pulls.

"Yes . . ." she breathed, when he bit gently down on the hardened crest, relishing as always the fierce need he had to devour her whole.

They moved languidly, in no rush. Every touch, caress, and murmur was a promise made. To forsake all others. To love one another, trust one another, and leave the past behind. Theirs was a union made for all the wrong reasons, but in the end it was one that could not have been more *right*.

Clothing fell away until their skin touched everywhere and he cupped her thigh and opened her, sinking the hard length of his cock into tight hot depths. Joining them more fully than the golden bands they wore ever could.

Gerard lifted his head and watched Isabel's face as he pumped deep into her. Her soft whimper filled the air, made his balls draw up, made his arms shake as he supported his weight. She tossed her head restlessly, her heels in his back, her nails in his forearms. The fiery skeins of her dark hair were spread across the Aubusson rug, releasing the heady scent that intoxicated him.

God, how he loved this. He doubted he would ever have his fill of the sight of her helpless to her desire or the feel of her cunt so tight and slick.

"Sweet Isabel," he crooned, freed for the first time from the desperation that had marked their past encounters.

"Gerard."

He groaned. His name was a tactile caress when spoken in that throaty voice. Lowering over her, he pressed his mouth to hers, drinking in her gasps as he worked her with his cock in exactly the way she liked, stroking her with long, deep, slow drives.

"Oh God!" she gasped, her depths rippling around him, her back arching in the throes of climax.

"I love you," he breathed, his mouth to her ear, his chest pressed to hers. Then he followed her, shuddering, spilling his seed in a rush of longing, giving her the promise of the life they would create together with boundless joy in his heart.

She met him stroke for stroke, his match in every way.

Epilogue

"I think he needs a stronger libation than tea," Lady Trenton whispered.

Gerard stood at the parlor window with hands clenched together at the small of his back. His stance was wide to better anchor him to the floor, yet still he felt wobbly and out of sorts. Like a colt struggling to gain its legs. He wished to be upstairs with his wife who was presently laboring to bring his child into the world, but the proliferation of visitors stayed him. All of his in-laws were present, as well as Spencer.

"I say, Grayson," Trenton called out. "You should sit, before you fall over."

A chastising noise preceded Lady Trenton's admonishment. "That was not very tactful."

Turning, Gerard said, "I am not in danger of collapse."

A lie of tremendous proportions. He felt the dampness of sweat at his brow and nape, and forced himself to breathe in measured rhythm.

"You are pale as cream," Lord Sandforth scoffed. His Grace's resemblance to his son was astonishing, differing only in the gray of his hair and the fine lines that rimmed his eyes and mouth.

Gerard straightened, his gaze moving from one end of the room to the other. The women sat on opposite chaises; the men stood at various points around the perimeter. All five pairs of eyes watched him warily.

It was deathly silent upstairs. While he was grateful for the lack of pained cries, Gerard wished desperately for any sign that Pel was well.

"Excuse me," he said abruptly, departing the room with an impatient stride. The moment his boots made contact with the entryway floor, Gerard sped up his pace. He rounded the staircase's curved handrail and raced up two flights to the third floor. He slowed only when he reached the nursery. After smoothing his hair with a rushed swipe of his hand, he turned the knob and entered.

"Papa!"

Gerard crouched just inside the room and opened his arms for the tiny, solid body that barreled toward him on chubby legs. Clasping his auburn-haired son tightly to his chest, he reminded himself that Pel had managed childbirth before with "envious ease and haste." Or so the midwife had claimed.

"My lord," the nursemaid greeted, curtsying. Her gaze was questioning. He shook his head to tell her there was no news to convey. She offered a reassuring smile and retreated to a chair in the corner.

Pulling back slightly, Gerard stared down into the face of his son and felt the now-familiar swelling of his heart. The past three years had been the happiest of his life. Pel's trust had unfurled like a flower, blossoming as time solidified his deep affection into a love that was unquestionable. Their first child—Anthony Richard Faulkner, Lord Whedon—had been born two years ago, bringing to the Faulkner household a joy and merriment such as Gerard had never known. Isabel was more beautiful now than ever before, her features kissed with a blissful glow he ensured never dimmed.

A soft scratching came to the open door. He glanced up and felt the weight of the world falling from his shoulders.

Lady Trenton would only smile so beautifully as the bearer of happy news.

Gerard rose and bore his son down to the second floor with him. He burst into his wife's chamber to the accompaniment of Anthony's helpless giggles and drew to a stumbling halt.

Isabel rested amid a proliferation of pillows, her glorious hair spilled across white linen, her cheeks flushed and eyes bright. She was radiant and without question the most beautiful creature he had ever seen in his life.

"My lord," the midwife said from her position at the washstand.

He nodded his acknowledgment of the salutation, deliberately averting his gaze from the crimson-stained towels in a large bowl near the bed. He sat gingerly on the edge of the mattress, his hand coming to rest atop Isabel's thigh. Anthony attempted to crawl over his mother, then paused with wide eyes as the bundle in her arms wiggled and mewled like a kitten.

"My love . . ." Gerard breathed, eyes stinging. There were no words.

"Isn't she beautiful?"

A girl.

With a shaking hand, he pushed the edge of the lace-trimmed blanket aside, revealing cloudy tufts of red hair and a face so precious he could scarcely breathe. He was madly, ferociously in love the moment his gaze settled on her. Her skin was petal-soft and touched with pink, like a . . .

"Rose."

Isabel smiled up at him. "How lovely, Gerard. And so fitting."

He stood, and rounded the bed. Setting first one knee then the other on the mattress, he crawled along the top until he reached Pel. Settling cautiously beside her, he drew her close with one arm behind her head and the other wrapped around a fascinated Anthony.

"We are four of us again," she said, leaning her head into him.

"Yes. The perfect four," he qualified.

"Perhaps four more?"

Gerard stilled, then he caught the mischievous gleam in her sherry-colored eyes. "Vixen."

"Ah, but I am *your* vixen."

"Four more, you say." Pressing his lips to her forehead, he sighed. "You will drive me to madness."

"I will make the effort worth your while," she promised in the throaty voice he adored.

He drew her closer, his heart so full it ached. "You already have, my love. You already have."

**Read on for excerpts of more evocative
historical romance from Sylvia Day.**

From *Seven Years to Sin*

She entered with a practiced smile, her gaze locating Captain Smith as he pushed to his feet at a long dining table, along with two other gentlemen who were introduced to her as the Chief Mate and ship's surgeon. She exchanged the expected pleasantries, then turned her attention to the violin player. He stood with his back to her before the large gallery windows wrapping the stern. He was sans tailcoat, which caused her to glance hastily away. But when the captain approached to escort her to the table, she risked another furtive glance at the scandalously semi-dressed gentleman. Without tails to block her gaze, she was afforded a prime view of the man's derriere, which was quite noteworthy. It was not a part of the male anatomy she'd had cause to study before. She found she quite enjoyed the ogling when the buttocks on display were so firm and well-shaped.

As she conversed with the ship's officers, Jess glanced frequently at the dark-haired musician who coaxed such beautiful notes from the violin. The fluid, practiced movement of his arm caused his back and shoulders to flex in a manner that had always fascinated her. The male body was so much larger and more powerful than a woman's—capable of fierce aggression while also being sleek and graceful.

The tune ended. The player pivoted to return the violin and bow to their case waiting on the chair beside him. Jess caught a quick glimpse of his profile. A frisson of awareness swept over her skin. He collected his jacket from the chair where it was draped, then shrugged into it. She hadn't thought it possible that the act of putting clothes *on* could be as arousing as watching them come *off*, but this man made it so. The graceful economy of his movements was inherently sensual, which suited his air of unwavering confidence and command.

"And this," the captain said, turning slightly to gesture at the gentleman, "is Mr. Alistair Caulfield, owner of this fine vessel and brilliant violinist, as you 'eard."

Jess swore her heart ceased beating for a moment. Certainly, she stopped breathing. Caulfield faced her and sketched a perfectly executed, elegant bow. Yet his head never lowered and his gaze never left hers.

Dear God . . .

Chapter 2

What were the odds that they would cross paths this way?

There was very little of the young man Jess had once known left in the man who faced her. Alistair Caulfield was no longer pretty. The planes of his face had sharpened, etching his features into a thoroughly masculine countenance. Darkly winged brows and thick lashes framed those infamous eyes of rich, deep blue. In the fading light of the setting sun and the flickering flames of the turpentine lamps, his coal-black hair gleamed with health and vitality. Previously his beauty had been striking, but now he was larger. More worldly and mature. Undeniably formidable.

Breathtakingly male.

"Lady Tarley," he greeted her, straightening. "It is a great pleasure to see you again."

His voice was lower and deeper in pitch than she remembered. It had a soft, rumbling quality. Almost a purr. He walked with equal feline grace, his step light and surefooted despite his powerful build. His gaze was focused and intense, assessing. Challenging. As before, it seemed he looked right into the very heart of her and dared her to deny that he could.

From *Pride and Pleasure*

"Mr. Bond," she said, after a slight delay. "I did not hear you approach."

One could blame the choir's singing for that. However, the truth of it was that he walked silently. He'd learned the skill long ago. It had saved his life then and continued to do so in recent years.

Standing, she moved toward him with a determined stride and thrust out her hand. As if cued, the singers below ended their hymn, leaving a sudden silence into which she said, "I am Eliza Martin."

Her voice surprised him. Soft as a summer breeze, but threaded with steel. The sound of it lingered, stirring his imagination to travel in directions it shouldn't.

He shifted his cane to his other hand and accepted her greeting. "Miss Martin."

"I appreciate your courtesy in meeting with me. However, you are exactly what I feared you would be."

"Oh?" Taken aback by her direct approach, he found himself becoming more intrigued. "In what way?"

"In every way, sir. I contacted Mr. Lynd because we require a certain type of individual. I regret the need to say you are not he."

"Would you object to my request for elaboration?"

"The points are too numerous," she pronounced.

"Nevertheless, a man in my position seeks predictability in others but fears it in himself. Since you state I am the epitome of what you did *not* want, I feel I must request an accounting of the criteria upon which you based your judgment."

Miss Martin seemed to ponder his response for a

moment. In the brief time of introspection, Jasper collected what his instincts had recognized upon first sight: Eliza Martin was intensely aware of him. Without her cognizance, her baser senses were reacting to him much the way his were to her: her delicate nostrils flared, her breathing quickened, her body swayed with the undercurrent of agitation . . . a doe sensing the hunter nearby.

"Yes," she said, with a catch in her voice. "I can see why that would be true."

"Of course it's true. I never lie to clients." He never bedded them either, but that was about to change.

"You have not been engaged," she reminded, "so I am not a client."

The man with the frightening hair intruded. "Eliza, marry Montague and be done with this farce."

With the voicing of that one name, Jasper knew why he'd received the referral and how little chance Eliza Martin had of dismissing him.

"I will not be bullied, my lord," she said firmly.

"Invite Mr. Bond to sit, then."

"That won't be necessary."

Skirting her, Jasper settled into the pew behind the one they occupied.

"Mr. Bond . . ." Miss Martin gave a resigned exhalation. "My lord, may I present Mr. Jasper Bond? Mr. Bond, this is my uncle, the Earl of Melville."

"Lord Melville." Jasper greeted the earl with a slight bow of his head. He knew of Melville as the head of the Tremaine family, a lot renowned for their eccentricities. "I believe you will find me to be highly suitable for any task in want of a thief-taker to manage it."

Miss Martin's blue eyes narrowed on him in silent reproach for attempting to circumvent her. "Sir, I am certain you are capable in most circumstances. However—"

"About the many points . . . ?" he interjected, circling back. He disliked proceeding when there were still matters left unaddressed.

"You are overly tenacious." She remained standing, as if prepared to show him out.

"An excellent trait to have in my profession."

"Yes, but that doesn't mitigate the rest."

"What rest?"

The earl's gaze darted back and forth between them.

She shook her head. "Can we not simply leave it at that, Mr. Bond?"

"I would rather we didn't." He set his hat on the seat beside him. "I have always taken pride in my ability to manage any situation put before me. How will I provide exemplary service if I can no longer make that claim?"

"Really, sir," Miss Martin protested. "I did not say you are unsuitable for your trade as a whole, only in regards to our situation—"

"Which is . . . ?"

"A matter of some delicacy."

"I cannot assist you if I am ignorant of the details," he pointed out.

"I do not want your assistance, Mr. Bond. You fail to collect that."

"Because you refuse to explain yourself. Mr. Lynd thought I was suitable and you trusted his judgment enough to arrange this meeting." Jasper would pay Lynd handsomely for the referral. It had been far too long since he'd felt this level of interest in anything beyond his need for vengeance.

"Mr. Lynd does not have the same considerations I do."

"Which are . . . ?"

"Sir, you are exasperating."

And she was fascinating. Her eyes sparkled with irritation, her right foot tapped against the floor, and her fisted hands moved often as if to rest on her hips. But she resisted the urge. He found her resistance most appealing. What would it take to break it and see her unrestrained? He couldn't wait to find out.

"I will compensate you for your time today," she said, "so all is not a complete loss to you. There is no need to continue this discussion."

"You overlook the possibility that I might have intended to assign a member of my crew to you, Miss Martin. I would, however, need to know what your situation is so I can determine whose skills would best suit your requirements." He intended to service her himself, but he wasn't above a little subterfuge when the prize was this delicious.

"Oh." She bit her lower lip again. "I hadn't considered that."

"So I noted."

Miss Martin finally sank back onto the pew in a movement of eminent grace. "Just so we are clear you won't do."

"It isn't clear." He set his cane between his legs and placed his hands atop it, one over the other. "At least, not to me."

She glanced at his lordship, then—reluctantly—back to Jasper. "You force me to say what I would rather not, Mr. Bond. Frankly, you are too handsome for the task."

He was stunned into momentary silence. Then, he relished an inner smile. How delightful she was, even when cross.

"Mr. Lynd was less conspicuous than you," she continued. "You are quite large and, as I said, far too comely."

Lynd was a score of years older and average in height, features, and build. Jasper looked to the earl and found the man staring at his niece with confusion. "I fail to see what bearing my face has on my investigative skills."

"In addition—" her voice grew stronger as she warmed to the topic of his faults, "—it would be impossible to disguise the air about you which distinguishes you."

"Pray tell me what that is." He was beginning to find it difficult to hide his growing enjoyment of the conversation.

"You are a predator, Mr. Bond. You have the appearance of one, and you carry yourself like one. To be blunt, you are clearly capable of being a dangerous man."

"I see." Fascination deepened into captivation. Perhaps she wasn't so innocent, after all. He spent obscene amounts of coin on his attire, deliberately crafting an appearance so polished very few saw past it to the rough edges underneath.

"I doubt you would be effective at your profession if you were not possessed of both predatory and dangerous qualities," she qualified in a conciliatory tone.

"And many others," he offered.

Miss Martin nodded. "Yes, I suspect the trade requires you to be well versed in a multitude of skills."

"It certainly helps."

"However, your masculine beauty negates all of that."

Jasper was ready to move forward. "Would you get to the point, Miss Martin? What—exactly—did you intend to hire me to accomplish?"

"Quite a bit, actually. Protection, investigation, and . . . to act as my suitor."